THE
Prophecy
OF THE
Stones

THE Prophecy OF THE Stones

FLAVIA BUJOR

Translated from the French by Linda Coverdale

MIRAMAX BOOKS • HYPERION BOOKS FOR CHILDREN • NEW YORK

First U.S. edition, 2004

5 7 9 10 8 6

Printed in the United States of America

This book is set in 13/19 Perpetua.

ISBN 0-7868-1835-2

Reinforced binding

Library of Congress Cataloging-in-Publication Data on file.

Visit www.hyperionbooksforchildren.com

TO JEAN LOSSERAND AND STEPHEN

CONTENTS

I LOVE THOSE WHO DREAM OF THE IMPOSSIBLE.

—JOHANN WOLFGANG VON GOETHE, *FAUST*

PROLOGUE

HE HAD BEEN AWAKE ALL NIGHT, THINKING. HE had gone without rest or nourishment. He did not need them. He had to devise his plan—that was the only thing that mattered. At dawn, he had once again summoned the Council of Twelve telepathically. The session had been brief. He had simply informed them that the matter was in hand, that the project could not fail, and that he would soon put it into execution. The council members had not dared to ask him what his plans were. They had complete faith in him. After all, he was their superior. He had ordered them to return at noon for a meeting of the utmost importance.

Now it was time to deal once more with those incompetents so hungry for wealth and power. He briskly straightened his long purple robe embroidered with gold thread, and strode off to the council chamber. When he opened the door with his usual abruptness, the room fell silent, as each councilor felt paralyzed by fear. Not one was bold enough to look him directly in the eye.

The terrified Council of Twelve watched him: the Thirteenth Councilor, whose existence beyond those walls was a mystery to all, and who imposed his will on everyone. His image was not reflected in any mirror. He cast no shadow. He was not human.

1

JADE

THE OLD MAN READ THE PASSAGE IN *THE PROPHECY* once more and nodded solemnly. "Soon, very soon," he muttered. Rising with difficulty from his chair, he turned to face the Duke of Divulyon, who was waiting anxiously before him.

"Well?" asked the duke.

The old man sighed deeply. He seemed exhausted. His face was etched with countless wrinkles. His back was bent, and he could barely stand on his trembling legs. Collapsing into an armchair, he said weakly, "I cannot change a thing. She will follow her destiny."

"Théodon, you are a wise man," said the duke, his voice rising in obvious distress. "You have devoted your entire life to understanding the Prophecy. You helped my father. You have helped me. You have advised me, supported me. Do not abandon me now! She must live. She must triumph, whatever happens. She is so young! To think that soon . . . What can I do to protect her, Théodon?"

Holding his head in his hands, the old man remained silent for a long time.

"I love her as much as you do," he replied at last. "I watched her grow up, and even though it goes against my better judgment, I have become fond of her. But she will not escape the Prophecy. Believe me, if I could have helped her, I would have been the first to do so. You ask me how she can be protected? You cannot protect her! Try to understand that! All you have to do is give her what is rightfully hers when the day comes. Now, go. Go and spend the few moments you have left with her."

"Fourteen years have passed much too quickly," murmured the duke in weary resignation. Then he left the room.

The old man stared at the flames blazing in the hearth. The Prophecy would be fulfilled. Now it was only a matter of days. He had waited for this moment, had longed for it impatiently. Soon all his questions would be answered. He shivered. It was foolish of him to have become attached to the child; he shouldn't have done that. The Prophecy had taken on another meaning: in those obscure pages where he had tried so hard to read the future and to understand the upheaval that was to come, he no longer saw anything except the fate of a girl named Jade.

That same girl was lying sprawled across her bed. She was feeling much too restless to read the book in her hands, and there was a faraway look in her eyes. Roused from her reverie by a sudden knock at the door, she leaped to her feet, calling, "Come in!"

A servant opened the door a crack, and said, "Your father wishes to speak to you. Will you receive him now?"

Surprised that her father was not busy at that hour, Jade gave her consent, and the servant retired.

Jade smoothed down her long black hair, then tossed it over her shoulders. She looked in the mirror and approved of what she saw. True, her smile revealed teeth with slight gaps between them; her eyelashes were perhaps a bit too thick; and she was constantly brushing back a few rebellious stray locks. Whenever she became irritated (which happened often), her cheeks grew red and she lost the self-conscious expression she usually wore. However, she knew she was tall, slender, and beautiful, and she always dressed with care. She was sure of herself. She knew that whatever she wanted, she could get.

While she was smiling knowingly at her reflection, her father entered the room. She went to him, and he hugged her with unusual affection. Although he loved his daughter, he did not normally show his feelings so openly. Reserved by nature, he was always cool and composed. And yet, that day, something was making him behave differently. Releasing Jade from his embrace, he studied her for a moment without speaking. Once again he admired the striking intensity of her green eyes. She is brave and tenacious, he reflected, trying to reassure himself, and she has a strong character. Her features betrayed that character: you could see in her face that she was proud and determined, but capricious and stubborn as well. Lost in thought, her father could not stop gazing at her.

It was Jade who broke the silence.

"Papa, is something the matter? Don't you have any important business to attend to? Why aren't you reading stacks of documents, or dealing with thousands of tasks as you do every other day? Is something serious keeping you from your work? Is it my fault?"

This last question was asked with feigned innocence, and her father answered with a forced smile.

"No, no, Jade, nothing's wrong. I've just got a bit of free time, that's all. I know it doesn't happen very often, but, as you can see, it does happen! So, how are you?"

"Not long now till the party," she replied eagerly. "It's

going to be absolutely fantastic! I still can't decide between the mauve silk dress or the white satin one. I ordered a third dress, a splendid one, from the county of Tyrel. If it arrives in time, I shall wear that one. I simply can't wait! Instead of counting the days, I count the hours—even the minutes! I've given instructions about how the banquet hall should be decorated, and what food and music we should have. Oh! It's such fun to be organizing everything myself! And I've arranged for musicians to come from a nearby town."

She kept on chattering enthusiastically, but her father was no longer listening. She's too thoughtless, he admitted to himself reluctantly. She has never encountered difficulties; she knows nothing of danger. She won't be able to survive. He reproached himself immediately for not having more confidence in Jade and tried to concentrate on what she was saying.

"It's going to be magnificent, superb, spectacular! I can hardly wait. I still haven't decided whether the ices should be served before the macaroons or afterward—perhaps after would be better, don't you think? By the way, I'm not sure if the Baroness of Carolynt will be coming. It seems she has a fever. She's the only guest who hasn't accepted yet. Anyway, I find her boring—"

"Jade . . . Do you know what fear means?"

Startled into silence, Jade was annoyed. Why had her father interrupted her, especially to ask a question that was quite beside the point? Wasn't he looking forward to the party?

"Fear?" she replied crossly. "Fear of what? I've never been afraid. It's a hateful feeling. Only cowards and weaklings are frightened. Why do you ask me that, Papa?"

Just then, Jade realized how pale her father was. How could she have failed to notice how tired he looked, with those dark circles under his reddened eyes? And above all, that haggard expression . . . Something had happened. Perhaps his business affairs had not been going well. . . .

"If only cowards and weaklings feel fear, then I am cowardly and weak," said the duke. "In any case, it doesn't matter."

"But, Papa! You're respected and admired by everyone, and for good reason! You are the Duke of Divulyon!" Jade's face lit up again, her green eyes flashing. "I would believe you if you said you were worried about matters of state, but you, frightened? No! If this is a joke, it's not very funny."

The duke did not reply. Jade's spirits fell again. "And now, Papa," she said gravely, "tell me why you don't think my birthday is at all important. In a few days, I shall be fourteen years old!"

"You are quite mistaken, Jade. I am very concerned about your birthday. But . . ." The duke bit his tongue. He had already said too much. She was not to know anything before it was time. Afraid that he might betray secrets he was not free to explain, he turned on his heel and left, going upstairs to his private suite, where he began to pace back and forth. Every second was bringing him closer to the moment when he would have to reveal everything.

Puzzled, Jade wondered briefly about her father's exceedingly strange behavior, then shrugged her shoulders and decided not to fret about it. Her thoughts returned to the festivities planned for her birthday, and a smile returned to her lips.

2

AMBER

INSTEAD OF KEEPING AN EYE ON THE SHEEP IN her care, Amber was daydreaming, as usual. Sitting on the grass, she imagined herself living near the sun, enjoying its warmth, chatting to the clouds and birds. The wind carried her along on marvelous voyages; at night, she was dazzled by the brilliance of stars she could reach out and touch, and—

"Briette! Briette!"

She returned to earth with a bump. She had forgotten that she was supposed to be looking after one of her little brothers as well as the flock of sheep. The child was sprawled under a tree, calling out to her at the top of his lungs.

"Briette! Come here! I'm bored. . . . Briette!"

Everyone had always called her Briette, even though her real name was Amber, which was probably too pretentious for a country girl and might have better suited a noble lady, someone from another world. She couldn't imagine why her parents had chosen that name for her, although she'd often wondered about it; but she loved the name for its originality, its air of mystery. It seemed to conceal a secret.

"Briette! Briette! Pretty-please, come here!"

Amber rose and went to rejoin her brother. She sat down beside him in the shade of the tree.

"Whatever is the matter?" she asked soothingly.

"I'm bored, that's what's the matter! I want you to tell me a story."

Smiling, Amber stroked his cheek affectionately.

"Later, perhaps, but not right now."

"Why not?"

"I'd like to be alone. I want to stay perfectly quiet and try to listen to the silence."

"I want a story! You're just saying silly stuff!" The boy clung to her arm. "Please, Briette," he begged.

Tenderly ruffling his hair, she freed herself from his embrace, then kissed him on the cheek.

"Later, I promise," she said. "You stay here for the moment. I'm going back into the sunshine—I don't like to be in the shade."

"But, Briette, it's so hot! How can you stand being out in the sun?"

"I just like it, that's all."

Amber returned to the middle of the meadow and sank down into the grass. Nobody wanted to go out in that stifling heat. The cloudless sky was almost too blue, too pure. The sun bathed Amber's face in light. Her hair was like red gold and gleamed like the sun, framing her lovely face with its tan complexion. Flecks of green flashed in her hazel eyes, giving them a natural sweetness and serenity. She loved to feel the sunshine caress her skin; she enjoyed the heat that everyone else found so unbearable. People in the village hoped the dog days of summer would end soon, without bringing on a drought, but Amber wished the hot weather could go on forever.

A silhouette appeared on the path and caught Amber's eye: a boy was running toward her. He crossed the pasture and staggered to a stop near her, out of breath. She knew him well—he was her childhood friend—and she smiled at him, peaceful and untroubled.

The boy could not return her smile, and looked sadly at her. Reluctantly, he gasped out his message.

"Briette, hurry—I'll stay with your brother and mind the sheep, but hurry, run! Your mother . . . She's not doing well."

Amber thought her heart would stop. Everything

collapsed around her. Mist floated before her eyes. Gripped by fear, she felt cold in the scorching sun. She could not move.

"Briette! Run! Go! You haven't much time—run, Briette!"

His voice reached Amber as if from far away. Her mind reeled as the whole world seemed to quake. With a desperate effort, she pulled herself together. She had to get there before it was too late. She scrambled to her feet and set out at a run. *Fast. Fast.* Tears blurred her vision, streaming down her face, but she never felt them. Only one thing still mattered—to prevent the unpreventable: her mother's death. That must not happen!

Her mother was very ill and had been suffering greatly for months now. No medicine could save her. But she mustn't die! Amber ran her frantic race against time and death. She could already see the village, and she ran and ran, unaware of how tired she was. She reached the village square at last, and then her house, where she burst into the single room, so dark and silent, and rushed to her mother's bedside. Kneeling, Amber took her mother's hand, squeezing it with all her might, cradling it, feeling its warmth. Her mother lay moaning on the bed, a mere straw pallet. She was already deathly pale, and her face expressed unspeakable suffering. Her mind seemed to be wandering.

"You're here, Amber, you're here," she murmured weakly in a quavering voice. "I have only a few days left to live," she went on after a moment, "and I will have fulfilled my mission."

"Mama, don't talk anymore. It wears you out."

"No. Only a few days. But I won't make it. I'm too sick."

Amber struggled to hold back her tears. As always, she had to be strong. Gripping her mother's hand even more tightly, she felt as though she were drowning in despair.

"Mama, Mama," she stammered helplessly, "everything will be all right."

She tried to believe her own words, wanted to convince herself they were true. More than anything, she would have liked all this to be only a nightmare and hoped she would awaken as usual, snuggled up with her sisters and brothers. But no, the nightmare went on and on, a horrible truth Amber did not want to face. She was used to conjuring up a dreamworld whenever the one in which she lived became too cruel. She would hide there, refusing to suffer. But her imagination was fragile, giving way easily to reality. Then the pain became even more intense, as if to take revenge on the girl who had tried to deny it.

"Amber . . . I must stay alive. A little while longer. A few days, only a few days. Soon I'll be at rest."

Amber trembled at the sound of her mother's voice and realized that both their faces were wet with tears. Her mother groaned, almost resigned to her fate, but Amber was not yet ready to give up. She would fight on until the end, even when all hope was gone and there was no future left. True to her nature, she was still looking for a gleam of light in the darkness.

"Amber. Amber. My mission, Amber . . ."

"Hush, Mama. Hush. Don't talk anymore. It's tiring for you, in your condition. But don't worry, you'll pull through. It's nothing more serious than a cold. You'll be up and about tomorrow. You'll see, it's a sunny day. The cherries are ripe. The grass is greener than ever. There isn't a single cloud. The sky is so blue! It's worth going outside for. Believe me, tomorrow you'll be better."

Amber's voice broke, and she could barely choke back a sob.

"Amber, I only want to live a few more days. After that, it doesn't matter to me, but I have my mission, and it's still too soon. If I die, who will do what must be done? Amber, it's my duty to stay alive for a few more days. But I won't be able to—I haven't got the strength."

"Mama, calm down. It's important to rest."

"Amber, when my last day arrives, and it's so close now . . . promise you'll believe me. Even if my words are those of a weak, sick woman . . . promise me."

"I'll promise you anything you want, Mama, but now, stop talking, it's wearing you out."

Thinking her mother was delirious with fever, Amber did not take seriously anything she said.

3

OPAL

"IF I WERE HER GUARDIAN, I'D BE WORRIED about her. She's so secretive, so fond of solitude. . . ."

"You're right. She isn't normal! She hasn't got a single friend, and no one can figure out what goes on inside her head."

"She never smiles, it's unbelievable! And her downcast eyes . . . She has a way of being so cold and stubborn—it's disturbing."

"Yes, there's something very unusual and puzzling about her. It makes you uneasy."

The two gossips stopped chatting at the approach of one of the oldest women in the village. No one knew her age, not even she herself: she no longer had the strength or the desire to count the years. Nobody paid attention to what she said anymore; people often thought she talked nonsense, but in spite of appearances, she was still lucid. Her back was bent, her face marked with a wrinkle for every path she had ever taken in life, and each of her slow steps seemed to cost her considerable effort.

After a moment, she reached the two busybodies. She could not possibly have overheard them, because they had stopped talking as she drew near. They greeted her with hypocritical smiles. The old woman stared at them contemptuously. "Of course Opal isn't normal," she said firmly. "Yes, she is different. And she will accomplish things you would never even dare imagine."

With that, she hobbled slowly away. Speechless, the two village women noticed for the first time how dignified and strong-willed Opal's great-great-aunt was.

For as far back as she could remember, Opal had always lived with Great-great-aunt Eugénia and her daughter, who bore the same first name but was called Gina, to distinguish her from her mother. Opal had never known any home besides the luxurious house where they all three lived. In spite of her advanced age, Great-aunt Gina was still a lively woman. She had always managed the housekeeping as well as Opal's education and had taught the girl everything she knew about literature and history. She had also passed on to the child her knowledge of plants and remedies.

Opal was a diligent and thoughtful student who never asked herself whether she liked learning things, but her tastes, feelings, and ideas were all rather vague. Many boys found the girl beautiful, but she was as cold as marble, and her stony indifference rapidly cooled any ardor she inspired. She was frail, a trifle too thin, with milky skin, and had the face of a china doll whose delicate features made her seem fragile. There was an absent look in her large, pale blue eyes, which sometimes appeared almost gray. Thick curls fell about her shoulders, accentuating her ethereal appearance. Her hair was blond, each strand seemingly of a different shade: flaxen, honey-colored, ash-blond. . . . She usually walked with her head down, staring at the ground. She wasn't shy, but did not care for the company of others. No one really loved her, and she didn't really love anyone either. Although Eugénia and Gina showered her with attention, she had never known true warmth or affection.

Opal was looking for something to draw. She drew a great deal, neatly and precisely, striving to create an exact copy of her subject. She had once heard that art was a different way of looking at reality, but that didn't mean much to her. She liked to reproduce what she saw, and above all, she wanted to excel, so she was constantly hunting for ever more difficult subjects. That day, she had rummaged through her entire room without finding anything that suited her. On a sudden impulse she went to Gina's room, which she never entered even though she had permission to do so. Once inside the room, she shivered and felt as if she were doing something wrong. This is ridiculous, she thought. I'm allowed to be in here! Gina has gone to the village, but if she were here, she'd be perfectly happy for me to come into her room!

Still, Opal felt ill at ease. She crossed the room and sat down on the bed. There was a wealth of complicated objects in the room she could have chosen to draw, but, moved by a strange desire, she tried to open the drawer of the bedside table—only to find it locked.

Opal was amazed at what she had just done. She had never felt such curiosity before. "Something's happening," she muttered. "I can't seem to control myself." The peculiar feeling persisted. "What is it about this room . . . ?" she wondered. Then, as if following some instinct, she pulled down the bedspread, looked under the pillow, and found a tiny key, which she slipped into the lock of the bedside table. Then she stopped and took a deep breath. What am I doing? she thought—and quickly opened the drawer.

The first thing she saw was a large, heavy book, its title written in gold letters: *The Prophecy*. Opening the volume to the pages indicated by a bookmark, Opal read a few lines, found them uninteresting, then slammed the book shut. She tried to make herself see reason: what was she expecting to find? Annoyed, she continued searching through the drawer and came across a black velvet purse. There's something inside, and it's calling out to me, she thought, untying the drawstrings. Inside was a solid object, warm to the touch. Opal had never felt this way before—it was as if she were experiencing a different reality. She took out the object and examined it: it was a precious stone—a gem—round, of modest size, and a very pale green color, glossy and smooth. Opal held it tightly. "It isn't a stone," she murmured to herself; "it's something else, something powerful. A message." She did not know why she was so certain of this, but she was sure she was close to the truth. She was in a trance, as though she were spell-bound, oblivious to everything around her. She felt that there was a connection, an almost palpable link between her and the stone, which was trying to tell her something.

Opal tightened her grip—and the stone grew cold, its surface roughening. A vast feeling of emptiness over-whelmed the girl, plunging her into melancholy. In a few seconds the stone was icy cold. Shaking, Opal was forced to let go of it. The connection she had sensed was brutally broken. She felt her forehead: it was burning. "I should never have opened the drawer," she reflected ruefully. "I wasn't supposed to discover this stone." She knew this, felt it with certainty. Hastily slipping the stone back into the purse, she returned it to its hiding place. She took the book lying on the bed and replaced it in the drawer as well, which she locked. She then concealed the key under the pillow and carefully smoothed out the bedspread. Just in time.

Her great-aunt Gina entered the room.

"Opal! Is everything all right? You look so pale. . . ."

"I'm fine. I was just looking for something to draw."

Although Opal tried to appear calm, she could not hide the tremor of distress in her voice.

At the very moment Opal touched the stone, he had started violently. A sneer twisted his evil face. Using his powers of telepathy, he immediately summoned the Council of Twelve. When he joined them in their vast council chamber, they all lowered their eyes in fear at his approach. His voice was chilling. "What we had ceased to hope for has at last happened. I was able to intercept something of great interest."

The twelve members of the Council understood what

he meant, and their morose expressions betrayed a glimmer of satisfaction.

"Should we command the Knights of the Order to bring her to us?" asked a councilor.

"No," came the curt reply. "I have a better idea."

"Which one of them is it?" asked another councilor eagerly.

"The third one. Perhaps the most dangerous. She has within her powers that are as yet unawakened—I felt this when she made contact with her Stone. This happened too soon, in her case, and we can be glad of that. Another few days, and we would have lost the advantage!"

"Which Stone is it?"

"The opal, the purest of the three, but I would also say the most fragile, now that I know everything about her. . . ."

Paris: Present Day

Dr. Arnon took off his glasses and beckoned the nurse.

"She seems to be resting peacefully, don't you think?"

He pointed to the bed where a sickly child was lying, apparently in a deep sleep, but the girl's face had a waxen pallor.

"She hasn't got much time left," he added. "Not more than a couple of days, in my opinion. You haven't grown fond of her, I hope?"

The nurse shrugged resignedly. "No, not really. Besides, she's already suffered so much. . . ."

The doctor carefully cleaned his glasses in silence for a few moments before observing gravely, "In any case, there's nothing more we can do for her. She has definitely stopped fighting since her parents died."

"She has no other family?"

"No brothers or sisters, just an uncle, who is now her legal guardian. But he hardly knows her. He's the one who pays for her care, with the parents' money."

"A rich family?" inquired the nurse.

"Yes. But that won't save her."

"And this uncle—he never comes to see her?"

"No," sighed the doctor. "Apart from one young man, once, no one has ever come to see her."

The nurse studied the frail form lying in the bed. She had no right to let herself grow so attached to someone, so close to the end. She turned her face away.

"You must have already heard more than your fair share of sad stories," said Dr. Arnon softly, "and you'll hear a great many more, believe me."

"I know."

"Well, then, come with me, let's forget all this. How about some coffee?"

The nurse nodded. Without a backward glance, she followed the doctor out into the hall, closing the door behind them. Now the only sound in the room was the wheezing of the machine that kept the patient alive.

4

THE PROPHECY OF THE STONES

JADE LOOKED STUNNING IN THE BLUE-GREEN gown that had been specially made for her in the county of Tyrel. Her green eyes sparkled even more than usual, and her face glowed with pleasure. She moved about the ball-room like a queen among her subjects. All eyes were on her: she was the star of the evening, and she was in seventh heaven. She danced, chatted with her guests, and laughed to her heart's content. The party was even more of a success than she had hoped. The refreshments were delicious, the decor was sumptuous, and the splendor of it all was dazzling. This, she thought, is perfect happiness.

Against all expectations, Amber's mother had managed to cling to life, and each extra minute she won from death was a small miracle. Ever since the moment when Amber had raced to her bedside, her end had no longer been in doubt, yet still she lived on. The girl stayed with her day and night, without sleeping, eating only a few morsels of bread when she felt hungry. Today her mother was worse. She had been unconscious since that morning. Fortunately, she was still breathing, but with great difficulty. . . .

The sun had already set. Her mother simply had to wake from this dreadful coma! "She's going to live, she's going to live," Amber reassured herself stubbornly. "There's always hope, always! As long as she keeps breathing. . . ."

"Amber . . ." Startled by her mother's hoarse voice, Amber realized that she had regained consciousness.

"Mama! Oh, Mama . . ."

"I'm going to make it, Amber, I'm going to make it. What time is it?"

Amber told her, cheered to find her mother more or less lucid, even though her eyes had begun to glaze over.

"I only have to hang on a little longer and I will have carried out my mission. Soon I'll be at peace."

"Mama!"

"You'll have to be strong and accept what you are destined to accomplish."

"Rest, Mama."

"Surely you haven't forgotten? Today you are fourteen years old."

"It had completely slipped my mind."

"Amber, I wish you a happy birthday."

* * *

Ever since Opal had found the stone, everything had gone badly. She had trouble sleeping and had been running a persistent temperature. She'd said nothing of this to Eugénia and Gina, fearing they would discover the cause of her illness, which her instincts told her was connected to the stone. She had secretly concocted medicines from plants, but nothing had helped. She was still running a temperature and had violent fits of nausea. She was afraid of giving herself away, of revealing that she had found that strange stone among Gina's belongings. "I didn't mean to do anything wrong," she kept telling herself. Since her discovery, she had not spoken unless it was absolutely necessary, and she'd become even more withdrawn. What possessed me that day? she wondered. I really don't understand. . . .

"Opal, a little more cake?" asked Gina, forcing herself to smile.

With a start, Opal emerged from her reverie.

"No, thank you," she replied coldly.

Although she knew that her great-aunt was trying to ease the tension in the air, Opal could not shrug off her guilt over what she had done.

Gina was so aggravated that her patience and tact failed her.

"For goodness' sake, it's your birthday!" she exclaimed in exasperation. "Eugénia and I tried to make everything nice, but you—you couldn't care less!"

"Gina—" pleaded Eugénia.

"Let me finish," continued Gina, growing angrier and angrier. "Opal, would a smile or a simple thank-you be too much to ask for after everything we've done for you? What have you got where your heart should be—a stone?"

Opal glanced sharply at her great-aunt. *Speaking of stones, you owe me an explanation!* she wanted to shout, but she remained silent, and bowed her head.

As he watched Jade, the Duke of Divulyon kept asking himself bitterly, "Why? Why her? Why now? Why must this be?" He knew his questions were useless and would change nothing. He himself was powerless, unable to affect or prevent anything whatsoever. Yet an inner voice kept tormenting him and cursing that prophecy. He would have liked to silence this increasingly painful voice, but he could not; he could think only of Jade. Sadly, he slipped his hand into the pocket of his elegant jacket and grasped the black velvet purse.

Amber's eyes were red, her hair tangled and dirty, her lips

dry, her every muscle stiff and sore. She neither knew nor cared. She had to watch over her mother. Her brothers and sisters had all been sent to stay in other households. She was the eldest, however, and was duty-bound to remain at her mother's bedside. The room was lit by the feeble gleam of a candle, its flame wavering and threatening to go out at any moment. Like happiness, she thought. *The other day I was sitting contentedly in that meadow, and all of a sudden, life has become a ghastly nightmare.*

"Amber," moaned her mother. "I'm in pain . . . such pain. . . ."

"Mama, don't talk, save your strength. Rest. Sleep, it's late. Soon you'll be much better."

"Yes, when it's all over . . . when I'm not suffering anymore . . . when I'm on the other side."

"Mama, I beg of you, be brave!"

"I'm almost eager . . . to go . . . rejoin my husband. . . . To forget the sorrow, the poverty, the feeling of having . . . done nothing . . . with my life."

"Mama! None of that is true! You've done so many things. Look at me—you made me, and without you, I'd be nothing!"

"If you only knew . . ."

*　　*　　*

After Gina had recovered her composure, an oppressive silence reigned in the room. Around the table, they avoided meeting one another's eyes. Eugénia and Gina consulted their watches nervously at regular intervals. Ordinarily impassive, Opal could not bear the tension. She wanted to go and shut herself up in her room, but she stayed miserably in her chair, feeling dizzy with fever. After half an hour, Eugénia gave a little cough.

"It's time," she announced.

Surprised, Opal stared at her.

"Time for what?" she asked uneasily.

With a sorrowful smile, Eugénia acquiesced. "There is still one hour left, but I think we had better begin without delay."

"Begin what?" asked Opal in bewilderment.

Gina cleared her throat discreetly. After apologizing to Opal for losing her temper, she looked at Eugénia and repeated, "Yes, it's time."

Then Gina placed an object on the table. Opal turned pale as her blood ran cold. The black velvet purse!

Gina knows that I found it, that I searched through her drawer, she thought in a panic, and she wants me to explain myself.

Strangely enough, however, Gina did not seem angry.

"It's a long story," she said, "and we cannot tell you all of it. You must discover the most important part for yourself. Do not open this purse right away. In fact, don't open it before midnight, because there might be serious consequences."

Opal listened in confusion, but having already felt the power of the stone, she did not doubt the truth of what her great-aunt said.

"It's already quite late," reflected the Duke of Divulyon. "Only half an hour left." He made his way toward his daughter, who was talking to her guests.

"Jade," he said softly.

She turned toward him with a radiant smile.

"Papa! I haven't seen you all evening. The party's going well, isn't it?"

The Duke of Divulyon felt a lump in his throat.

"Yes, the party is a great success," he managed to agree, "and you look lovely." His words brought another smile to the girl's face. "Jade, you have to leave your guests now. I must speak with you."

Taken aback, Jade protested. "What? But it's my party, Papa! My birthday! Whatever it is you have to tell me, it can't be that important!"

"Yes, actually, it is."

Jade did not hide her irritation and disappointment. Reluctantly, she took leave of her guests and followed her father, who led her to one of the private chambers of the palace, where he locked the door behind them. Annoyed, Jade sat down. The Duke of Divulyon sighed deeply. He had to begin, so that at midnight . . .

"Jade," he said, "I am not your father."

Amber's mother summoned the little strength she had left.

"Amber—I can tell that you don't believe me . . . but I am not delirious! Your real mother entrusted you to me when you were born, so that I might protect you until you were fourteen years old. Amber, I have loved you as though you were my own child."

Amber could not believe this. It was simply impossible. Her mother brought something out from beneath the folds of her tunic: a black velvet purse. She held it out to the girl. Intrigued, Amber took it.

"Do not open this purse before midnight. It is yours, and the contents as well. Your mother gave it to me . . . with you."

Amber felt her heart sink.

* * *

"There are two other girls," said Gina solemnly. "Your enemies. Never trust them. They, too, were handed over to others at their birth, to ensure their safety."

"Their safety?" cried Opal. "What is threatening us?"

"You mustn't know," said Eugénia quickly. "Not yet."

Opal sat quietly. She knew intuitively that everything would soon change, but she remained calm. She glanced outside at the dark and peaceful night. She was not afraid of the coming day, or of any day to come. She had only one question.

"Why did you wait so long before telling me all this?"

Jade leaped from her armchair in astonishment, shouting, "What?" Then she began screaming, "I don't believe it! I don't believe it!" Her cheeks were crimson and her eyes flashed with rage. It took her several minutes to recover a semblance of self-control. Somehow she knew that she must take this situation very seriously: her father—or rather, the Duke of Divulyon, whom she had believed to be her father—would never lie. Now she was pacing around the room, fuming with suppressed fury.

"I couldn't care less about this velvet purse and those other two idiots! I couldn't care less about my mother who abandoned me at birth, and I couldn't care less about knowing what you don't want to tell me!"

The duke tried to reason with her: "Jade . . ."

"I mean it! Why should this whole ridiculous story come crashing down on my head? I didn't ask for any of it!"

"Jade," interrupted the duke. "There's more."

"Now what! Another little surprise along the same lines? Well, no thanks, I can do without it!"

"At midnight, you are to meet the other two girls under a particular tree, which I will tell you how to find. You will not return until you have confronted many trials. Above all, do not reveal your identity to anyone, and keep the velvet purse carefully hidden. You will encounter many enemies along the way. Learn to recognize them and to be always on your guard."

"What?" said Jade, almost choking. "But I don't want to go away! I don't want anything to do with a future as horrible as that! I want to stay here! Please, Papa—I want to stay here. . . ." Jade burst into tears.

"Jade," whispered the Duke of Divulyon, "I love you more than I would have loved my own daughter."

"Now you must go. There is also a little money in the purse. You'll be all right, Amber."

"Mama, I don't want to leave you! You need me!"

"Not anymore, Amber. The tree is close by, between the village and the palace of Divulyon, in a meadow that belongs to no one and where flowers bloom all year round. It's one of the last enchanted places in the Realm."

"I know where it is, Mama," said Amber, whose heart was beating so fast, so hard, that it hurt.

"The tree is tall, with leaves that are always green, and fruit that is always ripe. There you will meet your enemies. Go, Amber. You must go. And so must I. . . ."

"Mama, I can't leave. You are and always will be my mother. I won't leave you. Not now."

"Be strong," replied her mother faintly. Then she closed her eyes and smiled.

"Mama, I'm staying," insisted Amber. She looked at her mother. "Mama! Mama!" she screamed, panic-stricken. "Mama!"

Her mother seemed to be sleeping peacefully, but she was no longer breathing. She had left this world, quietly, serenely, with the uncertain image of a freer place.

"Mama, Mama," moaned Amber, in an agony of pain and sorrow. She kissed her mother's forehead. Now she, too, had to set out into the unknown. I will be strong, she promised herself. Then, her heart broken, she disappeared into the night.

5

THREE ENEMIES MEET

UNDER A STARRY SKY, IN THE FOREVER FLOWER-
ing meadow, beneath the tree perpetually wreathed in
leaves, the girls looked at one another. They had met a few
minutes earlier, but had not yet spoken a single word. Each
one studied the others, all thinking the same thing: We are
enemies. Jade scrutinized the other two with disdain. Her
head high, an imperious look in her eye, she wanted them
to understand perfectly that they were of no importance to
her. A peasant and a commoner: I'm not impressed, she
thought smugly. But deep down she was extremely upset,
and determined not to reveal her feelings. She watched
Amber, her face crumpled, weeping quietly. Poor girl,
you're pathetic! thought Jade. She noted the humble clothing, dirty face, and hair spattered with mud. Jade felt no
hatred for Amber, even though she was supposed to be
her enemy. Then her eyes met Opal's—and she stiffened
immediately. She's not my type, she decided. We are
already and always will be enemies! Who does she think

she is, staring at me like that? She's getting on my nerves!

Actually, Opal was gazing almost absentmindedly at Jade. She didn't usually make hasty judgments, but she'd quickly realized that she and that snooty-looking girl were not going to get along.

As for Amber, she was too distraught over her mother's death to be thinking clearly. Try as she might, she could not stop crying. She glanced a few times at her two enemies, but was too wretched to do more than watch them without forming any definite opinions. She remembered scraps of phrases and envisioned herself at her mother's side: *Two other girls . . . your enemies . . . a meadow . . . people say it's enchanted . . . the purse . . . before midnight . . .*

Just one thing roused Amber from her thoughts. She made an effort to rise for an instant above the misery that weighed her down, and she recalled her mother's last words: *Be strong. Be strong!* She had to struggle against this suffering, to return to the present moment. Then she wiped away her tears and broke the silence.

"The black velvet purse! What time is it?"

Astonished that Amber had mentioned the mysterious purse, Jade and Opal looked at her with curiosity—and even though they would never have admitted it, they were pleased that someone had finally spoken up.

"What time is it?" repeated Amber.

Jade looked at her watch, proudly showing off its diamond-studded band.

"It's ten minutes past midnight," she announced haughtily.

Amber looked at Jade. She did not envy the girl her fine clothes, precious jewels, and flashing eyes, but in spite of herself, she admired the strength she seemed to radiate. Then Amber considered Opal. Motionless, emotionless, Opal possessed a coolness that Amber found impressive, considering the circumstances.

"My name is Amber. I asked you what time it was because my mother gave me a black velvet purse that I wasn't supposed to open before midnight."

"Me too!" exclaimed Jade. "Except in my case, it was my father who gave one to me—at least the man I believed to be my father for fourteen years . . . but isn't . . . anymore."

"Really?" marveled Amber. "My mother wasn't my real mother, either. I will always remember her as my mother, but . . . she just died. . . ."

Amber was overcome once more by grief. Opal, who had been silent until then, now spoke with unusual gentleness.

"Amber, I'm so sorry for you. It must be terrible to have all this happening to you in one day."

Amber nodded, somewhat comforted to hear a kind word. "And you—did you receive a purse, too?"

Opal nodded.

"At least the three of us have that in common. Well, my name is Opal." Then she added, in a harsh voice, "And apparently we are enemies—although I don't know why."

"That's right," agreed Jade sternly, looking at Opal.

"I don't believe that," said Amber. "How could we be enemies when we don't even know one another? After all, nothing's forcing us!"

"That's not true," insisted Jade. "My so-called father, the Duke of Divulyon, never lies. He said we're enemies, so we are."

"Your adoptive father is the Duke of Divulyon?" asked Amber.

"Yes. Until this evening, I was Jade of Divulyon. Now, I don't know who I am anymore. Not only do I know nothing about my family, but it seems I mustn't tell anyone my name because I have enemies everywhere."

"I was told the same thing," confessed Amber.

"Me, too," chimed in Opal.

"So what? Where does that get me?" Jade said huffily. "I don't know where I'm supposed to go, I don't know what

I'm supposed to do! And why am I here with you? Does anyone know what we're doing here?"

"No," replied Amber and Opal in chorus.

"What a mess we're in!" remarked Jade. "And why am I saying 'we'? You're my enemies, so there isn't any 'we'! Why should we stay together?"

"The three of us are stronger together than alone, especially if we have enemies in common," replied Amber. "Obviously, *they* are our greatest danger, right? As for me, I don't mean you any harm—I don't even know who you are."

"What if we opened these black purses?" said Jade firmly. "Perhaps there's something important inside."

"Good idea," agreed Amber.

"We're still enemies!" Opal reminded them.

Busily opening their velvet purses, the other girls didn't reply. Opal opened hers as well, unable to resist the desire to see the stone again. Amber stifled a cry when she found a stone the color of autumn, a dark, translucent orange with tints of red and chestnut: she felt as if she were holding a sunset. She felt a little more at peace, and although her grief did not disappear, it became less searing, giving way to a comforting warmth. Amber held tightly to the stone, which she could distinctly sense was not really a stone at all.

At that same moment, Jade was examining her stone, which was deep green, pure and intense. "A piece of jade," she murmured. The color was so rich, so striking, that she marveled at it for a few moments. Then, without knowing why, she, too, gripped the stone tightly.

Meanwhile, Opal examined the stone that had brought on her fever. This time she noticed its bluish, pearly reflections, which gave the pale green a complex and fascinating sparkle, as if the stone were flecked with glitter. Instinctively, Opal, too, grasped the stone with all her strength. The three girls felt their anxieties slowly ebb away. Everything inside them relaxed, and they began to have pleasant thoughts. They forgot that they were in the meadow, that they had been more or less driven from their homes, and that it was dark; they forgot everything, and felt a new freedom surge through them. All three girls closed their eyes at exactly the same time, and a bond formed between them. Their Stones seemed to communicate, to blend, to merge into one another, and the girls followed them. They felt as if they were one being and a thousand different beings at the same time. It didn't really matter: either way, they formed a whole, complete and indestructible. An image gradually appeared in their minds—an unknown, complicated symbol. It hovered for a while, long enough to pervade their memories, then faded away.

The three girls emerged slowly from their altered state. There was no doubt: they were to follow the sign they had been given, this strange symbol, composed of spirals, curves, and arabesques. The Stones had spoken to them by delivering this picture to them. The girls looked at one another with new and almost friendly eyes.

"These are not stones," observed Amber, her voice still dreamy and faraway. "They're something else. Something to help us. I really think so, don't you?"

"Yes," agreed Jade. "It was as if they were telling us what we must do: we must understand and seek out this symbol."

"It's the middle of the night," cut in Opal. "We'll see about that tomorrow. For now we have to find somewhere to sleep."

"Here!" suggested Amber.

"Here?" squeaked Jade indignantly. "I refuse to sleep anywhere but in a manor, in a spacious room, in a soft bed."

"Jade," said Amber in her gentle voice, "it's late. We're not going to walk for hours to reach the next manor house. What would we say? 'Yoo-hoo, it's us! It's three o'clock in the morning and we'd like to sleep here. Of course, we won't tell you our names, or anything about ourselves, because you might be our enemies, and anyway, it's completely acceptable to turn up at people's homes at three A.M. wanting to stay overnight, isn't it?'"

Jade glared at Amber.

"I will not sleep here," she repeated, pronouncing each syllable slowly and distinctly. She tried to come up with a convincing argument. "Besides, if we were told to leave and watch out for unknown enemies, it's because it must be dangerous around here."

"Not necessarily," objected Opal.

"Yes, it is!" insisted Jade. "We're not supposed to turn back, and we're certainly not to stay where we are. We must find out what this symbol means as quickly as possible."

Still dubious, Amber thought for a moment, then announced, "I know a small farm about an hour from here. It's very remote: an old woman lives there alone with her cats and her chickens. We could sleep in the stable. She'll never know we're there. We'll be safe."

"A stable! What next?" fumed Jade. "My dress will get all creased. And anyway, we're not going to find the meaning of the symbol in a stable."

"Why not? The old woman knows me, and even if she doesn't trust anyone anymore, she'll answer my questions.

In the morning, I'll go and see her as if I were paying a polite visit."

"And you'll tell her about us? Forget it!" said Jade curtly.

"Of course not! I'll pretend I've just arrived, and I won't mention you. I'll tell her that my mother died and that she drew this symbol before she passed away. I'll draw it for her and ask her if she's seen it before."

"Basically, you're going to feed her a big fat lie!" crowed Jade. "I like that! But what if, afterward, the old lady talks about it? What if our enemies find out we're looking for the symbol? Or what if the old lady is our enemy?"

"There's no danger of that," promised Amber. "She's not completely in her right mind anymore, and she lives cut off from the world. Listen, we're wasting time—shall we go there?"

"No, no, no!" Jade stamped her foot angrily. "I don't want to! It's out of the question. Look at my jewels! Look at the way I'm dressed! Think about it—can't you understand that I'm not a peasant girl who sleeps in stables!"

"We're going," Amber decided.

"No!" said Jade stubbornly. She couldn't bear having anyone stand up to her.

"Opal, what do you think?" asked Amber.

As was her wont, Opal had stayed out of the argument.

"I agree, let's go," she replied. "And if Miss High-and-Mighty doesn't want to come, she can just stay here."

"I am not high-and-mighty!" cried Jade furiously. "And to prove it, I'll come, too!" she blurted out.

She bit her lip, irritated at giving in like that to someone else's wishes. And to think she was going to have to sleep in a stable! But her pride prevented her from going back on what she'd said.

Opal rolled her eyes. "So, finally, you've changed your mind? We really could have done without all this!"

Unable to think of a stinging reply, Jade shot her a withering look.

"Enough!" demanded Amber firmly, stepping between the other two girls. "We have to leave."

Without protesting further, Jade and Opal fell in behind Amber. They walked swiftly, taking care not to dawdle, and said nothing more, lost in their thoughts. Jade tried to find a way to humiliate Opal. That village girl, thinking she was above Jade! It was intolerable! Jade trembled with suppressed rage. And on top of that, she would have to sink to sleeping on a farm. She felt like screaming, like hitting Opal, but the night was already too dark, and what lay before her was too uncertain for her to lash out like that.

For her part, Opal was wondering about the symbol they had to decipher, their mysterious enemies lurking in the shadows, and what the future would bring. She felt something awakening inside her—an interest in her new existence. She had been relieved of a burden: for her, leaving home had been like escaping from a prison, even though it had been a comfortable one. For too long now, she had felt trapped in a boring daily routine, in the certainty that tomorrow would bring nothing different. Her present freedom opened the door to a new life for her. She was going to discover the world, confront a danger she knew was not far away. She was neither excited nor afraid. She was curious: at last she would discover what "living" really meant.

As for Amber, she could think only of her mother. She saw once more her protective smile and heard her kindly voice, her merry laugh. She remembered the tender moments they had shared, and in her mind's eye she beheld her mother's plain face, marked by so many sorrows and too few joys. Her mother had lost her husband, carried off by a terrible illness, and she had never truly recovered from that blow. Amber had had to weather that loss as well, but it had been easier for her, as she had never really loved that boorish and brutal father who'd paid no attention to her at all. And she had been so young when he died, she hadn't actually understood what was happening. Today, however, everything was devastatingly clear, and now she had to bear this atrocious suffering. A few tears trickled down her cheeks. She could still hear her mother's voice: *Be strong. Be strong . . .*

Jade and Opal have more character than I do, she thought. They're strong by nature, while I—I have to force myself to be like that. I must put up a fight. If I can convince myself that I'm capable of winning—then perhaps I will succeed. With that, Amber quickened her pace. They had almost reached the farm. The three girls had crossed wide plains, fields, green meadows, and a few gentle hills. Behind one of these hills, remote and lonely, the derelict farm now appeared. "Follow me," said Amber in a whisper.

They entered a dark and tumbledown stable that had not been used in a long time. Beams sagged, cobwebs had invaded every corner, and the straw gave off a sickening smell. None of this bothered Amber: she lay down on the ground, yawned, and said good night. After a slight hesitation, Opal did the same, stretching out near Amber. Appalled by the place, Jade resolved not to join them.

"I will not sleep," she announced. "I will *not* sleep. . . ." Seeing that her words elicited no response, she added, "Oh, don't you worry about me! I'll just stand here. Really, it's no problem."

No reply. Suddenly, she had a bright idea. She went over to Amber, who had already closed her eyes, and shook her energetically. Amber stifled a cry of fright. Seeing Jade's face bending over her, she asked what was going on.

"Give me your clothes," answered Jade.

"What? Excuse me, what did you say?"

"We've got to swap clothes!"

"What on earth is she thinking?" mumbled Opal.

"I didn't ask your opinion," snapped Jade.

Then she turned back to Amber and said urgently, "Hurry up! I have a plan. Hand me your clothes. I'll lend you my dress. But be careful with it! Don't damage it, don't crease it, and *don't* get it dirty."

"Or else it's the end of the world," sighed Opal sarcastically.

"For once, you're right," Jade shot back in the same tone. "Amber—quick!"

"If you insist," said Amber, giving in, "but I'd really like to know why."

"Never mind that," said Jade.

Then, as if struck by a new idea, she added, "No, actually, this is fine. I'll stay as I am."

"But—"

"See you tomorrow!" replied Jade merrily.

"Tomorrow?" repeated Amber, now thoroughly confused. "Jade, wait!"

But Jade ignored her and slipped out of the stable.

6

AN UNWANTED GUEST

CROSSING A DESOLATE GARDEN WHERE BRAMBLES and nettles grew wild, Jade strode confidently toward the farmhouse. She rapped boldly several times on the rickety wooden front door, shouting, "Open up!" There was no response.

The peasant woman must be sleeping, Jade thought, and she knocked on the door again, twice as loudly this time. For a few minutes, she kept pounding away. Since no one had let her in and the woman was obviously still asleep, Jade tried something else: she let out a prolonged, high-pitched scream.

Amber and Opal heard this back in the stable and looked at each other in astonishment: what was she up to? Jade stopped for a moment, then screamed again, even more shrilly. That'll wake up the old woman, Jade thought. It certainly did—she looked terrified when she opened the door, and she was still only half-awake. Before her stood a girl, extremely elegantly dressed and adorned with priceless jewels. I must be dreaming, concluded the peasant woman. But Jade spoke up calmly in a voice that was far from dreamlike.

"Good evening. My name is Jade, and I want to sleep in your house, because your stable is most uncomfortable, and I do not intend to sleep out in the open. It's not exactly my style, you see."

The old woman was flabbergasted, her eyes as wide as saucers.

"I'm used to luxury," continued Jade, "but a clean bed would suit me well enough. I was driven from my palace, so I must make the best of things. Well, show me to my bedroom now, because I'm quite tired."

The woman shut the door. The girl is mad, she thought. But Jade began doggedly hammering away, yelling, "Open up!" Although the woman was deeply suspicious, she was curious to learn more, and slowly opened the door again. Jade looked her solemnly straight in the eye.

"I had planned," she announced evenly, "to wear peasant clothing and to make you believe I was a poor girl fleeing dreadful ill-treatment. You would have welcomed me immediately. But I decided to be frank with you, so do not disappoint me. I really am on the run, and even though I don't look poor, as of about an hour ago, I am."

The old woman shut the door again. She had never taken anyone in, and this girl was so strange! But she obviously wasn't lying; her voice had the ring of truth about it and her expression was perfectly sincere. The woman opened her door a third time, just a crack.

"Why are you running away?" she asked sharply.

"Not for the fun of it, believe me! I was forced to, and I have to say even *I* don't really understand why. You don't think I would ever have come to a farm as wretched as yours unless I had to, do you? And don't slam the door in my face again, it's not very polite and it's extremely annoying. Anyway, I shan't budge until you let me in."

Jade's hostile behavior left the old woman feeling flustered. This girl had something powerful and unusual about her.

"Come in," sighed the woman. "Follow me."

Jade almost smiled in triumph. The woman led her down a narrow hall to a tiny room, modestly furnished, but cool and pleasant.

"It was my son's room," she said sadly.

"It'll do," replied Jade.

"In any case, it's the only bedroom, besides mine."

"Fine. But I obviously need a proper nightgown."

"I'm not running a hotel," grumbled the woman.

She left the room without another word, returning in a few minutes to hand Jade a white nightgown yellowed with age, cut from material of middling quality.

"This isn't my palace, but it isn't the stable, either," said the girl by way of thanks.

"Make yourself at home," said her hostess grumpily. "Tomorrow, though, you'll be off."

"Oh, only if I feel like it. But don't worry, I can't stay long."

"So much the better! Now, go to sleep and leave me alone. You've got some manners, dragging honest people out of their beds in the middle of the night."

"But I had to! Don't you understand? Your stable is disgusting!"

The old woman gave a faint, fleeting smile. She had long ago forgotten how to smile. For years, she had lived alone, giving in to bitterness as she waited in vain for an end to her misfortunes. At last, someone had come, and even though it was only a willful young girl, bossy and probably mad, a few moments of excitement had done the old woman good.

Without another word, she trudged back to her room and fell asleep at once, with a feeling of satisfaction nestling deep in her heart.

As for Jade, she made a little face and put on the nightgown: it turned out to be a bit large, but warm, and not as scratchy as it looked. She climbed into bed where she tried to stay awake and mull over everything that had happened, but her eyes closed of their own accord.

In the morning, a cockerel crowed as sunlight poured into the bedroom. Jade did not wake up, however, and even slept rather late. When she opened her eyes after her long rest, her first thought was of the mysterious symbol, as if it had filled her dreams. She leaped out of bed and dressed quickly. She had brought with her a small turquoise bag, which she could never do without, and she now took from it a brush. After carefully arranging her hair, she removed her Stone from its black velvet purse. Holding it tight, she thought, "Tell me what I must do."

But nothing happened; the Stone remained a simple piece of jade. Irritated, she put it back in its place. I know perfectly well what I must do, she reflected. And this isn't what's going to help me. She looked around the room. The dirty white walls had nothing on them; there were a few dusty books lined up on a shelf, and a wooden desk stood against the wall near the bed. Jade went over to the desk: there was nothing on it, but the drawers were stuffed with letters. When she tried to read some of them, she couldn't make out the scribbled writing made illegible by the half-faded ink. Sighing, she put the letters back. Deciding that there was nothing of interest in the room, she left, and guided by the voice of the old woman talking to her cats, Jade made her way to the kitchen, which also served as a sitting and dining room.

"There you are," remarked the peasant woman sourly. "Sit down."

Jade took a seat at the rectangular table of solid, rough-hewn wood. "I'm hungry," she announced. "Give me something to eat, and then I'll leave."

The old woman placed a slice of stale black bread in front of her.

"Oh, no!" protested Jade, pushing away the bread. "I want something better. I'm warning you, I won't go until you've served me a proper breakfast."

"Foisting yourself upon me isn't enough for you—you're fussy as well!" cried her hostess.

"Naturally! What do you expect? Run along now and bring me some fried eggs, fresh bread, jam, hot chocolate, and milk."

"Will that be all?"

"No, you're right, that's not all: fix me a basket with enough food for several days. I'm on the run, remember, so

I must look out for myself. I don't want to die of hunger. If that happens, it will be your fault, because you won't have helped me! Hurry up."

"But—"

"Oh, and while you're at it," Jade told the dumbfounded old woman, "bring me a sheet of paper and a pen, too."

"What for?"

"Do you want my death on your conscience?" replied Jade melodramatically.

Realizing that arguing would be useless, the old woman gave in to Jade's demands. She served her a substantial breakfast, and afterward prepared several varied and nourishing cold meals, which she placed in a large basket. While Jade heartily tucked into her breakfast, she watched her hostess bustling about the kitchen. When the basket was ready and Jade had eaten her fill, having devoured everything on the table, she smiled at the woman and asked her again for a pen and paper. Now Jade had to concentrate only on the symbol and its meaning. The old woman cleared the table and brought writing materials. Jade drew the symbol with a steady hand.

"What are you doing?" asked the woman. "You're still not satisfied, you want something else? I've had enough!"

"Everything's fine," Jade assured her. "But come here, I

have something to show you. Tell me what you know about this sign."

The old peasant studied the drawing for a long time, then shook her head.

"I really don't know a thing about it. I can't help you."

"Don't hide anything from me," said Jade in a coaxing tone. "It's imperative that I find out what this symbol means."

"I've never seen it before."

"You're absolutely sure?"

"I couldn't be surer. But I know someone who would know how to decipher it. He lives a few hours from here, in a city called Nathyrnn."

"I've heard of it, of course," Jade said smugly, "but I've never been there. Who is this man?"

"He sells old books. He has traveled a great deal, but . . ."

The old woman fell silent. Jade did not notice how upset she was, and pressed her further.

"Do you know this man well? Can he be trusted? I mean . . . can *I* trust him?"

"He's my son," blurted out the old woman, her voice overcome with sorrow.

"Oh, I see. Why does speaking of him make you cry like this?"

Sure enough, a tear was sliding down the old woman's wrinkled cheek.

"I can't talk about it."

"I've told you my name and I've not hidden from you the fact that I'm in serious danger. Now, it's your turn to trust me. You should know by now that I'm not the kind to give up easily. I'll make you talk to me, because I'm very curious!"

"My son has many enemies, and you might be on their side."

"Don't be silly! I have my own impressive collection of enemies—it seems they're everywhere, and I don't even know who they are! But what do you expect, these days," said Jade flippantly.

"I think I'll have to tell you my son's story or I'll never get rid of you," sighed the woman.

"There's no doubt about that," agreed Jade.

"My son is very special. He has always had a desire to learn: even as a child he loved nature and had such a generous spirit—"

"Oh, spare me the corny details and just tell me what's so special about him."

"We were very poor, much more than we are now," began the old woman, ignoring Jade's rude interruption.

"At sixteen, my son set out to discover the world. He craved freedom and adventure. One night he disappeared, leaving behind a letter of farewell."

"Just one question," interrupted Jade. "What's your son's name?"

"Jean, Jean Losserand. So Jean became a wanderer. He traveled all over the world, brave and alone. He often wrote to me. One day, he returned from a very strange land, the only country in the world not dominated by the Council of Twelve."

"Dominated!" exclaimed Jade. "You're exaggerating. 'Ruled' is more like it."

"The only country that is not *dominated* by the Council of Twelve," insisted the woman. "Under the Council of Twelve, anyone born a peasant will always remain a peasant. Anyone who is weak will be despised and crushed. Anyone who thinks differently will be forced to conform. Anyone trying to step out of line will be beaten back and trampled. Anyone who is creative will be limited to routine copy work. Anyone who is gifted will be compelled to become ordinary. Anyone who revolts will be killed. Anyone who dreams of liberty will be imprisoned immediately. Anyone who—"

"Be quiet!" shouted Jade. "You're talking nonsense.

Anyway, if freedom is forbidden, how could your son be a wanderer?"

"Exactly, just let me continue. I was saying that Jean traveled to the most extraordinary country. 'This place is ruled by no one,' he wrote to me, 'and the people all live as they please.' But not many travelers can cross the magnetic field that surrounds this territory. To cross, you must believe in the beauty of every individual being, in creativity, in freedom. You must believe in a better world, in the magic of each instant, and in fantastic dreams. You must be able to imagine the unimaginable. Only then can you enter this land. That is why it is inaccessible to the Council of Twelve."

"What's inside this country? What is it called?" asked Jade.

"It's called Fairytale. Magic creatures and warmhearted people live there. . . . But I can't tell you more about them, because I've never been there. You'll have to ask my son. I only know all this because of his letters. He told me that any child may enter this land, because what is unreal to adults is real to a child."

"What did your son do there?"

"What did he do? He helped people, he had unbelievable adventures, risking his life and battling against evil forces."

"It sounds like something out of a storybook!" said Jade incredulously.

"Anything can happen in Fairytale. But my son began to miss his own country and, turning his back on the glory and happiness of Fairytale, he decided to come home. Not many people just decide to leave like that. Some simply stop believing in everything that surrounds them and wake up one day back in their own beds. They can never return to Fairytale. But with Jean, it was different. He simply wanted to see his childhood home again. Now, it so happened that the Council of Twelve decided to outlaw traveling. Jean was arrested by the Knights of the Order and spent three long years in prison. Afterward he was obliged to find a profession. Since he could no longer travel except through reading, he became a secondhand-bookseller. Ten years ago, however, the Council of Twelve forbade all communication by letter, and since then I've received no news from him. He is not allowed to leave the city of Nathyrnn, where he is constantly being watched."

"I was going to give you one of my priceless pieces of jewelry to thank you for your hospitality," said Jade, "but I think I can do better than that. Although it might take a while, I promise I'll send you news of your son."

7

A Message for Opal

ONCE MORE, THE THREE GIRLS FOUND THEM-
selves walking across the dukedom of Divulyon. To avoid
drawing attention to themselves, they made a detour
around the villages and avoided fields where peasants were
working. Nathyrnn was still very far away.

Amber carried the basket filled with provisions that
Jade had brought. During the night in the stable, she had
been so worried! She and Opal had spent a long time
wondering what Jade was up to. Amber's active imagination had invented a thousand different scenarios, and she
shivered at the possible consequences of what Jade might
have done. Opal had remained her usual calm self, however, explaining to Amber that she lived only in the present, never looked back on the past, but did not fear the
future, either. Jade could do whatever she wanted, and
worrying about it wouldn't change a thing.

Gradually the conversation had taken another turn.
Amber had spoken freely, describing with feeling the

world she had left behind. She re-created her daily life for Opal, who was astonished at the love Amber showed for everything. Amber talked about how she watched the moon and the stars, breathed the perfume of every wild-flower, ran barefoot in the cool grass, swam in the clear water of a lake. She also explained how much she loved sunshine, and making up marvelous stories, listening to other people and helping them, and reading tales (which were forbidden, it was true, but which she had secretly enjoyed in the home of a generous and learned man). Opal drank in every word. Amber had been happy, she admitted, even though she had lived in the most abject poverty. She had suffered, it was true, but that had only made her happiness more precious. And then, her mother had died. . . . Amber did not tell Opal about her sorrow; it was still too soon for that. But she thanked Opal for listening to her, and realized that by confiding in Opal, she had established a bond, albeit a fragile one, between them.

Now that they were on their way to Nathyrnn, Amber studied Opal. She was certain the girl was not as heart-less as she seemed. The night before, Opal had been awakened by a nightmare, and Amber had seen terror in her eyes, as if she were hoping to be rescued. Opal had murmured feverishly about dark, threatening faces and a danger that was very near.

"They're out there and they're getting closer! I'm the one they know about—I should never have gone into the room. And now it's too late."

Amber had soothed her in a soft voice, and the two girls had quickly fallen asleep again.

Now Amber turned wearily to Jade.

"Have we still got far to go?" she moaned.

"Yes," came the curt reply. "I've already explained three times that we have to go to Nathyrnn to find Jean Losserand, talk to him about the symbol, and make him tell us about his journey to Fairytale."

"I don't believe in tales or in that magic land," said Opal bluntly. "The Council of Twelve has outlawed fairy tales. I've never read any, and I've done just fine without them!"

"Well, I believe in that place," declared Amber. "I've always made up stories like that, and I love to tell them. I'd really like to go there—to Fairytale! Jade, what about you?"

"Of course I've read fairy tales! In my palace, there was an old philosopher named Théodon. He obeyed the Council of Twelve—in his own way—but I don't think he was afraid of them. He's the one who gave me tales to read and who taught me so many things."

"He taught you many things?" jeered Opal. "You'd never know it!"

Jade was about to reply when Amber intervened.

"Calm down! We can't start squabbling like children every time we talk. Jade, you hadn't finished. You believe in this country, in magic, in the unreal?"

"I'd like to believe," answered Jade, after a moment's thought. "This land does exist, I'm certain of that. But who lives there? I need to hear about Jean Losserand's experiences, and then perhaps I'll be truly convinced."

Since no one could think of anything to add, the conversation was over. Once again a stubborn silence reigned.

Jade tried to imagine what Nathyrnn and Jean Losserand were like. She really had no idea what he would tell them, so she started thinking about the questions she would ask the former traveler. She was consumed with impatience and exasperated at having to walk so far—too far, in her opinion.

Amber was thinking back to that morning, when she'd been so worried about Jade, only to see her turn up with a basket laden with food and announce, with a disconcerting smile, "We're leaving for Nathyrnn."

Questioned eagerly by Amber, Jade had told them everything. Opal had listened quietly, but Amber had caught her breath in surprise: the old woman at the farmhouse had behaved so cordially—that didn't sound like her at all!

Jade had spoken at length about Fairytale. During that part of her report, Amber had drifted into a daydream: she saw herself crossing the magnetic field of that wondrous land, in a truly magical setting, and she began to imagine detailed adventures that drew her into this enchanted world.

"Amber!"

Startled from her reverie, Amber gave Jade a puzzled look.

"Amber, haven't you noticed that something's wrong with Opal?"

Amber turned toward Opal, who had stopped a little way behind them: her face was frozen in fright, her eyes fixed and vacant.

"I tried to shake her—she didn't move," continued Jade. "And you just kept on walking!"

"My mind was elsewhere," protested Amber.

"Opal seems to be elsewhere as well. Personally, I couldn't care less, but I suppose it might be serious."

The two girls spoke to Opal and tried to rouse her from her trance. In her distress, Amber felt overwhelmed with remorse, even though Opal's plight was hardly her fault. Then all of a sudden, Opal seemed to come to. The mask of terror vanished, but when she tried to say something, she abruptly fainted. With a cry, Amber fell to her knees beside her. Jade merely stood there watching, but her eyes betrayed a concern she would rather not have felt. Luckily, Opal regained consciousness a few minutes later.

"What happened to you?"

Opal hesitated, trying to find exactly the right words to describe everything she had experienced.

"Someone sent me a message, but he did not reveal his identity. First, a dreadful pain flooded through me, and I felt helpless as my body grew rigid. I was numb with suffering. Then a man's voice spoke to me: it was harsh, and echoed inside my head, saying that I would be the first to die. Each word hurt me. Then the voice said that I was under its control and that there was nothing I could do to change things."

"One of our enemies who hadn't anything better to do than torment a poor girl," interrupted Jade. "How pitiful!"

"No," disagreed Amber. "This is serious: someone has contacted Opal using telepathy."

"The voice also sent me images," continued Opal. "First, a vision of a city. I'm certain it was Nathyrnn. And then, on top of all that incredible pain, I started to feel unbelievably sick. The voice said, 'We will meet in this city.' Next I saw an enormous book with gold letters stamped on it: it was called *The Prophecy*. It was covered in blood. The voice invaded my mind and said: 'The Prophecy will not come to pass the way others would have wished, but on one point, it tells the truth: you will die! As for the Chosen One, he will fall as well. But you will be the first to succumb, and it will be you who betrays them all. You are in my power and you have no choice but to obey me.'"

"It has to be a lie!" cried Amber.

Suddenly Jade felt she couldn't hate Opal anymore, and she didn't want to humiliate her with a cutting remark. Perhaps Opal was not as unfeeling as she tried to appear— in fact, at that moment, Jade found her almost touching, for Opal was quietly crying.

"I know that every word is true," Opal said in a muffled voice. "I'm convinced of it."

"Not at all," replied Amber reassuringly. "Opal, you know perfectly well that voice wanted to hurt you and was certainly lying to you."

"No. I'd like to believe that, but I know it was all true. And there's more."

Opal's tears were flowing faster now. She had managed to calm down a little, but she was too terrified by the message to be completely in control of herself.

"Let's hear!" demanded Jade brusquely. "Tell us what else the voice said."

"If it doesn't upset you too much," added Amber quickly.

"The rest of the message was absolutely true. The voice tried to use a softer tone, but it was hoarse and rough. It told me that it knew me better than I knew myself and that I had never excelled in anything at all, that I'd never felt love, or sadness, or joy, or compassion, or fear. It added that I had never been considerate of other people, or taken an interest in anything. That I had been a burden for those around me, that I was nothing. Nothing! Its last words were that no one had been able to love me and that no one ever would. Everything the voice said is true. It's all true!"

Surprisingly, Opal did not burst out sobbing. On the contrary, she choked back her tears and held her head up with dignity.

"I'm not that girl," she declared. "If no one loves me, that's too bad! But at least now I don't need to pretend anymore that I have no feelings."

Impressed and a little embarrassed, her two companions were speechless. Jade's earlier compassion vanished, and she almost laughed at this whole scene, but Amber silenced her with a warning look.

Unable to keep quiet any longer, Jade finally said, "It doesn't change a thing—we're still going to Nathyrnn! And we should get going straight away. We'll deal with this message later. In any case, there's nothing more we can do about it now."

"I'd like to consult our Stones," replied Amber. "I'm worried about this voice."

"You're scared!" said Jade mockingly.

"Yes, I am—so what? Don't you think I should be? I think I have good reason to be scared, and anyway I'm not like you."

"Like me?"

"Yes, so high-and-mighty that I never admit how I feel."

"Excuse me? Are you criticizing me?"

"No, I'm simply making an observation. Fine, let's get out the Stones. End of discussion."

Jade's green eyes flashed for a second as her fury began to kindle, but then it quickly died down. Each girl took her Stone from its purse and held it tightly. Nothing happened. Disappointed, Amber and Opal wondered what had gone wrong, but Jade's anger flared up again.

"We have no choice: we have to go to Nathyrnn," insisted Jade.

Amber agreed, but Opal protested immediately.

"No! Absolutely not! Whoever sent me the message told me I would meet him there. I can't go. It's impossible."

"That's right," admitted Amber. "Perhaps you're in real danger. Let's avoid that city."

Jade held her tongue for a moment. She could have been stubborn, explaining once more her desire to meet Jean Losserand, to understand the mystery of Fairytale and the meaning of the symbol. And yet, she kept quiet. Even if she was incredibly selfish (which she would never have believed, let alone admitted), she did not want to put Opal's life at risk. No matter how shallow she was, Jade was also intelligent. She realized that there was something odd about what the voice had said. She stood there, lost in thought, and all at once found the flaw in the message.

"We're going to Nathyrnn," she announced confidently. "Trust me, no one is in any danger."

Satisfied to see his authority respected by the Council of Twelve, the Thirteenth Councilor began to speak, and the walls trembled at the hollow sound of his voice.

"Opal is under my control," he announced calmly. "It all went just as I had wished. She believed every word I said."

Admiration now joined the fear felt by the councilors. He stared at them haughtily for a moment, considering their greedy faces, their white hair and dull eyes. He himself did not know what old age was.

"What will happen now?" the Third Councilor ventured to ask. He was an elderly man, but still naive and easily influenced.

"There is no need for you to know."

"Of course not, naturally," stammered the Third Councilor.

At last the councilors dared to look up at their leader. His towering form loomed in the dim light. In the darkness that concealed his face, only his eyes could be seen; piercing eyes that gleamed harshly.

"That is all. You will be informed of further developments."

With these words, he left the chamber.

8

THE GATES OF NATHYRNN

AMBER ADMIRED JADE: SHE SEEMED THOUGHT-less and spoiled, but had just shown them that she could also be quite shrewd. She had quickly guessed what Amber would never have imagined: "If the voice threatens to find you in Nathyrnn," she'd said with cool assurance, "it's certainly because it hopes you won't go there." Opal had been hard to convince. Her pretty, pale face was distorted by fear and she was shaking all over. Each step that brought her closer to the city cost her tremendous effort. At first she had begged Jade not to go on. She had shrieked with such despair that she had succeeded in terrifying herself even more. Jade had lost her temper and ordered Opal to follow them, and when that failed, she had finally grabbed Opal's arm and given her a resounding slap. Jade was not given to patience or moderation, and Opal was suffering the consequences.

"You're not yourself! On any other occasion, I would have had no qualms about leaving you here, but as it seems you're at the mercy of any old telepathic enemy with nothing better to do than terrorize young girls, you're coming with us, whether you want to or not."

Reluctantly, her cheek burning, Opal finally gave in to Jade.

"Opal, are you feeling better?" asked Amber after a while.

Opal refused to talk about it. She felt more humiliated than frightened now, and the last thing she wanted was pity.

"I'm fine," she said in a steady voice.

"You're sure?" insisted Amber.

"Yes."

"Jade," asked Amber, "how far is it to Nathyrnn? Opal is still quite weak."

"I feel fine," repeated Opal, who was finding Amber's concern rather annoying.

"We're an hour or two away from Nathyrnn."

"You're sure we're on the right road?"

"Absolutely," snapped Jade.

"I'm hungry," announced Amber. "We hardly touched our supplies this morning. We should stop again, to rest and have another meal."

"No," said Jade.

"We're stopping!" declared Opal.

Jade glanced at her more in astonishment than irritation—she hadn't expected any argument.

"Looks as though we're stopping," said Amber.

"All right," sighed Jade.

They sat down beside the path, surrounded by dry grass and wildflowers. Amber smiled to see the sun shining with all its might, and began eating ravenously. She looked at Opal, who now seemed like a different person after receiving that telepathic message. There was dismay in her big blue eyes, and all the color had drained from her face. Amber was secretly hurt by the fact that Opal hated Amber's fussing over her. Amber needed to be liked by others, and she wished Opal were more friendly toward her, but she understood that Opal was on her guard and that she considered both her companions potential enemies.

"I'm not hungry," said Opal, pushing back the basket Amber was offering her.

"Let's try the Stones again," suggested Amber.

"That doesn't help," said Jade, but she undid the drawstrings of her black purse anyway, and took out the Stone.

Amber and Opal did the same. This time, the effect was instantaneous. The three girls became queasy, and felt as if they were caught up in a whirlwind. They were seized with a nameless dread. The Stones seemed to be vibrating, and the girls were shaking. The sensation stopped as suddenly as it had begun, leaving the girls reeling on their feet. Amber and Jade felt utterly exhausted, but all Opal's anxiety had vanished, and she seemed like her old self again. She was ashamed of the weakness she'd shown, and wanted to make up for it.

"Let's head for Nathyrnn. It was stupid of me not to want to go with you. I was under the spell of that message and I was talking nonsense. Just forget what I said."

She wanted Amber and Jade to understand that the emotional girl of before, who had spoken under the influence of the voice, wasn't really her. She was furious with herself for the frightening ease with which she had let the voice overwhelm and disorient her.

"Jade," said Amber as they all walked along, "when we're in Nathyrnn, you ought to sell your gown and your jewelry so you can buy more ordinary clothing. The way you're dressed, people will notice us."

"I like being noticed," Jade shot back, exasperated. "And I don't want to look like a peasant! If you can't afford to buy jewelry and a dress from the county of Tyrel, just shut up and let me wear what I want."

Amber felt like snarling back at her, but she controlled herself. It was best not to aggravate Jade. It was true that her dress, delicately made by skillful artisans, suited her perfectly. Carried away by her imagination, Amber pictured Jade as a woman warrior, holding a saber dripping with blood, riding a wild-eyed stallion as white as sea foam. Then she thought of Opal, whom she saw as a storybook princess, wearing a golden diadem nestled in her curly blond hair and a pearl-gray dress that set off her pale skin and light blue eyes—which were demurely downcast, as always. This last thought made Amber smile. She finally woke from her reverie when Jade cried, "Here is Nathyrnn!"

The three girls had arrived without incident outside the city. Along the way they had met only country people, who'd been surprised to see them and had not dared to look at them openly. Now fields and meadows had given way to the impressive ramparts that completely surrounded Nathyrnn.

"How do we get into the city?" asked Amber in dismay.

"I hadn't thought about that," replied Jade with a wry smile, attracted by the prospect of danger and the unknown.

The walls of the city were guarded by the Knights of the Order. Three of them manned the entrance. They bore sharp swords, wore gray uniforms, and were mounted on horses of the same color. Fearsome and pitiless, they were merciless in their pursuit and punishment of the guilty, enforcing the dreaded law of the Council of Twelve everywhere they went.

Signaling her companions to follow her, Jade went up to one of the knights. Amber and Opal stood warily behind her.

"What do you want?" demanded the knight rudely. He was an imposing figure, with a coarse and unattractive face. His voice was cold.

"We must enter Nathyrnn," replied Jade boldly, not in the least intimidated.

"Your pass!"

"What pass?" said Amber without thinking, and earned a stinging look from Jade.

"Don't listen to her," she told the knight with a flirtatious smile. "She's one of my servants, and not too bright."

"Hand over your pass," repeated the man. "No one enters Nathyrnn without a pass issued by the Duke of Divulyon, who governs this territory by decree of the Council of Twelve."

"I know that," said Jade promptly.

She'd been going to add that she was the daughter of the Duke of Divulyon, but caught herself: she was not to reveal her identity to anyone. She smiled at the knight again. The man seemed rather disconcerted by her appearance; he could tell she was rich and belonged to an influential family. He had his orders, however, and could not let anyone enter without a pass.

"The Duke of Divulyon is my uncle; my name is Coralie of Mordorais, and these two girls are my servants."

Jade had a cousin of that name, the daughter of the duke's sister, a girl of about her own age.

"I have heard of your illustrious family, Lady Mordorais," replied the knight in a more gracious tone. "But without a pass, I may not allow you to enter."

"You will feel the wrath of my father," declared Jade calmly.

"The Count of Mordorais?"

"The very same. You must surely be aware that he is under the command of the Duke of Divulyon. He has great influence with him, and thus with the Council of Twelve as well."

"I do not doubt it."

"My father asked me to come to Nathyrnn to see someone, a certain Jean Losserand. He is to return an object belonging to my father, a book of great value."

"Why did the Count of Mordorais not send a page on

this errand, or else have you accompanied by an escort?" asked the knight doubtfully.

"I wanted to see Nathyrnn, and I do not like to saddle myself with an escort. My father did indeed give me an entry pass, signed by the Duke of Divulyon, but I seem to have mislaid it. He will be seriously vexed if I return empty-handed."

The knight was very suspicious, and said nothing.

Jade spoke coaxingly. "How can you doubt my words when you see my jewels? Aside from me, the only person in this entire dukedom who may wear such gems is the daughter of the Duke of Divulyon. They prove that I am Coralie of Mordorais and that you should let me enter the city."

"I cannot."

Jade lost her temper.

"Let me enter Nathyrnn immediately or I swear that my father will drag you through the mud until you beg for mercy!" she hissed, her eyes spitting fire. "He'll have you tortured in the public square like a common criminal, and you will suffer a horrible death. If you do not open this gate right now, you will regret it!"

"I . . . I really cannot, Lady Mordorais."

"Obey me!" yelled Jade.

"Ja—uh, Coralie," suggested Amber in a low voice,

"perhaps you should offer one of your jewels to this knight so that we may enter. . . ."

The knight's eyes gleamed. "Your servant is not such an idiot after all, Lady Mordorais."

"You shall have nothing!" fumed Jade. "I do not have to pay to enter."

"And you shall not enter," concluded the knight.

"That's what you think. Open this gate."

"No."

"Open it!" roared Jade.

The knight instinctively placed his hand on the hilt of his sword. That was when Opal stepped forward majestically, pushing aside Jade, who stumbled in surprise. Opal turned her icy gaze on the knight and addressed him in a determined voice.

"Enough lies. This girl is not Coralie of Mordorais, and I am not her maid."

Taken aback and impressed by Opal's self-command, the man asked her, "Then who is this so-called Lady Mordorais?"

"She is my own maid. We exchanged roles to ensure my safety."

"Your safety?" exclaimed the knight, growing increasingly bewildered. "But who are you?"

"My family is too noble for its name to be pronounced

before you," replied Opal coolly. "The Council of Twelve has entrusted me with a mission of the gravest importance. I must keep it secret and travel with the greatest discretion."

The knight gazed at Opal in admiration.

"Why do you not have a pass to enter Nathyrnn?" he asked. "And what is your mission?"

"Alas! We have come a long way and were traveling with a guide who betrayed us, unfortunately. He stole our pass and fled. By the time we realized this, it was too late to do anything about it. As for my mission, I ought not to speak of it, but since you have proved so understanding, I will reveal something to you. . . ."

"I'm listening," replied the man eagerly.

"My mission concerns the Prophecy and three enemies of the Council of Twelve."

A light dawned in the knight's eyes.

"So it's true? The rumors do speak of . . . the subject you mentioned."

Opal shivered. So, her intuition had proved correct.

"You understand," she continued, "that it is vitally necessary that you assist me in my mission. The Council of Twelve must not be thwarted in such an urgent enterprise!"

Opal had spoken solemnly, her big blue eyes staring without blinking into the knight's gaze.

"I understand com-completely," he stammered.

He summoned the other two knights, and together they opened the gates of Nathyrnn.

Without a word of thanks, Opal walked with great dignity into the city, followed by Jade and Amber.

"Good luck!" the knight shouted after the three girls.

And the heavy gates of Nathyrnn swung shut behind them.

9

THE BOOKSELLER

FOR TEN YEARS, JEAN LOSSERAND HAD TRIED desperately to hold on to his thirst for life and adventure, but as time wore on, he became bitterly aware that he was losing interest in his quest for happiness. He had long dreamed of escaping this city that was like a prison, but as his hopes faded, so, too, did the strength to struggle against his fate. Now and then, he thought sadly of his aging mother and reflected that he would never see her again. His monotonous existence had stifled even his love of freedom, and his beloved books had finally lost their charm. Fairy tales, fantastic stories, and all novels had been forbidden. Only biographies or technical works were allowed, because they did not offend the Council. Jean Losserand could no longer find comfort anywhere; he was under constant surveillance and now lacked the willpower to fight back in any way. His life had been reduced to an endless, helpless sigh. Until the day he heard a knock on his shop door.

Since he had so few customers, he no longer bothered to take care of his bookshop, which looked neglected. Dusty, torn volumes were stacked everywhere in untidy piles, and the shop door was always closed, so he was surprised when someone came knocking. He shuffled slowly to the door, opened it, and stood gaping in astonishment at the three girls, who gazed back curiously at him.

"Are you Jean Losserand?" inquired Jade.

The bookseller studied her for a moment, noticing the liveliness and determination that danced in her eyes: the color of jade, he thought.

"Excuse us for disturbing you," said Amber softly, "but are you really Jean Losserand, the son of the old woman who lives in a remote farmhouse?"

"With a disgusting stable," added Jade.

"I am indeed Jean Losserand," said the startled man. "Do you know my mother?"

"Yes!" said Jade gaily. "She's very hospitable."

"My mother?" he repeated in disbelief.

"Yes," replied Jade. "We've come here to ask you for help. May we come in?"

"Of course."

Jean Losserand led the unexpected visitors to an adjoining room, where he invited them to sit down in some very worn, red velvet armchairs. He fussed around them, offering them biscuits, preparing mint tea, all the while studying them intently. Their clothes seemed quite ordinary, of good quality but not luxurious. In all other respects, however, the three girls were most unlike one another. When he looked into Amber's face, he seemed troubled, and his left hand began to shake the way it always did when he was overcome with emotion. Amber noticed that he had trouble setting the teapot down on a low table, and she served the mint tea for him, pouring it into chipped china cups.

"Thank you," he murmured gratefully. "And now, tell me what I can do for you."

"It's a long story," replied Jade.

Then she quietly and carefully inspected their surroundings. Taking a sip of piping hot tea, she spilled some on her trousers. Her sumptuous attire had been attracting unwelcome stares of amazement from the citizens of Nathyrnn, and Amber had finally convinced her, to sell her dress and some of her precious jewelry. Jade had used some of the money to buy more suitable clothing, and Amber had used a few small copper coins from her black velvet purse to purchase a plain, simple outfit, because even her peasant clothes had been attracting attention. She had also washed her face at a public fountain to get rid of the smudges of dirt, straw, and tears. Nibbling on a biscuit, Amber felt better, refreshed, even though she was exhausted; their communication with the Stones had sapped all her energy. She was relieved to have arrived at last at Jean Losserand's shop, which had been hard to find in the dark and narrow street. Amber had regretfully concluded that she did not like Nathyrnn: the people appeared surly and uncommunicative and the streets were too quiet, without many shops. Everything was shabby and deserted. She felt reassured to be in the bookshop, with this man who seemed friendly and attentive. She had observed him closely, as was her habit. He was impressively tall, but his shoulders drooped a little, as if he carried a heavy burden. Amber guessed that he was between thirty and forty years old. His face was stamped with wisdom and kindness, yet his eyes expressed a kind of resigned despair and regret.

"Explain how I can help you," he repeated. "Who are you? What are you doing in Nathyrnn?"

He seemed to be speaking to Amber, but it was Jade who replied.

"We come from the area around the palace of Divulyon, and we are here to see you. We were able to enter Nathyrnn thanks to Opal's brilliant lie."

Jade jerked her chin at Opal with a hint of disdain, and Opal returned the favor with an icy look.

"We know you are on our side," continued Jade, " and we have enemies in common." In a low voice, she added, "It seems the Council of Twelve is meeting to talk about us. And what they have to say is not good. . . ."

"If you are enemies of the Council of Twelve, then welcome to Nathyrnn. This city is really a prison where those who have visited Fairytale are held captive," explained Jean Losserand.

"We don't have any idea why the council is concerned with us," confided Amber, "and we have enemies whose identities we don't even know. Just today Opal received a terrifyingly powerful and evil telepathic message. Do you know who could have done this?"

"Only the members of the Council of Twelve know how to practice telepathy. In Fairytale, of course, many magicians can perform it as well, but they could never have sent a message from such a great distance."

"Then the Council of Twelve really is against us," observed Jade. "I can't believe it. I've never heard anything bad about the Council of Twelve. My own father was chosen to govern a territory and was made a duke by the council. He obeys the laws and the orders of those twelve old men."

Seeing Jean Losserand's puzzled expression, Jade explained herself.

"I am Jade of Divulyon. I shouldn't really tell you this, but I trust you. I found out just recently that I'm not the duke's daughter after all, and I've been driven from the palace."

The bookseller was beginning to understand. So, the rumors that had already been circulating in Fairytale ten years before had been well founded. All his doubts about Amber suddenly became certainties. He had recognized her—she was indeed who he thought she was. He had studied every feature of her face, and his suspicions were confirmed. Jean Losserand was filled with joy: *she* was alive! The sun rose in his heart, as hope and an infinite love of life flooded back into his soul. He told himself once more, *She is alive!* He was burning to shout out those wondrous words, but he knew that he must not, and managed to hold his tongue.

Meanwhile, Jade was looking in her bag for the paper on which she had drawn the symbol. When she finally found it, she gave it to Jean Losserand, who examined it with interest.

"What is it?" asked Jade breathlessly. "Can you understand it?"

"It's a sign written in one of the ancient languages of Fairytale," he said immediately.

"Really!" exclaimed Amber. "And what does it mean?"

"It's rather complicated—it concerns wisdom and the power to read what is hidden deep within the heart, but at the same time, the symbol can be read as a name: Oonagh."

"Oonagh?" repeated Amber, instantly enchanted by the lilting sound of the name.

"Oonagh is someone who lives in Fairytale," continued the bookseller, "someone whose people have been largely decimated by the Council of Twelve. Oonagh is a magic creature renowned for her wisdom, and she can read the secrets of the heart. She is spoken of with the greatest respect."

"Oonagh lives in Fairytale!" breathed Amber, her imagination catching fire.

"Yes, in a crystalline grotto."

"I think we'll have to go and visit this Oonagh," observed Jade. "But tell us a little about Fairytale. I thought it was a legend."

"Not at all," Jean Losserand assured them. "I really did go there."

"Well—what's this place like?" asked Jade.

"I'll tell you everything I know. But, most important,

to be able to cross the magnetic field surrounding Fairy-tale, you must believe wholeheartedly in the impossible. You girls are no longer naive children trusting in fantasy, so this may be difficult for you."

"I'll manage it," said Jade haughtily, because she couldn't conceive of anything in the world that she would not be able to do.

"Who lives in Fairytale?" asked Amber. "Damsels in distress, knights in shining armor, wizards?"

"Among others. A long, long time ago, when the Council of Twelve did not yet have the power it wields now, hundreds of people with magic powers lived freely in the world. Human beings were merely one of many advanced species, and everyone respected their mutual differences. Yet despite the many advances humankind had made—technological progress, huge towering cities, travel to the stars—the Council of Twelve feared the immense power these kindly magic creatures held. The council gained power by sowing hatred in men's hearts against the other races. Gradually, by abusing the trust of those peoples who were so different from us, the council succeeded in destroying them. It was a lawless time, and a shameful one, too."

A shadow of fear passed over Amber's gentle face.

"What happened next?" she asked haltingly. "Why didn't anyone rise up and try to save them?"

"No one really understood what was going on. People trusted their neighbors and were used to living in harmony. It all happened in a confused and secretive way. Finally, the magic creatures, who were peaceful beings, decided to avoid further bloodshed. Their survivors withdrew into a distant land, far from civilization, but rich and fertile. There they combined their powers and created magnetic fields to protect themselves. Thus was born Fairytale, which has now become a prosperous country of entrancing beauty, where humans and creatures endowed with supernatural powers live side by side with the same tolerance as before. Unfortunately, evil does rage there as well. Wherever there is life, there cannot be only goodness. But at least the Council of Twelve is unable to impose its law there. It is a free place."

"That story is so beautiful," murmured Amber, deeply moved.

"Yes," said Jade matter-of-factly. "Is Fairytale far from here?"

"No, it's not far at all," replied Jean Losserand. "Nathyrnn marks the limit of the dukedom of Divulyon. The border is less than fifteen minutes away, but heavily guarded. Few succeed in crossing it. And just beyond lie the magnetic fields surrounding Fairytale."

"That close?" cried Jade. "Then it will be easy to get there."

"No, it won't. To begin with, you need an exit pass to leave Nathyrnn. Then comes the hardest part: crossing the border."

"Getting out of Nathyrnn shouldn't be a problem: Opal thought up a very plausible lie," remarked Jade acidly. She was still disgruntled at failing to win over the Knight of the Order through her own scheme.

"Yes," agreed Amber enthusiastically—"Tell him, Opal!"

Reluctantly, Opal did.

"Some instinct led me to say that I was working for the Council of Twelve," she related in an indifferent voice. "I was suddenly convinced that the telepathic message had come from them. I knew, I sensed, that we were their enemies."

At these words, Jean Losserand shivered.

"It is true that when a message is sent telepathically, the mind of the person sending the message must be linked to the mind of the person receiving it. However, that does not mean that they can read each other's thoughts," he said. "Unless—unless the purpose of the message is to instill fear or inflict pain."

There was an uneasy silence.

"The voice also spoke of a prophecy," said Amber faintly. "And an enormous book covered with blood. Do you know what that's all about?"

Jean Losserand weighed his words carefully, afraid of revealing what it was vital to conceal. Before he replied, he considered Amber for a moment, with her sweet face and kind eyes.

"*The Prophecy* was written centuries ago by a philosopher named Néophileus, who was a member of a strong and unconquerable fairy race called the Clohryuns. Néophileus had the gift of seeing into the future, and he had a premonition that many of his kind would be destroyed, a few hundred years later, by the Council of Twelve. Unfortunately, no one believed him, because everyone thought that they had learned to live in peace forever."

The three girls were transfixed by his words: Jade's eyes gleamed with curiosity, and Amber's reflected interest and understanding, while Opal's remained inscrutable.

"Néophileus also felt that a day would come when times would change and the world would be transformed. He foretold a deep disturbance, but for the first time in his life, his powers failed him, and he was unable to decipher any details."

"I don't understand," said Amber.

"In other words, at a certain place on the curve of time, the future was unclear to Néophileus. He saw that instead of following a single, distinct line, the future divided at that particular point into several paths. Only one path would be taken, and all of humanity would follow a course that would change the world as we know it. And so, Néophileus wrote *The Prophecy*."

Jean Losserand stopped. He had said enough.

"We absolutely must go to Fairytale to consult Oonagh," said Amber. "How can we cross the border of Divulyon?"

"I don't know what to advise you," confessed the bookseller. "When I went to Fairytale, the border existed only in theory. Now, it's quite a different matter."

"We'll get across," said Jade confidently.

"How?" insisted Amber.

"I cannot help you," replied Jean Losserand, "but go and see a young man called Adrien of Rivebel. He is only sixteen, but he has already spent three years in Nathyrnn's dungeons. And he has just been set free."

"But why was he locked up?" cried Amber.

"This young man lived in Fairytale, where he was born the son of a noble family of knights. When he was thirteen, Adrien wanted to explore the outside world, so he left his homeland. The Knights of the Order seized him at the border of Divulyon and threw him in prison."

"That's not fair!" exclaimed Amber.

"Of course not," agreed Jean Losserand. "But rumor has it that he isn't like the other prisoners. Locking him away hasn't broken his spirit at all. In fact, people say that he's indomitable and that the bars of his cell, far from destroying him, have toughened him instead. He has been condemned to spend his life here, in this grim and hopeless city, yet everyone is saying that he's trying to incite a rebellion to liberate the citizens of Nathyrnn."

"I love rebellions!" crowed Jade. "What a good idea."

"Unfortunately, it's impossible," sighed the bookseller.

"No," said Amber. "Nothing is impossible."

Jean Losserand smiled sadly. He no longer had the heart to dream of the impossible.

"Go and see Adrien of Rivebel," he repeated. "Perhaps he can help you."

Jade tossed back a stray lock of black hair and said, "We don't need any help, but we'll go and see this Adrien of Rivebel. Nathyrnn must be liberated."

"I'm telling you, it's impossible," groaned the book-seller.

"Your mother is waiting for you, Mr. Losserand," replied Jade, "and I promised to send her news of you. The best thing would be if you took it to her yourself, don't you think?" And she added defiantly, "Nothing is impossible!"

10

ADRIEN OF RIVEBEL

AMBER EXPECTED TO SEE A CHARMING PRINCE straight out of a fairy tale, gallant and poetic, but Adrien looked more like a young knight with hard, chiseled features. He seemed thoughtful and self-possessed, and only his grave eyes revealed the courage and fire that burned inside him. His tousled chestnut hair added to the aura of brooding mystery that surrounded him. Adrien knew how to feign indifference and disguise his deepest feelings: that was what had enabled him to withstand those three years of prison. He had not committed any crime, but rather than allowing himself to be overcome by fury, he had survived by holding on to the knowledge that his conscience was clear. Realizing that anger was useless, he had ignored it, even though in his heart he cried out for justice. Now that he was free again, he had let his true nature reassert itself. He had planned the revolt of Nathyrnn down to the last detail, and now he was seeking allies to join his cause. He was sure that his plan would succeed, but he had yet to find anyone who could help him carry it out. Almost all the inhabitants of Nathyrnn had been "broken," either by prison, or simply by habit and submissiveness. There were not many left who held on to their hopes and dreams. Only a few approved of Adrien's revolt, but even they did not dare to join him. They were not won over—yet.

So Adrien of Rivebel had not despaired, but he was still waiting for help. It came to him in an unlikely form when he met Jade, Opal, and Amber. He was not in the least surprised to see them burst into his tiny room at the inn where he was staying, and he welcomed them cordially, waving them toward some rickety chairs. Adrien of Rivebel was educated and intelligent: he had known at once who his visitors were, for he had heard many stories about them in Fairytale. He himself, on his tenth birthday, had consulted Oonagh to learn what path he should follow, and the magic creature had advised him: "You are not the Chosen One. But you cannot remain in the shadows. Your heart is proud and passionate: find water to dampen that devastating ardor, not fuel to kindle its flames."

"But why?" Adrien had asked in disappointment.

"You are capable of provoking great danger. You must be extremely careful, or other lives will be placed in peril. Do not listen to your heart—it is too impetuous.

Open your eyes and be guided by your reason."

"This is all very confusing," Adrien had murmured.

"One day you will encounter those whom all are waiting for, and you will understand."

Now that the three Stones of the Prophecy were standing before him, he was not sure what lay ahead, but he had a clear sense that together they would be able to take a step in the right direction. Of course, he said nothing of all of this to them.

At first the girls studied him in silence. They each soon recognized him as someone they could trust: the one person who could help them escape Nathyrnn and enter Fairytale.

Jade understood immediately that she had found an ally, someone like herself. In his eyes she read the revolt of Nathyrnn that she might organize with him. She paid no attention to the intensity with which Adrien returned her gaze, but it did not escape either Amber or Opal.

Amber was impressed by the young man. She guessed that he was headstrong and determined, like Jade, but capable of much more self-control. Opal's reaction had been different: the very instant she laid eyes on Adrien, a profound change came over her. She was deeply affected, and experienced a sudden warmth spreading through her being; she could not resist this feeling and, if the truth be told, she did not wish to. She felt pleasantly strange, and wondered vaguely what was happening to her. She stared openly at Adrien's face. And then it came to her: she understood, she knew, that she was made to love those gray-green eyes. She was certain that she and Adrien should be together—it could not be otherwise. She, who was normally so cold, was flushed with warmth. But Adrien's eyes were riveted on Jade. Opal saw this, yet felt no jealousy, no resentment. It's a mistake, she thought calmly. Adrien cannot look at Jade that way. And if he's feeling for her what I feel for him, then . . . he'll have to change his mind.

Meanwhile, delighted at the prospect of stirring up a revolt, of defying the law and proving her bravery, Jade had launched into an excited discussion about the uprising in the city.

"A friend has told us that you're plotting revolution in Nathyrnn!" she told Adrien, flashing him a knowing smile.

She addressed him with easy familiarity. He was only two years older than she was, and politeness had never been her strong point.

"I don't want to spend my life within the walls of this horribly sad city," replied Adrien. "I've come up with a plan of escape, to return to Fairytale. But I want *all* the inhabitants of Nathyrnn to be free. And I know I can do it, although it's quite complicated. We would have to use magic, but I haven't found anyone in this city capable of accomplishing what I have in mind."

"And what's that?" said Jade impatiently.

"Someone must cast a spell, and all those who find themselves outside the magic circle must be put into a deep sleep."

"What is a magic circle?"

"It's a small protective spell circle that forms around a sorcerer when he recites magic formulae, to shield him from the effects of his own magic. When he casts a sleep spell, the circle helps him to stay awake. Once the circle is formed and the recital is finished, the sorcerer may leave the circle without being affected by the spell."

"I see the problem," mused Jade. "The Knights of the Order would fall asleep, but so would the inhabitants of Nathyrnn!"

"Exactly. And only an experienced sorcerer could conjure up a vast magic circle. It would have to be huge to contain all the people in the city."

"And then everyone could escape without being in any danger," added Jade.

"Not quite. The enchantment would not last longer than

ten minutes, which barely leaves us enough time to open the gates of the city and flee. But to reach the border of the dukedom of Divulyon, we'd have to renew the spell several times. And that's the insurmountable problem: it's already exhausting enough to use such powerful magic, but casting the same spell repeatedly in such a short time is almost impossible."

"*Almost,*" said Jade meaningfully. "Therein lies the difference."

Suddenly, Opal spoke up.

"Adrien, you said you haven't found a sorcerer who can carry out your plan?"

"That's right," confessed the young man.

"*We* could do it—well, I think we could," she said.

"Us? How?" asked Amber.

"The Stones!" replied Opal. "Since we need a source of powerful magic . . ."

Adrien didn't bother to feign amazement at Opal's words, because he had been waiting for just such a moment to arise.

"Let's suppose that this is possible," he said. "There's still a second problem. We also have to let everyone in Nathyrnn know exactly when the escape is going to happen, so that they'll be ready."

Adrien knew that the revolt could not succeed without some bloodshed, but he did not want to frighten his new allies unnecessarily.

"When will the escape take place?" asked Amber.

"Let's say, in one month."

He watched for Jade's reaction. It was the one he had hoped for.

"No!" protested Jade. "I'm not going to wait a month. I want to reach Fairytale as soon as we can."

"What do you mean by 'as soon as we can'?" asked Amber uneasily.

"Tonight."

"Tonight?" cried Amber and Adrien in unison.

"It should be possible," replied Jade. "Our enemies contacted Opal using telepathy. Let's use this same method to alert the people of Nathyrnn!"

"To reach every mind in the city," began Adrien, "we'd have to—"

"We'd have to try!" interrupted Jade. "If we let ourselves be held back by doubt, we'll stay in this place for ever, and that is out of the question!"

"It's not that simple," warned Adrien. "It will take a huge effort. . . . Oh, well—you're right. If you've managed to get in here, you'll manage to get us out of here!"

he concluded, carried away by Jade's enthusiasm.

Amber took a deep breath. She wasn't completely convinced, but Jade and Opal had already taken their Stones out of their black velvet purses. Amber hesitated, wondering whether the trust they placed in Adrien had been a bit premature; after all, they had only just met him. But she took out her Stone anyway. Actually, the prospect of remaining imprisoned in Nathyrnn didn't thrill her any more than it did Jade.

"Just concentrate on your objective: to warn the citizens about the escape," said Adrien. "If your message is clear enough, and your will strong enough, people will be convinced. Concentrate all your strength on that."

Opal nodded in assent, but Amber grew tense without knowing why. Holding tight to their Stones, the three girls focused their thoughts on liberating Nathyrnn. They had no idea how deeply they were concentrating, and their cheeks flushed with the effort. Then something completely unexpected happened. The girls closed their eyes simultaneously, and before Adrien's astonished gaze, out of nowhere a translucent sphere materialized around them and began to rise into the air, while the girls floated lightly inside. The sphere seemed as fragile as a bubble about to burst, but in reality it was more solid than metal armor. The girls themselves noticed nothing. An image had come to them of a crowd streaming out of the city gates. The girls murmured words they did not know, saw visions they did not understand. Something had possessed them, and yet this something seemed to come from their innermost being. Without knowing it, they were sending these thoughts to the entire population of Nathyrnn.

Impressed, Adrien watched the scene unfolding before him. He heard the words that Jade, Opal, and Amber were emitting telepathically, and was certain the inhabitants of Nathyrnn would now join the revolt—such was the persuasiveness of the girls' voices echoing in his mind.

After a quarter of an hour, the sphere containing the three girls slowly descended and landed on the ground, vanishing as suddenly as it had appeared.

Jade and Opal did not seem at all affected by the miracle they had just performed, and quietly returned to their chairs. Jade smiled, proud of herself, but Amber's eyes had a vacant look. She sat down heavily on the floor and began to cry.

"Never . . . I'll never see her again. . . . I never should have . . . and without a word of apology . . . I won't survive. . . ." Then, abruptly, her tone changed, and she shook her fist threateningly. "I don't want to!" she shouted violently. "No! I want to be free! Stop!"

"Amber!" cried Jade. "What's going on?"

Adrien sighed and said, "This can occasionally happen, although I assumed with your powers you would be immune to it. In making contact with every single inhabitant of the city, Amber has absorbed all their thoughts. She will have to experience each person's emotions before she can get rid of them. It will take several hours."

"Why didn't it happen to Opal and me?" asked Jade.

"Amber must be very sensitive," explained Adrien. "But don't worry. She'll come out of it, and she'll just be left with a few bad memories."

"You're sure?" said Jade.

"Absolutely. The most important thing is, you succeeded! It's quite a feat, and it means that we have a real chance. Well done!"

"Thank you," said Jade smugly. "That wasn't so hard."

"So much the better. What's ahead of us will be."

"We'll see," said Jade, and added rather loftily, "I'm not afraid."

PARIS: PRESENT DAY

I woke up: after what seemed like an eternity, I had finally emerged from my deathlike slumber. For the first time in a long while I could hear my heart beating; I felt alive, and happy that I was. I could just make out, barely visible, a glimmer of light at the end of this black tunnel of pain and sorrow, this hopeless daily gloom.

Before that night, I had not been able to forget that death was stalking me, and would snatch me away without pity. I was frightened. I was cold. My life had no meaning. I wasn't dead, but might just as well have been. The days were all alike: desperate, useless, and filled with suffering. My disease was eating away at me. I couldn't take it anymore. I had run out of tears, and courage; I had nothing left. Everything had turned out to be in vain. In the end, my existence had been reduced to nothing, and I hadn't even enough strength left to see the injustice of my own despair.

Just another night, exactly the same as those that had preceded it and those that would follow. At least I had thought so as I drifted off to sleep. Usually, I never dreamed. I slept very little, and badly. But that night something extraordinary happened. I had a fantastic dream—about an unbelievable reality. I had the feeling that somewhere, in a distant world, the dream was being lived out. How could I be sure that dreams weren't actually messages from some other real existence, while my senseless life was in fact just the imaginary reflection of that unknown world?

I was overcome by a fit of coughing. The dream—I clung to it as hard as I could, with every thought. Jade, Opal, and Amber . . . Strange! The initials of their names formed my nickname, Joa. Before, everyone had always called me that; it is short for my real name, Joanna. I tried to swallow the lump in my throat. I had thought I was through with the time when tears of longing and regret would well up in my eyes without warning. That belonged to the past. Over and done with. From now on, I had no name anymore, because no one bothered to talk to me. I was nothing, just a body, almost motionless, on a bed in a room. Nothing.

I closed my aching eyes. Hope would get me nowhere. But I would go on dreaming.

11

REBELLION!

JADE AND ADRIEN HAD PREPARED A DETAILED
escape plan and were convinced it would succeed. After
feverishly searching for a particular magic formula in the
few books of sorcery hidden in the city, the young man
had at last waved in triumph a yellowed sheet of ancient,
crumbling paper, which Jade had examined. Together they
had agreed on their plan of action. Now the time had
come to cast the spell.

"It's too late to go back," thought Opal. She would have
to go through with it. And yet something inside her kept
trying to persuade her otherwise.

Amber had emerged from her torpor, but still felt weak.
Jade and Adrien were anxious to begin.

Jade picked up the formula. Opal went over to her. Still
feeling dizzy and a little muddled, Amber joined them.

"Right," said Adrien, his heart pounding, "this is it.
You have to recite the formula over and over, without
stopping. The magic circle is invisible. The magic will

draw strength from your own energy."

The three girls took out their Stones.

"If all is well," continued Adrien tensely, "the people of Nathyrnn should be gathering at this moment before the city gate. I will go and join them. While you recite the formula, I will open the gate. Then you will join me, and everyone will be freed."

"We know," said Jade. "It's simple."

"It will be hard for you to walk," warned Adrien. "You'll surely be greatly weakened by the strength of the spell. Let's hope the exhaustion doesn't hit you until after we leave Nathyrnn."

"No problem," Jade cut in impatiently.

"Remember to concentrate," continued Adrien, ignoring her.

"Yes, yes, you've already explained everything to us," grumbled Jade.

There was no more time for talking. Adrien left to join the inhabitants of Nathyrnn. The three girls held their Stones and began to recite the magic formula. Nothing happened. The words didn't make any sense at all. They read the formula over again and again. Then suddenly they began to feel the weariness Adrien had warned them about. After a few minutes, realizing that the spell had been cast successfully, they all stopped at the same time. They weren't physically tired, but they were no longer able to think or speak; they had become mindless bodies. And yet, as if controlled by an unknown power, they knew what they had to do. They rushed to the entrance to the city, where they found Adrien waiting by the open gate. The people of Nathyrnn were overjoyed at the prospect of regaining their freedom.

"There you are!" exclaimed Adrien when he caught sight of the three girls. "Everything seems to have gone smoothly. Now we have to evacuate everyone; some will come to Fairytale with us, while others will go back to their place of birth."

Jean Losserand was among that last group. He was finally going to see his old mother again, and his real home. In the throng of people hurrying to leave, he waved to Jade, Opal, and Amber with tears of happiness and disbelief in his eyes, but the girls didn't see him: he was unrecognizable in his newfound joy.

"You're going to have to press on without me," Adrien told the girls. "I must release the prisoners from their cells. I know where the keys are, but I'll have to move quickly. Go toward Fairytale for about ten minutes, then stop to rest and wait for me."

Without a word, the girls left the city, following the crowd returning to Fairytale. Their minds were still blank, and they showed no surprise at the unbelievable scene: the entire population of Nathyrnn was streaming through the city gate, while the Knights of the Order were spellbound in sleep.

The girls and some of the rejoicing crowd marched together into the darkness; after ten minutes, they stopped, following Adrien's instructions. A few moments later, the spell was broken, and the three girls fainted. The magic had sapped all their strength: while the spell was working, the girls had been sustained by its power, but now they were completely drained, and could not be roused from their torpor.

Some ten minutes later, Adrien arrived at the head of more than a hundred and fifty prisoners.

"For the moment, everything's going fantastically well," he exulted.

Then someone showed him the three girls laid out unconscious on the bare ground. Adrien knew that their condition wasn't serious, but when he saw Jade lying sense-less and unmoving, he felt a pang.

"We're continuing on," he announced. "I'll carry one of the girls, and two of you will take the others. They must awaken before we reach the border. These are the girls who cast the spell, and it's thanks to them that we've got this far."

The crowd murmured in astonishment. Adrien waved for silence.

"They will not be strong enough to cast another spell and put the knights who guard the border to sleep. We have no choice: we'll have to prove that our dreams are worth living for, that our courage is not an illusion. We will have to fight."

A clamor of fear went up, but Adrien remained calm.

"Each prisoner has taken the sword from a knight in Nathyrnn. Since some prisoners are too young or too weak to fight, their weapons will be given to the most valiant among us. We have not escaped in vain! We have one goal, and it is close. Let those courageous enough to fight step forward. Hope is invincible!"

The border of the dukedom of Divulyon was very well guarded, but Adrien's passion and unshakable will inspired every sturdy, brave man to come forward. Adrien took charge of handing out the weapons.

"Hope is invincible," he repeated softly, as if trying to convince himself.

The people of Nathyrnn set out for the border again.

Two men had picked up Jade and Amber, so Adrien found himself carrying Opal. The young man noticed that there was a nobility about her, and as he held her in his arms, he became aware of the warmth of her body. Looking around him, Adrien noted the fierce determination shining in everyone's eyes: women, children, old men, all were pressing forward bravely. It was a dark night, but the hard and rocky road they were taking was the path to freedom. The crowd was quiet, savoring the fleeting tranquility all around them.

Soon Jade, Opal, and Amber regained consciousness. They felt sore, quite feeble, and their heads ached, but their minds were clear. They walked unsteadily and had to be helped along for quite a while. Realizing the gravity of the situation, they tried to cast a new spell, but they were too weak, and their efforts failed.

In about a quarter of an hour, the troop reached the border of the dukedom of Divulyon. The darkness concealed them from their enemies, who stood before them in the hundreds: the Knights of the Order. And behind them lay the magnetic field, forming a dome over Fairytale. Although the field was opaque, it gave off a dazzling light.

"Fight fiercely," Adrien urged his armed men. "Create a diversion so that the weakest among us may cross first, and don't fall back until we are the last ones left. Stir up as much trouble as you can."

With these words, he ran forward brandishing his sword, followed by every man fit enough to do battle. Some had no weapons and went into combat barehanded, shouting valiantly.

At first they had the advantage of surprise. As mothers and their children ran helter-skelter toward the magnetic field, the Knights of the Order, busy defending themselves against the attack, were able to stop only a few of them. The children entered Fairytale without any difficulty, and their mothers managed to follow them. But on the battlefield the attack quickly turned into a disaster. The Knights of the Order triumphed easily over their adversaries; only about a dozen men, including Adrien, were really able to challenge them. Many of the former inhabitants of Nathyrnn now lay gravely wounded or dying. Hanging back in the darkness there remained only a handful of frail youths, some frightened old men, many middle-aged women, and Jade, Opal, and Amber.

"If we wait, we won't get through," said Jade urgently. "We have to try our luck now and take advantage of the enemy's confusion. Run! Save yourselves! Don't stop—dash in between the ranks. There's still some hope left, so run for it!"

Gathering up what little strength she had regained, Jade rushed fearlessly toward the battlefield, where she seized the sword of a man lying on the ground in a pool of blood. Her thorough education had included training in the arts of war. Drawing on her knowledge, Jade raised the sword. At that moment, the din of clashing arms died down, then ceased altogether. Both the Knights of the Order and the fugitives could not help but be struck by the sight of the proud fourteen-year-old girl with raven-black hair. Her image seemed completely out of place on that blood-soaked field. Uncertain how to react, the Knights of the Order hesitated. This was a mistake. Jade, swift and agile, sprang to the attack. Amber, Opal, and the other unarmed fugitives then hurried toward the magnetic field. Amber passed through it easily, while a few others, after encouraging one another nervously, managed to follow her, but most of them, including Opal, were unable to cross into Fairytale.

Suddenly, Adrien, who was fighting passionately, shouted to Jade and the last men who remained, "We must fall back! If we don't, we won't survive!"

But Jade didn't listen to him. Such was her prowess that she was triumphing over the most experienced Knights of the Order.

"Jade! Come on! There are too few of us—we cannot win!"

Almost with regret, Jade retreated toward the magnetic field with Adrien and the other men. Hastily grabbing her Stone, she tried to cross the barrier of Fairytale. "I believe in it," she told herself, "and I must go and see Oonagh. Fairytale exists—and the impossible as well." She felt a tremendous pain as she hit the magnetic field: her entire body was violently repulsed. An icy wind blew through her. She tried to advance, but could not. Then she clenched her fists and closed her eyes, and when she opened them again, she understood that she had passed into Fairytale.

On the other side of the magnetic field, things were going very badly. The few surviving combatants had crossed the barrier after Jade, leaving on the other side only Adrien and those who could not manage to believe in the impossible, with Opal among them. Realizing that their opponents were fleeing the battlefield, the Knights of the Order began to pursue them. Some of the last fugitives were weeping in despair, others shrieking in terror, and Adrien could not bring himself to abandon them.

"All you need to do is believe," Adrien pleaded. "Just try, remember a childhood dream, it doesn't matter which one. You'll get through. . . ." But he knew his words were useless and that it was too late. Then something staggering happened: Opal walked out to meet the approaching enemy.

"Knights!" she called out in a firm, strong voice. "I do not ask you to spare me. But be compassionate enough to judge my companions fairly. Their only crime has been to seek their freedom. Do they really deserve to die?"

Adrien stared at Opal in admiration. She, whose eyes were always modestly downcast, was gazing unflinchingly at the enemy. She held herself with such majesty, and looked, at that moment, invincible. And she was so beautiful. . . . Adrien realized that he'd been blind. He loved Opal. He ran toward her to protect her, to tell her how he felt, but a Knight of the Order was faster than he was. The knight had sneered at Opal's words, which carried no meaning for him; he had been taught to take lives, not to save them. He drew his keen sword and with a brutal smile, plunged it pitilessly into Opal's heart.

Adrien arrived only in time to catch Opal's lifeless body in his arms. As he held her, his garments stained with her scarlet blood, he thought she had never looked so beautiful, serene even in death. With tears in his eyes, he pressed his lips to Opal's still warm, soft mouth.

"I loved her," he said simply.

The Knights of the Order looked at one another. They were used to weeping and lamentation, to shouts of accusation—none of that could touch their hearts anymore. Enough: it was time to get the job done.

But Adrien continued, in a sad, steady voice that did not seem to belong to him: "It's not your fault."

The knights stiffened in surprise.

"You were trained to fight and to kill. It's your job, and you do it well. You are men who know how to bear arms better than anyone else."

The knights grew more and more astonished.

Quietly, Adrien took Opal's Stone from its black velvet purse and held it tightly, as she had done before.

"And yet," he continued, "you have forgotten the most important thing. You all have hearts; you can feel love. And that is what makes you real men."

His audience nodded slowly and, strangely enough, not one of them ventured to raise his sword again.

"You have killed the one I loved," said Adrien, "but I do not reproach you for it."

Was it Adrien's words that moved the knights, or the vision of the young man bearing Opal's dead body? Or did the Stone release some kind of magic? No one would ever know.

Then Adrien said with great dignity, "If you are men, you know what you must do now."

And a Knight of the Order, hesitantly, sheathed his sword. The others followed his example. They were not sure they had chosen correctly, but something deep inside them had impelled them to make this decision.

Turning his back to them, Adrien walked toward the magnetic field. He held tight to the Stone, choking back tears. He was now one with Opal. She had loved him. He loved her.

He passed easily through the magnetic field of Fairytale. Although hope had failed, love had triumphed over the impossible.

12

THE NAMELESS ONE

THE WOUND WAS DEEP: A BLOODY GASH ON HIS left forearm. The day before, he'd had to fight off the Bumblinks, wicked creatures who were rife in the northern forest of Fairytale. He had tried to travel through the woods instead of spending long, arduous days going around them, a decision he now regretted. The forest was teeming with evil spirits who resented any human presence. In just the last three days he had already fought two battles, and his horse had been killed in one of them. Luckily, night was falling, and the inhabitants of the forest were settling down to sleep.

He had halted in one of the few clearings, and he felt completely drained. Suddenly he heard a sound, and with his good hand, swiftly drew his gleaming sword. A form appeared. The young man waited, on his guard. The stranger drew near: short, stocky, he wore an ample dark green tunic and at his waist, a sword. It was impossible to tell his exact age, for although a few lines furrowed his brow, his expression was still youthful. An unruly shock of light blond hair fell over his forehead. His nose was small and flat, his lips pale but full. His eyebrows, like his hair, were fine and almost white, while his large, dark eyes seemed merry, yet at the same time wise with experience. Although he was smiling broadly and seemed friendly, something about him hinted that he could prove a formidable foe if the situation demanded it. Was he human? At first glance, his appearance was very much that of a man. But on closer inspection his skin revealed a slight silvery sheen.

"Sheathe your sword, stranger!" cried the creature. "My intentions are peaceful."

The young man with the wounded arm hesitated at first, unconvinced, but after a moment's reflection he complied with the creature's request and put away his weapon.

"I've traveled a long way to find you," continued the newcomer. "My name is Elfohrys, and I've come not to fight you, but to seek your help."

Elfohrys stepped closer and studied the young man before him: he was about eighteen years old, with dark brown hair and deep blue eyes flecked with emerald green. His face was grave, and his intense gaze was imbued with melancholy.

Elfohrys caught his breath: "At last," he told himself.

"Tell me," he asked, "aren't you a hovalyn, or a knight errant, as the common folk say?"

"I am," confirmed the young man.

"And what is your name? You may tell me, have no fear," Elfohrys assured him, in mounting excitement.

"I have no name," confessed the young hovalyn. "Or at least, not that I know of. Two years ago, I awoke in a field without any memory of my past. I decided to become a knight errant and go in search of my real name."

"The Nameless One!" exclaimed Elfohrys admiringly. "Your reputation is known throughout all Fairytale! Everywhere, people speak of a gallant hovalyn seeking his own name. Are you truly the Nameless One?"

"Unhappily, yes. My quest seems to have led me nowhere."

"It is within my power to assist you. I can help you travel through this forest, and will accompany you even farther on your way."

"But why should you wish to help me?"

"I, too, am on a quest, but I may not reveal to you either its purpose or my destination." I am seeking the Chosen One, added Elfohrys to himself, and I believe I have found him.

The hovalyn asked no questions; after all, he welcomed

a traveling companion, even a mysterious one. The silent young man's thoughts turned, as always, toward his dream: to have an identity. He had wandered in vain through most of Fairytale asking everyone if they knew anything about him. En route he had fought many monsters that had been terrorizing the population, and admittedly he had been richly rewarded, but glory was not what he wanted. At night, after having faced a thousand perils, he never fell asleep without wondering what his name was and where he had come from. He had invented hundreds of pasts for himself, depending on his moods; but this brought him little comfort, and frustration continued to eat away at him as he wandered on his fruitless mission.

It was growing late, and he was getting hungry. The youth opened his heavy leather bag and took out some bread, a gourd of water, some smoked turkey, and a strange-looking fruit. He offered to share his food with Elfohrys, who declined politely, producing an extraordinary-looking meal from his own bag: a sticky purple mass, which he devoured. Quickly satisfied, he waited patiently while his companion ate his own repast. Without a word, the Nameless One made a crackling fire, and sat down beside it to ponder his unexpected situation. All of a sudden he had found himself in the company of a stranger about whom he knew absolutely—or almost—nothing. Could he trust him?

Elfohrys had stretched out and was already fast asleep.

The young hovalyn could not manage sleep himself and lay staring up at the twinkling stars. He tried to recognize the different constellations and remember their names. He was overcome with anguish . . . What was he? Who was he? Nothing but a body, a soul in pain, with no memory, nothing that would make him a human being. He was a stranger even to himself. He drew his sword from its scabbard and studied its long, glossy blade, so smooth and sharp. He imagined the blade piercing his own heart. Would he feel cold? Perhaps not; he already carried winter inside him, an eternal winter of questions without answers. Of what use was he in this world?

The stars shone more brightly than usual. He got up, sword still in hand, and began to walk without knowing where he was going, without worrying that he might become lost. What did it matter? He took a winding path and plunged into the darkness. He walked on and on without stopping, oblivious to his surroundings, arriving at last in a moonlit clearing. Spying a lake, he went to its edge and sat contemplating his face in its clear water. This face of his—what did it represent if he did not have a name? Alone with his thoughts, he sat there for a long time, his sword lying by his side. Suddenly, his reflection was disturbed, and from the lake rose a beautiful creature like a mermaid, with a woman's body and two tails of equal size covered in golden scales. Her features were delicate, her blue eyes glinted with gold, and her skin was almost too white, too flawless. Her black hair, tumbling in heavy, silken curls to her shoulders, did not seem wet from the waters of the lake from which she had just emerged. In her slender hands she held a golden casket encrusted with pearls.

"Mortal!" she said fearlessly. "You have dared to approach the Lake of Torments! Only those who suffer may gaze at their reflection in its waters; all others drown themselves, having sought here a consolation they did not deserve. My sisters and I are the guardians and mistresses of the lake. We show ourselves rarely, and only to those worthy of us. I have come to speak to you, mortal, for I must give you something that belongs to you."

"You are mistaken. I possess only my body, my soul— nothing else belongs to me. . . . I am nothing, and do not even have a name. I am called the Nameless One."

"I know your identity, your past, and even some of your future. There are many who know as much as I do, without knowing you. But even if you were to ask me, I would not reveal to you the name you received at birth, for that is not my mission. The only thing I have the right to give you is this casket. It was entrusted to us, to my sisters and me, many years ago, and we promised to give it to a particular person, destined to appear at this lake one day. That person is you, mortal. Those who entrusted the casket to us had one wish: that you guard its contents carefully."

The Nameless One seized the object. Without a sound, the mermaid with the jet-black locks sank back into the depths of the lake. Dumbfounded, but curious, the young man slowly opened the casket, holding his breath, his heart pounding wildly.

In an instant he snapped it shut violently, his intense disappointment shaking him to the core.

The casket was empty.

The Thirteenth Councilor did not often fly into a rage. This time, however, he was in an indescribable fury; he was shaking, and his features were distorted with anger. When he shouted, his voice echoed through the rooms of the palace of the Council of Twelve.

"What?" he roared. "You tell me that all the inhabitants of Nathyrnn have escaped? Do you take me for an imbecile?"

The image of a Knight of the Order, quaking with fright, appeared on a large, thin plaque of gold floating in the air.

"Uh . . . Yes, everyone has escaped," confessed the man in a voice that was barely audible.

"And how do you explain that?" bellowed the Thirteenth Councilor. "Are you going to tell me, perhaps, that you just happened to be asleep when they escaped?"

"Well, actually—yes," stammered the Knight of the Order, confused and ashamed.

"You dare to lie to me? Do you not know the fate that awaits you? Death! And dishonor! In the public square!"

"But I assure you, I am not lying."

"Give me the border of the dukedom of Divulyon—at once!"

The image faded instantly, replaced by the face of another Knight of the Order.

"Commander-in-Chief of the Knights of the Order guarding the border of Divulyon, at your service!" he barked.

"Commander," snarled the Thirteenth Councilor, beside himself with rage, "did you arrest a large number of fugitives a few hours ago?"

"The thing is . . ." replied the commander, suddenly humble and hesitant.

"What happened?" cried the councilor. "Don't lie to me!"

"We did in fact intercept a number of people. We neutralized most of them. We fought valiantly. Our troops were hard pressed. We—"

"I want to know if anyone crossed into Fairytale!"

"Yes," admitted the knight miserably.

"But that's impossible!" shrieked the Thirteenth Councilor. "Who was leading this revolt?"

"Apparently, a young man we have not been able to identify."

"Were there three girls, about fourteen years old?"

"I believe so. One of them in particular was an extremely fine warrior."

"Don't tell me she's dead, or you'll meet the same fate!"

"No, not her. A different one."

"Which one? Describe her!"

"Blond, milky skin, pale eyes, simple clothing . . ."

"What? You've just signed your own death warrant, knight!"

With a wave of his hand, the Thirteenth Councilor made the golden plaque vanish. He clenched his fists furiously—all had not gone according to plan. If he had managed to prevent the girls from reaching Fairytale he could have destroyed them quickly. Now Jade and

Amber were beyond his reach . . . for the time being.

It was time for a new plan. True, Opal had died too soon for his liking, but together, the Stones were a threat, they were powerful. Without Opal, the other two were vulnerable—and he would show them no mercy.

Before long, the Prophecy would be nothing but a waste of paper, a meaningless book. At that thought, his face twisted terrifyingly into a grimace of joy.

13

DEATH

THE COUNTRYSIDE WAS SHROUDED IN DARKNESS,
but they could vaguely discern wooded hills and plains of
dense, wild grasses.

The former inhabitants of Nathyrnn hugged one
another joyfully, their faces transformed by happiness.
How could they not believe in the impossible after seeing
the merciless Knights of the Order sheathing their
swords?

Speechless with sorrow, only Adrien, Jade, and Amber
did not share in the general euphoria. Opal's death had
shocked and overwhelmed them. She was gone, never to
return, and she had left them so suddenly that they could
not quite believe it, although Adrien held her lifeless
body in his arms. Her blond curls tumbled in the breeze,
a thin smile was frozen on her pale lips, and her face had
a waxen pallor. In spite of everything, even in death, she
was still beautiful, and seemed all the more untouchable.

Adrien held back his tears and put on a brave face to

hide his grief and bitter regret. Still carrying his sad burden, he led Jade and Amber to a modest but handsome manor, the home of his friend Owen of Yrdahl. The front door to the manor always stood open in welcome, so Adrien simply made his way through dark corridors to a guest room he had often used, paying no attention to the few late-night revelers, who looked at him curiously.

When he reached the room, he laid Opal down gently on the clean white sheets of the bed, knelt in front of her, took her still-warm hand in his, and gazed at her in silence.

Standing slightly behind him, Jade and Amber no longer knew what was happening, where they were, or what they were doing. They couldn't think, let alone move. They could not grasp that Opal was dead.

Amber couldn't help crying. Blinded by tears, she wondered why life was so incomprehensible and why it relentlessly pursued those whom it had decided to destroy. She had thought that nothing could touch Opal, that she was in some way immortal. Why had Opal disappeared in such a cruel and untimely way?

Jade felt bad: she hadn't been able to feel real sorrow at Opal's fate. She had shed a few tears, but they'd been inspired more by her horror of death itself, by her dread of plunging one day into an endless void, of not being able to think and dream, of being erased from the world, forgotten. A little ashamed, Jade admitted to herself that she had absolutely detested Opal. Even now that she was dead, Jade couldn't summon any affection for her, only a hint of compassion. Jade was aware, however, that she, Opal, and Amber had belonged together in some vague way, forming a whole that should not have been wrenched apart. Opal was not supposed to have died, she was certain of that. Her feelings were in turmoil: she wasn't really sorry that Opal had died, but she felt guilty because of her callousness. She remembered the dead girl's chilly disdain for her, but a voice reproached her for being hardhearted and arrogant, reminding her that Opal had been vital to their quest.

Just then a man entered the room. Well built, with broad shoulders, he was simply dressed and seemed about twenty years old. He had a frank and engaging smile and appeared to be beside himself with happiness.

"Adrien!" he shouted. "You've come back! I jumped right out of bed when I learned you were here! Tell me, who are these charming ladies?" Turning to Jade and Amber, he announced, "Let me introduce myself: I am Owen of Yrdahl, an old friend of Adrien's, and I'm delighted to meet you! Welcome to my home!"

Adrien rose, and now Opal's body could be seen lying on the bed.

"Look, Owen! She's dead! Dead! It's my fault. A Knight of the Order murdered her, but I could have stopped him! And I did nothing. . . ."

Owen's smile vanished instantly. He rushed to Opal's side, seized her wrist, and looked at the blood still flowing from her wound. Then he dashed from the room without a word. Jade and Amber stared at each other in astonishment. A few minutes later, Owen of Yrdahl returned with a short, stout, middle-aged man who examined Opal without a word.

"This is Lloghin," explained Owen, "one of our most experienced healers. Of course your friend's case is not really serious, Adrien, but it would be better if she didn't lose too much blood."

"Owen," replied Adrien miserably, "don't make fun of me! Opal is dead, and I don't see how a healer can change that! It's not something to joke about."

"Joke?" Then Owen hit his forehead and cried, "That's right, you haven't heard!"

"Heard what?" asked Adrien, who felt an insane glimmer of hope return to his heart.

"Death is on strike! She hasn't done that for two

centuries, and it's very annoying. Your friend is alive."

"Very annoying?" repeated Amber. "I don't see what's so annoying about a miracle! What is Death on strike for?"

"Everyone knows that Death lives in Fairytale—in an inaccessible area, obviously. And just a few hours ago, she decided to stop working. So, for now, no one can die."

Jade and Amber were stunned. Adrien, who was used to Fairytale, could only weep tears of relief.

"Death is depressed," continued Owen. "She claims that no one loves her, which is true, naturally. But she would like to be appreciated for her true worth. They say she wants to kill herself. Since that's impossible, she's become even more depressed. Her advisers are at their wits' end."

"So Opal is alive!" rejoiced Amber.

"Yes, but it will be some time before she is completely well again. That's why we must stop the flow of blood."

Lloghin the healer was now applying balms and compresses to Opal's wound as he chanted strange words over her.

"The last time Death went on strike there were terrible consequences," continued Owen. "The strike lasted about ten years. People who hurt themselves or became ill during that time got rapidly better, but those who had already been sick or injured continued to linger in that state with no hope of deliverance through Death. In the end, her advisers managed to make her see reason, but I have the impression that this time, it's more serious."

"What a story!" marveled Amber.

"Now that your worries about your friend—Opal, is that right?—have been put to rest, perhaps we might be introduced to one another?"

"Well," replied Jade, yawning with fatigue, "we've known Adrien for less than a day, but we did liberate a city with him, and we've come to meet Oonagh, who reads people's hearts or something like that. By the way, I'm Jade, but that's all I can tell you about myself, except that I was driven from my palace by my own father and I have enemies everywhere, which isn't my idea of a nice life, but what can you do. . . ?"

"I'm Amber," said Amber simply.

"Jade, Opal, Amber," murmured Owen, as if struck by an obvious thought.

Jade yawned again. She was so exhausted she no longer knew what she was saying.

"Sleep," she mumbled, feeling her eyelids growing heavier and heavier.

"Ah—yes, of course, I'll show you girls to a bedroom,"

said Owen, adding to Adrien, "Wait here for a few minutes—I'll be back."

When he returned, Owen was bursting with excitement.

"The Stones of the Prophecy! You've brought the girls everyone in Fairytale is talking about! You owe me an explanation!"

"They're unbelievable girls," said Adrien, "and don't hold it against Jade if she was asleep on her feet. A little while ago, she fought the Knights of the Order."

"But it's so rash of her to reveal her name and her story—doesn't she realize the risk she's running?"

"No, I don't think she does," replied Adrien. "She doesn't seem to know much about the Prophecy."

"Then it's not for us to enlighten her. Now, tell me what the Outside is like!"

"It's so different from here," sighed Adrien. "You just can't imagine—the two worlds are almost complete opposites. Outside is huge, beautiful, just as you've heard on this side, but it's also hard, violent, and primitive. Life there is rough and archaic. The people don't know what freedom is; they live in an unjust and class-ridden society."

"You must be exaggerating."

"Maybe . . . no, I don't think so. How about you, tell me: what has changed over here?"

Owen's face grew solemn.

"We've begun to despair," he confided in a low voice.

"No . . . Don't tell me that . . . the Chosen One . . ."

"Yes. He still hasn't been found."

"This is getting serious. According to the Prophecy, it won't be long now until the battle. And if the Chosen One hasn't turned up, how will we fight? The army will begin to assemble soon, but without him, it won't help us at all."

"That's what everyone is worried about," said Owen glumly. "They're losing heart. Oonagh is waiting, but nothing is happening. The Chosen One has not revealed himself."

"And if he doesn't come?"

"That will mean that Néophileus was wrong, that the Prophecy is false, and that our hopes are in vain," Owen finished with a sigh. "But that can't be possible!"

"If the Chosen One doesn't exist, then perhaps the Stones don't have the power they are supposed to possess."

"And all will be lost," concluded Owen grimly.

14

THE GHIBDULS

THE NAMELESS ONE RETRACED HIS STEPS WITH great difficulty, but dawn found him back in the clearing, lying asleep next to Elfohrys. The forest was bathed in sunshine, clear and bright in spite of the magnetic field around Fairytale. The rustle of leaves in the warm breeze mingled with the day's first notes of birdsong as the forest awoke. The young man and Elfohrys opened their eyes. Stiff and aching, and still drowsy, they were nevertheless determined to be on their way.

Shrill cries sounded in the distance: the inhabitants of the forest were waking as well. Two races shared these woods, the Bumblinks and the Ghibduls.

Elfohrys belonged to a group of magic creatures that were few in number, but much respected, the Clohryuns, a race from which Néophileus himself was descended. The Clohryuns did not possess true supernatural powers, but Elfohrys knew how to defend himself and did not shrink from fighting adversaries more agile than he. A trusted friend had told him of a path leading out of the forest, and even though he had never taken it before, Elfohrys now proposed it to his companion. They would have to be on constant guard, of course, because there was always the risk of encountering some Bumblinks or Ghibduls.

The two travelers set out briskly, with Elfohrys confidently striding along winding paths bordered with brambles and stunted shrubs. The Nameless One felt no fear, for he attached so little importance to his life that he was not afraid of losing it. After a few monotonous hours, Elfohrys left the paths to head into the thick of the forest.

"There's no other way," he told his companion, who simply nodded.

Now the woods seemed even more threatening. The bare, scraggy trees loomed up against a cloudless sky.

"The closer you get to the heart of the forest," explained Elfohrys, "the more you can sense the presence of evil beings. I'm surprised that we've come this far without any trouble."

As time passed and the sun rose higher, the atmosphere became muggy, despite the shade beneath the forest canopy. The young man felt strangely tired and would have liked to stretch out under a tree for a nap. He stared blankly into space and began dragging his feet. Sounds became muffled, and images blurred. He was gasping for breath. Finally all grew dark around him and he collapsed. He heard a reedy voice intoning, "Nothing, nothing, nothing, you are nothing, nothing, nothing. . . ."

Then Elfohrys forced him to listen by sending a pleading telepathic message: "Don't give up, Nameless One! It's a mental attack from the Ghibduls! Wake up, all you need is a little willpower. Don't let them defeat you!"

But Elfohrys's voice irritated the young hovalyn, who wanted to get rid of it. His mouth was dry, and he struggled to tell Elfohrys to be quiet. But instead, without really wanting to, he said clearly, "The casket, in my leather bag!" It was as if someone had put these meaningless words into his mouth. Then he immediately lost consciousness and would gladly have remained in that state for ever.

A few moments later, though, he felt Elfohrys place the pearl-encrusted casket in his hands. Driven by a powerful instinct, he opened it—and was instantly bathed in a refreshing feeling of well-being. He leaped to his feet.

"You've come to!" exclaimed Elfohrys. "I thought you were lost—the Ghibduls' powers of mental persuasion are very strong. I shook you, I shouted, I even used telepathy to help you, but I couldn't rouse you."

"Thank you," said the young man. "If you hadn't been here, I would not have survived."

"Yes, you would have, but the Ghibduls would have captured you and taken you back to their lair to torture you."

"Thank you again," repeated the hovalyn, at a loss for words.

"It was a good thing you mentioned that casket! I found it in your bag, but I just couldn't open it no matter how hard I tried. Tell me, is it enchanted? Does it obey only you?"

"I'm not too sure, I found it along the way. . . ."

Elfohrys let the matter drop, but wondered why his friend had asked for the casket from the depths of his stupor, and how it had managed to save him.

"Nameless One," said Elfohrys abruptly, "when we get out of the forest, where do you plan to go?"

"We aren't out of it yet," replied the young man evasively.

"True, the Ghibduls won't give up easily. You've eluded them, so they'll do everything in their power to take revenge."

"They're formidable enemies," agreed the hovalyn, relieved to see that the conversation was taking a different turn.

But Elfohrys was not so easily put off.

"Be that as it may, you still haven't told me where you're going next."

"I—I was planning on heading for the city of Thaar," came the reluctant reply.

"Thaar?" repeated Elfohrys incredulously. "The City of Origins? How can it possibly interest you, a hovalyn? It's a most dangerous city, very hard to get into, and it has no connection with your quest!"

"I don't know where to go," confessed his companion, "and Thaar is one of the few places I haven't visited yet. It's as simple as that."

"Have you already been to see Oonagh?" asked Elfohrys, hoping he knew what the answer would be.

"No, never. What do you think that creature could tell me? I know only too well what's in my heart: questions, worries, but nothing of my past."

"That's where you're wrong. A long time ago, I went to see Oonagh myself. I learned things I had never suspected, and yet they were written in my heart."

"I'm almost certain her words won't help me at all," insisted the young man. "And anyway, Oonagh lives so far away, in that grotto lost inside a steep mountain. So few people undertake that journey. . . ."

"Trust me. Take my advice: go there. If you don't learn anything about your identity from Oonagh, we'll go to Thaar."

"All right, if it means that much to you, I'll go and see Oonagh," the hovalyn agreed.

Far away, in the very center of the forest, stood the dismal and terrifying lair of the Ghibduls. No one had ever understood them: among themselves they behaved in a manner far superior to that of men, for they never waged war among their own kind, they tolerated one another's faults, and never had family disputes. People mistakenly believed their customs to be backward and their society primitive. The Ghibduls felt love and pity just like any other creatures—perhaps even more so. They lived freely and happily; they made their home in the forest, and never left it. Because of their repulsive appearance, many legends had arisen concerning their cruelty, when in fact they were naturally affectionate and loyal, although fierce in battle. Since they were stronger than other species, they ruthlessly killed any intruders they found, suspecting them of wanting to take over the forest for themselves.

In their eyes, such intruders were savage beasts, a challenging prey doomed to a violent death. The Ghibduls positively enjoyed the feeling of warm blood their hands, and they delighted in its rich, sweet odor. The Ghibduls believed that to die at their hands was a privilege and a blessing for inferior beasts, who were incapable of thinking or loving—which was exactly what those same beasts thought about the Ghibduls.

Now the Ghibduls had just suffered the most stinging insult within living memory: there was a man in the forest, and that man had outwitted them. They had attacked him after his defeat of their friends, the Bumblinks, when he had valiantly defended himself and managed to wound most of his attackers. He wielded an apparently enchanted sword with uncommon skill and, above all, he did not fear death. Until then, the Ghibduls had encountered only men who clung desperately to life. They had been forced to admit that this hovalyn was different, and they had retreated in humiliation. Their pride had been wounded and they were set on taking revenge, but somehow they could not suppress a grudging feeling of admiration for the hovalyn. They had even tried to overthrow him using their mental powers, which they employed only against their most valiant enemies—but the human had triumphed again.

Mortified, the Ghibdul warriors sought counsel with their wise men, the strategists and councilors in charge of matters of the utmost importance. These wise men were themselves taken aback by the warriors' reports, but one of them came up with an astonishingly clever solution. There was violent opposition at first, but the plan eventually won everyone over. The human being who had beaten them had no idea whom he was up against, and the Ghibduls had more surprises in store for him—they could promise him that!

Paris: Present Day

I was frightened by the impenetrable, unchanging silence. All I could hear was the constant hum of the machines I was tethered to, that my flickering life was connected to. I had always been scared of the dark. Why pretend otherwise? And to me, that's what death was: complete darkness, eternal and unfathomable. I imagined myself falling into an abyss without anything to hold on to; I saw myself engulfed by nothingness, in a world without feelings, thoughts, colors, lost forever in a void. There would be no more pain. . . . I would dissolve in this emptiness, forget everything, lose everything, every trace of my existence. Actually, if that was what death was, then perhaps I had already left this life. But no, I was still lying here, motionless, pale, trembling convulsively, awaiting the end. I was afraid, so afraid, that I thought my fear might triumph and kill me before my illness could. I had more or less accepted the pain, understood that it would remain until the end, slyly gnawing away at me, but I had never been able to forget this fear always lurking inside me, relentlessly devouring, haunting, and overwhelming me. I was frightened of silence, darkness, time, oblivion, eternity. Death. I wished that I could stop time, order it to halt in its course. I pleaded with it to go backward, to give me back my life, my future. I had nothing left that could help or comfort me. There was only anguish, growing ever worse.

Then the dream had come. It had disrupted my waiting, hurled me outside time, outside the life I'd been leading or the absence of life that was my world. I wanted the dream to go on forever, to make me forget everything else, to wipe it all from the face of the earth. . . . I believed I could live in my dream, making it my reality and turning my sad reality into a distant and impossible dream. Without knowing it, I had timidly begun to hope again. But in the end, it was only a dream, and this grim realization destroyed all my illusions.

Even my dream wouldn't stay with me. I had to face facts: it was just an illusion. So I took a deep breath, and I faced the truth——the one I could see in the furtive glances of the nurses, the desperate truth that *hid deep inside me. I could not continue to believe that I could ever have my old life back again: I had neither the right, nor the strength, to hope for that. Joa, always spoiled by her parents, the successful, accomplished girl with so many friends—Joa had ceased to exist.*

I reined in my fear; I shattered the shell of fantasy I had tried to construct around myself thanks to that dream. And I said out loud, so I could hear the truth I was trying to escape from: "I'm fourteen years old. And I'm going to die."

15

FAIRYTALE

WHEN SHE WOKE UP, AMBER WAS DISORIENTED and panicked for a moment. Where was she? What had happened? Then the events of the previous day, so charged with emotion, came flooding back to her.

She took her time getting up and had a nice hot bath in a small private room adjoining her own. She sniffed the delicate scents lined up on a shelf and dabbed some perfume behind her ears. Then she dressed, combed her hair, and set off down the corridor outside her bedroom without any idea where she was going. She passed several ornately carved wooden doors without daring to open them, went down many corridors that all looked alike, and finally realized that she was walking around in circles. At last, to her great relief, she met a woman of about fifty, who laughed heartily when Amber explained her dilemma.

"My dear girl," she replied, "this manor isn't big enough for you to get lost in! Come along, follow me, I'll show you the great hall, where you can have a bit of breakfast."

"Actually," said Amber timidly, "I'd like to find Jade, Adrien, and Opal. We arrived together last night. . . ."

The lady's face suddenly looked serious.

"So you're the ones," she said thoughtfully. "Come, I'll take you to your friends."

As Amber followed her, she noticed that the woman was not walking: her body glided along an inch or so above the ground.

"Are you—are you working magic?" she asked awkwardly.

"Magic? That's what I dreamed of as a child, actually, but I couldn't do it. I didn't have the gift."

"But your way of walking without walking . . ." said Amber in confusion.

"That? But my dear girl, I'm a Dohnlusyenne. How else would I get around?"

"Oh, right. Sorry," replied Amber, utterly befuddled.

Just then the Dohnlusyenne opened a door and ushered Amber into a room where she found Adrien at Opal's bedside with Jade and Owen of Yrdahl.

"Amber!" cried Owen. "There you are! How about coming on a ride around Fairytale with us?"

"Wonderful!" she replied eagerly.

"I'm staying behind," announced Adrien. "If Opal

wakes up, I want her to find me right by her side."

Jade, Amber, and Owen left the manor. Three horses were tied up in the courtyard, and as the girls drew closer they noticed subtle differences between these horses and the ones they were used to: these animals had a soft and rather thick brown coat, golden manes that almost seemed to be made of glistening flames, and blue eyes gleaming with intelligence.

"Here are the horses we'll ride," said Owen. "They're real thoroughbreds—you won't find more magical beasts anywhere."

"Magical?" said Amber, disconcerted. "Do they fly, shoot fire from their nostrils, or something like that?"

"Of course not," laughed Owen. "I didn't say that a wizard had enchanted them!"

"Then how are they magical?" asked Amber.

"You're disappointed? If you like, I can give you a more ordinary horse," said Owen with a hint of mischief.

"No, no," said Amber quickly.

They mounted and rode out, Owen leading the way. The two girls were soon puzzled to find there was nothing extraordinary about the landscape of Fairytale: an endless sky of immaculate blue above a few distant peaks crowned with everlasting snows. Amber looked around at the white-capped summits and rolling hills.

"Over there," said Owen, "where those mountains are, that's where Oonagh lives. If you didn't really need to go there, I would advise against it, but, well . . . And never go to the city of Thaar. Don't even try, that's the last thing you should ever do."

"Why?" asked Jade, intrigued by his comments.

"It's more than dangerous," continued Owen. "It's just plain deadly. That city is cursed. They've renamed it again and again, but nothing helps—that city will never change."

"But why?" repeated Jade.

"It doesn't matter," said Owen curtly, suddenly uneasy.

Amber had been only half listening to the conversation; she was stroking her horse's coat, and was surprised to find it rough instead of smooth, as she'd expected.

That reflection had hardly crossed her mind, however, when the texture of the hair changed beneath her finger-tips, becoming silky and pleasant to the touch, exactly as she had imagined it. Curious, she stared down at the animal's coat. White would have been so pretty, she thought—and her wish came true: she saw the horse's coat grow paler until it reached the color she'd had in mind, a dazzling, pure white.

"Owen," cried Amber, "I get it! The horse guesses the

wishes of his rider, and then makes them come true! It's magical. . . ."

"Imagine that!" said Owen teasingly. "Aren't you pleased? These horses have always seemed like excellent mounts to me. . . ."

"They're wonderful!" cried Amber happily. "I just can't believe it, that's all!"

The three young people were traveling along a dull road, past ordinary houses and meadows of no interest, and Amber's suggestion that they run a race was immediately accepted by her companions. Amber concentrated on wanting her horse to gallop as fast as possible—and felt giddy with speed as the wind whipped her face and the ground flew by beneath her horse's hooves. She had never felt anything like it. After a few fantastic minutes, she looked back to see Jade and Owen lagging far behind. She mentally ordered her horse to stop, and waited for her friends.

"I've never seen that before!" exclaimed Owen. "It usually takes a while for the horses to get used to their riders, and long months of training before they will carry out their wishes—and even then the riders must have lots of experience with them. I had to work hard with the horse you're riding before he understood me as well as he does you!"

"Does he have a name?"

"How would I know it? Obviously, he must have one, but naturally a horse never speaks to a person, even if he's able to."

"And you haven't given him a name?" asked Amber.

"No, he wouldn't be pleased, that's not their custom."

"Ah," was all Amber said, because she'd run out of words to express her astonishment.

Since the ride was becoming tiring, the girls readily agreed with Owen's suggestion that they turn back. Jade questioned their host about how the citizens of Fairytale lived.

"We're free," he said simply. "We have responsibilities, of course, but we are all individually responsible for our own actions. We work, we amuse ourselves, we live. . . ."

"But the fairy creatures?" insisted Jade.

"They live among us."

"But then, what's so magical about life here?" asked Jade, who was running out of patience.

"It's just a name, Fairytale—a vague idea, not a way of life. It's a word; it doesn't illustrate reality or try to represent it. And our existence isn't a fairy tale—we all have sorrows, problems, even though we live among magical creatures. . . ." Owen broke off. "Wherever there's life," he said softly, "wherever there are men, there is also evil."

Soon the manor was in sight. The three riders took their horses to a small stable. While Amber fondly admired the stallion she had ridden, a graceful animal whose golden mane stood out against the creamy white of his new coat, his lively blue eyes observed her without a flicker of emotion. Amber left him with regret to follow Owen and Jade.

There was a great disturbance inside the manor, and the three young people had barely set foot inside when a man rushed over to Owen. Jade and Amber recognized him: it was Lloghin, the healer they'd met the night before.

"Something serious has happened," he announced, visibly upset.

"What's wrong? Calm down, Lloghin."

"I can't. . . . A messenger arrived after you left."

"A messenger? The news must have been important!"

"Oh, yes," sighed Lloghin miserably. "Owen, the worst has happened."

"*What* has happened? Tell me!"

"The city of Thaar has fallen."

"What!" shouted Owen of Yrdahl, thunderstruck.

"The messenger is in the great hall," added Lloghin. "I advised him to await your return."

Deeply worried, Owen went off with the healer. The

two girls had no trouble finding the room where Adrien had been watching over Opal, but they stood outside in the corridor for a moment.

"Thaar," murmured Amber thoughtfully. "What's so dangerous about that city? Who has taken it?"

"It's very strange," said Jade. "Owen and the healer look really terrified. And I thought war didn't exist in Fairytale."

"I feel as if I'm living in a dream," mused Amber. "So many things seem unreal to me."

"Well, I've had enough! I want to know what these Stones are, what I am, and why I was chased out of my home," declared Jade. "I want someone to explain to me what the Council of Twelve can possibly have against us. I want to live in a world where things are definite, where I'm not surrounded by mysteries and impossible dreams! As soon as Opal wakes up, we're leaving to go and see Oonagh."

With that, they entered the room to find Opal alone and shaking violently. The two girls rushed over to her. She was still unconscious, but was muttering vague sounds that didn't make any sense. She abruptly fell silent, and lay motionless.

"Where is Adrien?" cried Jade crossly. "He just goes off without any warning, and here we are, with Opal out of her mind, stuck in some manor in the middle of blasted Fairytale!"

"Adrien must have had a good reason to leave the room," replied Amber quietly. "We can go and get Lloghin."

"Where is he? I feel lost here! I'm out of my league, it's all too magical for me!"

"There's nothing magical about the manor," said Amber, "and surely we can manage to find the great hall!"

Suddenly Adrien appeared, wearing a blue-and-gold uniform. He looked particularly determined, but his face was pale.

"Adrien!" cried Jade indignantly. "Where were you?"

"Thaar has fallen," replied the young man.

"Yes, we know," said Amber.

"So there's a war?" asked Jade.

"Yes and no," answered Adrien gravely. He sat down in a wooden chair before continuing. "I'll tell you everything— you ought to know, so that you can tell Opal why I abandoned her."

"You only left while we were riding," said Amber. "It's not such a big deal."

"I don't mean that. I'll be leaving soon. For good."

"But—" interrupted Jade.

"Let me finish, listen to me, both of you. Thaar is not an

ordinary city. Some say that it's haunted by evil. Thaar belongs to the past, and reflects it. Thaar has been called the City of Origins and is the only city that has remained intact for thousands of years, as if it were outside time. This city has never truly been a part of Fairytale and, strangely, even though it lies beneath the magnetic field, Thaar is not protected by it. For a long time the Council of Twelve has been able to reach it through telepathy. That's one of the reasons why this city is so dangerous. There aren't many people living there, and some of them are hungry for power and have betrayed Fairytale by helping the Council of Twelve control the minds of all the inhabitants of Thaar.

"Some citizens did manage to resist, with difficulty, but the dark force of the Council of Twelve has invaded the city and now holds it in its power. From there, the evil could spread throughout Fairytale. The members of the Council of Twelve or even the Knights of the Order can now materialize in the city by using teleportation, thanks to a complex spell that has been cast only a dozen or so times throughout history. It's highly unlikely, however, that they will use this spell. It's almost certain what their plan is: using their minions in Thaar, they will invade the minds of others and enslave or destroy them. And they will succeed in this. Everyone in Thaar has finally stopped resisting. We don't know exactly what's going on there at the moment but, luckily, one of the inhabitants managed to escape. Messengers have been dispatched throughout Fairytale."

"How will everyone fight back?" asked Amber, shivering.

"The plan is simple: regiments of volunteers will encircle the city. If the Council of Twelve tries to take over more of the inhabitants, the soldiers will put up a fight— mentally. In any case, our army will attempt to contact the minds of the inhabitants, to help them, which is almost impossible, given the strength of the Council of Twelve. We will also try to enter the city to fight, to push back the mental attack."

"Wait a minute," said Jade. "Why are you saying 'we'?"

"I've just joined the army," announced Adrien in a voice charged with emotion. "I leave tomorrow."

"You're risking your life?" cried Jade.

"I want to be useful, not to hide shamefully, waiting to see what happens," replied the young man. "They need volunteers. My life or another's, what does it matter?"

"But you'll come back, won't you?" asked Amber.

"Perhaps," said Adrien evasively. "When it's all over. But perhaps not. At least I will have died fighting."

"Adrien, don't be so melodramatic," cried Jade. "You

make it sound as if it's the end of the world!"

The young man gave a faint, strained smile, and said, "I haven't finished. And don't ask me any questions. What I'm going to tell you is very important. Believe me, I'm serious when I say that. . . . I shouldn't say anything, but . . ."

"Oh, just get on with it," snapped Jade.

"You must go and see Oonagh. Now, without delay. We're running out of time."

"What about Opal?" asked Amber.

"Lloghin has given me a potion he has concocted that will bring her round for a few brief moments so that I can say good-bye to her. Then she will fall back into her coma. You'll have to arrange for her to be transported with you. She'll be all right without me."

"But how will we find our way?" asked Amber indignantly, and somewhat fearfully.

"You'll manage. It's crucial. Now, leave me alone with Opal for a few moments. Then you must. Owen will give you the magical horses you rode earlier."

The girls went out into the corridor and closed the door behind them.

"Everybody wants to get rid of us!" fumed Jade. "We're always being chased away!"

Amber said nothing, but Jade was right, and she, too, had had enough.

In the bedroom, Adrien was gazing longingly at Opal. "I'm so sorry," he murmured. From the pocket of his tunic he took out a beautifully carved flask containing what looked like a bubbling blue liquid. As he opened it, a heavy smell of blood, rotting flesh, and death filled the air. Wincing with disgust, the young man held the repulsive mixture close to Opal's nose. When she opened her lips, Adrien poured the miraculous draught into the girl's mouth, and she swallowed it obediently. Slowly, she came around: her nostrils flared; then her lips curved in a smile and she said faintly, her eyes still closed, "I've had such a lovely sleep. . . ." She yawned and opened her eyes.

"Opal!" cried Adrien, his voice thick with emotion.

The girl's vision was still blurred, and it was a moment or two before she came to completely. Then her pale, almost transparent eyes brightened and she breathed softly, "Adrien! You're here. . . . What happened?"

The young man felt tears come to his eyes, but he held them back as he reflected sadly that he was seeing Opal for perhaps the last time.

"I love you," he confessed shakily. "I will always be

thinking of you, until I see you again. I will be near you whenever you think of me."

He could not continue. Her huge eyes fixed on Adrien, Opal seemed overjoyed and miserable at the same time. Sitting up, she flung herself into the young man's arms and whispered, "Don't leave me, don't go, stay with me—it's dangerous, you're risking your life. . . . And I love you."

She tried to say something else, but all at once the light in her eyes died, and she fell back senseless against the pillow.

Adrien never understood how Opal had known that he was going off to fight, but what mattered most to him was the knowledge that she returned his feelings. Now, with love as his shield, he could leave fearlessly to confront the Council of Twelve.

16

GOOD VS. EVIL

AMBER AND JADE MADE THEIR WAY IN SILENCE on horseback toward the snowcapped mountains. They rode past houses, some modest, others imposing, and fields of crops that lined the road. There were only a few laborers, who were singing and laughing merrily instead of cultivating the land. They seemed human, but their long hair looked like spun silver.

Supporting the unconscious Opal as she rode, Jade was wondering where she would sleep that night and what insane adventure she was getting herself into. "Don't laugh," she burst out, "but I get the feeling everybody in the world knows what we're supposed to do—except us! Amber, you know what I've been thinking?"

"No," replied Amber absently.

"If the Council of Twelve is against everyone who knows about Fairytale, it's because it's frightened of them."

"Yes, that seems logical," said Amber.

"Listen, imagine if everyone knew about Fairytale—

there would be rebellions all over the place! Everybody would want to come here. Now, think about it: no one rises up against the Council of Twelve, because no one is brave enough, but it would also be totally useless—there are Knights of the Order everywhere. But, do you know, I bet the main reason no one's doing anything is that most people don't even realize what's going on! You see?"

"Yes," agreed Amber. "The people are deprived of their liberty, their dreams, their ambition. . . . From the moment they're born, they're given a future with no surprises. My parents were peasants, so I was destined to be one too, and I had no choice in the matter. The Council of Twelve robs people of their freedom under the pretext of giving them a stable society, but no one realizes this. They follow the rules without a second thought because they're used to them from birth."

"Before I left home I definitely saw the world only the way I'd been taught to see it. What about you, did you figure this out a long time ago?" asked Jade.

"I always knew it. I grew up freely, on my own, and I took refuge in reading forbidden books and learning about life through them. Look at the world under the Council of Twelve: the sick and weak are considered feeble, useless, and contemptible. People never notice those more unfortunate than themselves—except to make fun of them," Amber replied.

"It's true, people do only what they're ordered to do, they never question anything, they don't give a thought to friendship, affection. . . ." Jade mused. "Anyway, as I was saying, if the Council of Twelve has something against us, that's because it's frightened of us, as unlikely as that may seem. Ever since our births, it's had plenty of time to destroy us, to send Knights of the Order to hunt us down. So if the Council of Twelve is afraid of us now, it must have a very good reason—but I just can't figure out what it could be."

It was now early afternoon and the two girls had not eaten at the manor, so they decided to stop. Before their departure, Owen had given them enough supplies for their entire journey.

Jade and Amber sat down in the cool shade of an oak, and gently laid Opal down beside them. Their companion was still unconscious, but Lloghin had managed to stanch the flow of blood from her wound and it was now healing.

The two girls unpacked their supplies and hungrily attacked the fresh bread, dried meat, and creamy cheese, leaving aside the unfamiliar and less appetizing food.

"You know, Jade," said Amber, "I'm not sorry I came

here, after all. What kind of a future did I have? I didn't really have one at all. I was about to leave childhood behind and see what lay ahead of me: nothing."

"Ye-es," conceded Jade, "but it wasn't the same for me. Only a few days ago I would have proclaimed to the world that I was the daughter of the Duke of Divulyon, I would have told you all about my sumptuous palace, and unlike you, I believed that my future would bring me everything: fame, fortune, whatever my heart desired. Now I feel a little guilty that I didn't know enough to look beyond appearances."

Jade stopped talking and felt her cheeks flush. She would never have imagined that one day she would talk to someone about her feelings! And yet, the Duke of Divulyon had assured her that Opal and Amber would be her enemies, which had turned out to be true for Opal, but not for Amber. Why had he said that? Jade had the unpleasant impression that she had changed since leaving the palace. And Amber was coming dangerously close to being her first friend—a word that had always seemed mysterious to Jade, and yet attractive, too.

No, it wasn't possible! She, Jade, the daughter of the Duke of Divulyon, thinking such things! It was so strange—and she'd only left home a few days ago! She would have sworn that years had passed, perhaps because she sensed that her past was over and done with.

"I've got an idea," said Amber out of the blue. "Why don't we see if we can revive Opal with our Stones?"

"All right, let's try."

Amber took the black velvet purse from Opal's pocket and folded the girl's fingers around the Stone. Then she took out her own amber Stone and squeezed it tight, while Jade did the same with hers. They waited a moment, and then Amber squeezed even harder. The two girls felt that the Stones were trying to reach Opal through their energy, but it was no use: since she was unconscious, it was impossible to reach her the way they had before.

Disappointed, they soon set out on their journey again. Amber took Opal this time, apologizing mentally to her horse for this extra weight. She was sure that her mount understood, even though he didn't answer her.

"I'd really like to give you a name," Amber murmured telepathically, "even though Owen claims you wouldn't like that."

The horse instantly became agitated, and Amber felt a mild discomfort; she guessed that her mount was using telepathy to dissuade her from opposing his wishes.

"Fine, all right, don't get upset! I won't give you a name.

But I wasn't aware that you could communicate feelings and sensations to me. It's astounding!"

The horse stopped. Amber realized that she had annoyed him and wounded his pride.

"I'm sorry! It's just that I'm not used to Fairytale. Many things here are so different from where I come from."

Satisfied with her explanation, the horse walked on.

The girls rode for a long time without knowing whether they were on the right path. They were heading toward the mountains, but were still so far from Oonagh.

Twilight veiled Fairytale in shadows, and then night fell. The travelers weren't tired, but they decided to stop because the countryside seemed more threatening in the dark and the girls were afraid of getting lost or being attacked by an unknown enemy. Adrien had advised them against seeking anyone's hospitality, fearing they might encounter some danger. The girls knew that their enemies could be everywhere. Before, they had felt safe in Fairytale, but now, in the darkness, they didn't know what to think. They sat down under a tree by the side of the road and ate their supper. Then they stretched out on the prickly grass, laying Opal down beside them.

"I've been thinking," said Amber.

"Me, too."

"The inhabitants of Fairytale are believers. They believe in the impossible. They're free. Not necessarily happy, as Owen said, but free to choose their lives. I don't think that war can exist here, in such a peaceful country. In the rest of the world, ruled by the Council of Twelve, people don't believe anymore, they don't dream anymore. They don't know whether they're happy or unhappy. They don't even want to know. There isn't any war out there, either—but there are many things that are forbidden—"

"You're mistaken," cut in Jade. "There's evil here, too—Owen said so. There must have been wars and violence. You can't always live in peace. And over there, on the Outside, war has existed for a long time and still does today. The Council of Twelve fights against freedom and happiness. It won't ever conquer them completely. Wherever there is evil, there must also be goodness. So there is war. There, and here."

"You must be right," replied Amber admiringly. "Good and evil, the eternal battle. . . ."

They both laughed.

"On the Outside," continued Amber, "most people hardly ever think about others. They forget to look around them, they forget about people's feelings. And they don't even realize it! Who would rebel, out there? Who would dare to be different from everyone else? And who would show these others how to change?"

"That's why it's up to Fairytale to help the Outside," concluded Jade. "Here, everyone understands what goes on out there, and they can help them. And we certainly haven't the right to pretend that none of this is happening."

Carried away by her speech, Jade was about to say something else when a faint voice interrupted her, startling both girls.

"Where are we?"

Opal was awake.

"I don't feel well," she said weakly.

Amber crouched down beside her reassuringly. "We're in Fairytale," she explained. "You were hurt, but it isn't serious."

With a stifled cry, Opal touched her wound, which was still painful in spite of Lloghin's expert care.

"Let's get out our Stones," suggested Jade.

Opal and Amber promptly obeyed and, as they all concentrated, they felt a pleasant warmth. For an instant they thought of nothing: they felt relaxed, and their problems melted away. Then the communication slowly faded, and a wave of tiredness enveloped Jade and Amber, as though they had given part of their strength to Opal.

"Thank you. I feel better," sighed Opal. "My wound hardly hurts at all anymore. But I need to rest a little before we set out again. And by the way—where are we going?"

"To see Oonagh, of course," replied Jade tartly.

"But we're in no hurry," added Amber. "Tonight, we'll sleep. Tomorrow, we'll tell you everything."

And the three girls closed their eyes, forgetting all their troubles.

17

THE GHIBDULS' PRISONERS

ELFOHRYS AND THE NAMELESS ONE HAD stopped for the night in a small clearing. There had been no further incidents along the way after the mental attack from the Ghibduls. At one point Elfohrys had become disoriented, but after an hour the two travelers had managed to set out in the right direction again.

Before they lay down to sleep, the young hovalyn had asked how long it would take them to get out of the forest.

"Alas," Elfohrys had replied, "it's not up to me. If we don't run into any more obstacles, perhaps we'll be out of the forest in two days, but it could also take weeks."

After eating and chatting for a little while, they had lain down to sleep. The Nameless One, who'd had almost no rest the night before, had fallen into a deep slumber, unaware that the Ghibduls had been studying him all day long. When they were sure he was asleep, they insidiously entered his mind and numbed it for several hours. They did the same to Elfohrys, so that now even the end of the world would not have disturbed the two companions.

Satisfied, the Ghibdul wise men rubbed their clawlike hands together. Cackling loudly, they sent a dozen warriors to fetch the sleeping travelers back to the Ghibdul lair.

These magic beings could fly for short distances at low altitudes of less than three meters from the ground, and now they swept through the forest searching for their prey. When they found them, they tied them up roughly with strong vines and sneered at their victims. How could such pathetic creatures ever have seemed like a threat?

Two Ghibdul warriors grabbed the travelers as if they were nothing more than packages, and the creatures flew merrily back to their city.

The room seemed to spin around him. Where was he? What was happening? The young hovalyn had no idea. He tried to remember recent events, but his mind was still in a fog. He forced himself to keep his eyes open. He did not remember losing consciousness. Then he realized that his wrists and legs were bound, and that he was tied to a sort of chair covered with a greenish moss like lichen. Still drowsy, he did not even try to free himself. He was in a strange room with dirty white walls, along with Elfohrys, who was unconscious and also tied with the same dark vines.

Slowly the young man's mind cleared completely. This experience was like the one two years before, when he had woken up in a field in the middle of nowhere, except that this time, thank goodness, he could still remember everything that had happened before he'd fallen asleep in the clearing. He studied the room more attentively. The light was dim. Besides the two bizarre chairs, the place had no other furniture and told him nothing about his captors. He tried to wriggle free, to break his bonds, but in vain. On the contrary, the vines gripped him all the more tightly.

Then Elfohrys woke up, just as confused as his companion.

"Where are we?" he asked groggily.

"I don't know. You can't remember how we got here either?"

"I can't recall a thing."

The young man heaved a sigh of relief. So he wasn't alone in having no recollection of their capture, and there must be some explanation for their loss of memory.

The door opened with a sudden crash. Treading heavily, a Ghibdul haughtily entered the room. He was short and stooped, but this did not make his appearance any more reassuring. A kind of natural armor like a dark green shield covered his body. The only parts not concealed were his repulsive hands, sharp-clawed feet, and his purplish neck and head. His wrinkled face was particularly frightening: his nose had three nostrils, and his eyes, two folded slits, were an unclean, muddy color, glittering with intelligence and cruelty. His mouth, of the same green as his armor, was twisted and so translucent it was almost invisible. Unruly hair, like the vines binding the two prisoners, stuck out from under the Ghibdul's rusty helmet, and from his back grew two flimsy, blackish wings, now folded.

He was terrifying.

"A Ghibdul," Elfohrys observed aloud.

"Do you have a problem with that, prisoner?" growled the creature.

"Where are we?" asked the Nameless One. "What do you want from us?"

"Be quiet, vermin. It is beneath my dignity to speak to beasts such as you. No one, no prey, has ever had that honor."

"I would willingly have done without it," grumbled Elfohrys.

"Shut up! I speak; you listen. If you do not obey me, I will behead you here and now, and you will have to wait until Death's strike is over for me to kill you for good!"

The prospect of waiting with their heads cut off to be dispatched at some uncertain date by this gruesome creature persuaded the two captives to remain silent.

"Right," continued the Ghibdul in his hollow voice. "This is the situation. You are our prisoners, and you have no chance of escaping. First, you should know that you are within our city, which I am sure must seem breathtaking to you inferior animals, unaccustomed as you are to our refined civilization. In a few hours, you will be fed. Then we will bring you to a place that will delight your uneducated minds—"

"What place?" asked Elfohrys without thinking.

"Silence!" thundered the Ghibdul. "How dare you defy me, inferior being!"

"I didn't mean to," replied Elfohrys placidly.

"You miserable creature! If you only knew how much I long to tear you limb from limb this very moment. . . ."

The Ghibdul went over to Elfohrys and passed his hand lightly across the Clohryun's cheek, slicing it open with curving claws. Golden blood welled up on the prisoner's silvery skin, but he never made a sound.

It was the Nameless One who spoke to the Ghibdul.

"You'll be sorry for that, I promise you."

"You dare threaten me?"

Surprisingly, their tormentor seemed almost thoughtful, even curious.

"It isn't an empty threat," continued the young knight. "I always prefer to give fair warning."

"I'll show you on the spot what I'm capable of," declared the Ghibdul.

"That's fine with me," said the hovalyn firmly.

"We'll fight barehanded, but I will spare your life, so as not to disobey my orders."

"Very well," replied his adversary, not in the least intimidated.

The Ghibdul uttered a few unintelligible syllables, and the vines binding the young man untied themselves. Elfohrys glanced uneasily at his friend.

The Nameless One knew that one or two swipes from those fearsome claws would be enough to defeat him, yet he stepped forward serenely, almost nonchalantly.

The Ghibdul's expression changed hideously, stretching his face with what could only be interpreted as an evil smile. Without warning, he lunged at the young man, who seemed so frail and harmless in comparison, and his hands slashed repeatedly through the air, but whenever his opponent seemed within reach, the agile young knight would evade his attacker. The Ghibdul gradually ran out of breath, but not wanting to admit defeat, he kept trying to wound the hovalyn.

Elfohrys watched his nimble young friend with admiration as he skillfully dodged every blow.

At last, the panting Ghibdul muttered a few incomprehensible words that propelled the hovalyn back into his chair, where the vines twined around him once again.

"Man," said the Ghibdul in a harsh voice with a hint of grudging respect, "if you have managed to avoid my attacks barehanded, that does not make you in any way superior to me."

"I never claimed I was," replied his prisoner evenly, "but you have no reason to think me inferior to you, either."

"Wait and see what we Ghibduls can do! Our telepathic strength is unequaled and, armed, we are formidable!"

"Very interesting," observed the young knight.

Visibly offended, the magical creature left without another word.

"Why did you challenge the Ghibdul?" asked Elfohrys reproachfully.

"I wasn't going to let him attack you without saying anything."

"A rash reaction to a few drops of my blood! I have strong natural defenses, and my wounds will swiftly heal without leaving any marks. But you, you've just earned the enmity of that Ghibdul, which won't vanish so quickly, believe me!"

"Well, he didn't seem particularly well disposed toward us from the beginning," replied the hovalyn lightly.

Frustrated by the bonds imprisoning them, the two captives tried in vain to free themselves as the minutes ticked by, and they could not help wondering anxiously what fate lay in store for them.

When the door finally opened, it was a woman who entered. Elfohrys and the Nameless One stared at her in amazement. She was human! Clothed in a clumsy patchwork of fabrics made from forest plants, the woman was dirty, and her bare feet, like her hands, were covered with scars. Her face, although disagreeable, nevertheless showed clearly that she was human. She had high, prominent cheekbones, an aggressive gleam in her slanting black eyes, and thin lips. Her complexion was dull and her flat nose seemed to take up most of her morose face. Tangled brown hair stuck together with mud and filth fell to her broad shoulders.

Setting down a wooden tray bearing a few fruits, she undid the vines binding the two prisoners' hands, complaining all the while.

"Eat," she said in a gravelly voice, "but don't be thinkin' 'bout escapin'! You can do as you like, but those ties round your feet, they won't come undone!"

"You're human?" asked the young knight politely.

"Yeah, but the Ghibduls need servants like me. Women lost in the forest—they take them into service. They ain't mean to me, not 't all."

"What's your name?" asked the hovalyn, trying to strike up a conversation with the woman and gain her confidence.

"Naïlde. Eat, don't ask questions! I ain't to speak to you. I 'ave it good 'ere, and I don't 'elp prisoners. You think I'd run 'way, maybe? Well, sorry—nah."

"You let people of your kind die? You don't feel bad hearing them scream under torture?" asked Elfohrys.

"The Ghibduls treat me better 'n humans did, so me, I serve 'em right, that's all."

With that, Naïlde swore and spat contemptuously at the young hovalyn's feet. Then, with a strand of spittle still on her lips and a sour, disdainful look on her face, she turned on her heel and left, slamming the door behind her.

"Unbelievable," marveled Elfohrys. "That woman has even adopted the Ghibduls' charming customs!"

"Who knows what her life among her own kind was like," replied the Nameless One kindly. "Before becoming an inhuman woman, she must have been a simple soul, perhaps misunderstood. She has probably suffered a great deal. We cannot say what comfort she has found among the Ghibduls, but judging from what she says, she's satisfied with her life here."

Elfohrys looked at his friend curiously. He was speaking sympathetically about a woman who had just refused to set him free! The nature of humans, concluded the Clohryun, is definitely even more incomprehensible than I've been told.

The young man was quietly eating some of the fruit brought by Naïlde. When he'd had enough, he handed the tray to Elfohrys, who devoured everything that was left. Since his hands were still free, the hovalyn tried to remove the bonds around his legs, but with no success.

"Ah, you humans," sighed Elfohrys, almost resignedly. "Ever hopeful! If you ask me, it's what ensures your survival. No matter how many times you're told it's no use, you keep trying anyway."

When Naïlde returned to collect the tray, the Nameless One held his breath, wondering if the servant might have changed her mind, won over by pity. Elfohrys noticed the gleam of hope in his eye and thought, Still just as naive, still trusting in others. Humans are convinced that they're filled with goodness even when they're striving to do one another in. Strange. . . .

Naïlde let loose another barrage of insults at the young man, whom she seemed to take a personal satisfaction in humiliating. Clearly she had not changed her mind one whit, and the disappointed hovalyn realized he'd failed to convince her to set him free.

Grumbling, the servant left the room.

The two prisoners began to feel apprehensive again after Naïlde had gone, and almost immediately, four imposing Ghibduls appeared, one of whom muttered a few words that released the captives from their bonds.

"Follow us," ordered a Ghibdul gruffly.

As they were led through somber rooms toward an exit, the two companions were able to observe the building where they had been imprisoned: its bizarre architecture lent it a dark air of isolation, and yet, inside, the gloomy place was swarming with Ghibduls.

The captives were escorted by their jailers through narrow, winding streets. They soon discovered what no outsider could have suspected: the active and organized Ghibdul capital, hidden away. Its location had clearly been carefully chosen, for this small city was surrounded by huge trees that formed a natural defense.

An immense building gradually appeared before them, and the Ghibduls escorting them smiled proudly when they caught sight of it. It was built of stones painted black, decorated with embellishments, and resembled a theater.

The small party entered a crowded hall where striking sculptures and paintings revealed the Ghibduls to be capable of fine and original art—a talent that would have astonished any outsider.

The jailers escorted their prisoners through the throng and up endless stairs until they reached a copper door. Opening it, they thrust in their charges, slammed the door shut, and left.

Without even the vaguest notion of what was happening to them, the two companions tumbled into a void. After falling through a sort of spongy bubble, they landed unhurt—to a wave of applause.

Dumbfounded, they rubbed their eyes at an incredible sight: the interior of a gigantic theater, very elegant and well lit, where thousands of Ghibduls were comfortably ensconced in seats covered with dark velvet. Newcomers were streaming into the audience from all directions. The theater was elliptical in shape with countless rows of spectators leading up to a ceiling that depicted the forest beneath an azure sky. In the center of the theater was a spacious stage atop a short, wide marble column surrounded by transparent glass, enabling the spectators to see the stage from any direction.

The only problem was that Elfohrys and the Nameless

One found themselves on this very stage. Looking up at the ceiling, they could see the almost invisible trapdoor through which they had plummeted into the heart of this theater.

"Elfohrys, where are we?"

"I have no idea, and it wouldn't help a bit if I did."

"But this is incredible!" said the hovalyn. "Everyone says the Ghibduls are barbarians, and here we are in the middle of an unimaginable place!"

"You know, Nameless One, it's a shame, but I don't think we're ever going to get a chance to tell anyone about it."

Ghibduls were flying around the theater offering refreshments to the audience. The concept of money was alien to them: buying, selling—none of that existed. Nature provided them with everything.

The young hovalyn noticed that a small section of the theater was a standing-room area reserved for a few dozen coarse women, some of them human, and even at a distance he recognized Naïlde among them, screaming and shaking her fist, perhaps at him.

The lights went out. A powerful voice echoed through the theater.

"Welcome, my dear Ghibdul friends! Today I have the honor of presenting to you an authentic Clohryun and a man—a hovalyn, would you believe! Who will be the victor? How long will they hold out? The betting is open. As usual they will undergo the trials we have prepared for your entertainment. And so I wish you a pleasant afternoon—and I hope you enjoy the show!"

The audience clapped enthusiastically.

Elfohrys and the Nameless One exchanged worried looks. Before they could say a word, while the spectators were still applauding their entrance, they both felt a sharp pain stab them in the left arm. The young hovalyn already had a wound inflicted in battle by the Bumblinks, and now this wound reopened and began to bleed. He stifled a cry, but almost at the same time came another attack, this time battering his whole body. It caused no wound, but he could hardly keep himself from collapsing and writhing in agony on the stage.

The Ghibduls laughed, commenting on the scene with amusement.

The expression on Elfohrys's face showed that he also was in atrocious pain, and at the third assault, directed at the left leg of the two victims, the Clohryun fell fainting to the ground.

The audience booed him disdainfully.

The young hovalyn was staggering, seriously wounded in

the leg. The unbearable odor of his own blood was choking him, strangling him; he was drowning in it, and his eyes rolled upward with anger. Why were these Ghibduls so savagely eager to see him suffer? Determined to behave with dignity, he stayed on his feet while his left arm was lacerated by an unseen power. Murmurs of astonishment began to ripple through the crowd.

A fresh barrage of bodily pain was launched at the hovalyn, knocking him down, to shouts of disappointment from the audience.

The Nameless One immediately plucked up his courage and strength, however, and staggered to his feet once more. His eyes shone with such determination that the spectators were shaken.

When he felt an invisible dagger pierce his abdomen, the hovalyn did not flinch. After all, he wasn't risking anything, because Death was on strike. All he had to do was resist the attacks. But he was exhausted, and when agony surged through his body again, he had to lean against the glass wall surrounding the stage. With a last effort he tried to draw himself up, to shout a threat, something brave and dignified that would restore a little of his pride but everything was growing hazy around him: images, sounds, smells—all of his perceptions were fading, vanishing, leaving only suffering.

Still he resisted, when all of a sudden the same voice from before resounded throughout the theater: "The moment has come—it is time to choose."

A thrill of excitement swept through the crowd. The Nameless One made a superhuman effort to stay on his feet. Everything seemed so distant. . . .

"Hovalyn!" continued the voice. "Kneel, renounce what you are, give up the fight. You can never vanquish us. If you submit, your torture will cease, you will be one of us. We know the identity you seek so desperately. We will reveal it to you. You will have a place among us. But if you defy us and refuse this offer, the pain will torment you to the point of madness. And when Death ends her strike, we will kill you. So, do you admit defeat? Will you serve us?"

"Never," gasped the Nameless One.

A new wave of pain flooded instantly through him.

A distant voice, solemn and harsh, but filled with admiration, then echoed through the theater.

"It's him. . . . It's him! Stop, it's him!"

The Nameless One fell unconscious.

18

THE NALYSS

THE SUN HAD BARELY RISEN WHEN THE THREE travelers woke up. They ate a meager breakfast; Amber tried tasting a strange fruit that turned out to be delicious. No one spoke, for they were still quite tired.

Opal was the first to see the two girls coming toward them. Their fresh, dainty faces seemed quite carefree, yet Amber could not help noticing their conceited, almost disdainful expressions. It was impossible to tell how old they were. They both had short brown hair, attractively tousled, but one had liquid brown eyes while the other's eyes were periwinkle blue—with a gleam of malice. They looked very much alike: small, narrow, slightly upturned noses; full lips set in an innocent pout. Their features and attitude suggested that the girls were charming and angelic, but they could not disguise a certain arrogance.

At first the two newcomers simply studied the three travelers in silence. Then the blue-eyed girl piped up, "Loorine! Do you think they're humans? Real live humans?"

"Could be," replied the other in a rather snooty tone. "What luck!"

"I'm definitely alive," announced Jade dryly. "You might take that into account while talking about us."

"You're right, Mairénith," said Loorine. "They are humans!"

"Thanks for noticing," snarled Jade.

Amber and Opal examined the strange girls attentively, feeling more irritated than intrigued by the contempt in their voices.

"How happy I am!" cried Mairénith, batting her long, curving black eyelashes.

"We're so pleased to meet you," declared Loorine, with a smile that revealed her perfect white teeth.

"I think you're pretty!" said Mairénith merrily. "Don't you agree, Loorine?"

"Yes, very pretty."

"Thank you," said Jade, "but would you please stop making fun of us?"

"Very pretty," repeated Loorine. "We've never seen the like before, have we?"

"No," said Mairénith. "Jade, tell me, do you find me pretty?"

"How do you know my name?"

"I just do. I'm a Nalyss, and nothing less. So, do you think we're pretty?" she continued in a wheedling voice.

By now Jade, Amber, and Opal were wondering just who these visitors could possibly be.

"Why do you ask?" said Amber.

"I really want to know," replied Mairénith fretfully.

"Yes, you're pretty," said Jade in exasperation. "But you're very weird, and if I were you, I wouldn't be so conceited."

Amber and Opal smiled fleetingly to hear Jade mention her own greatest flaw.

"She thinks we're pretty!" crowed Mairénith in delight, as if she hadn't heard anything but that.

"Of course we are!" agreed Loorine.

A third girl then appeared. She was as lovely as the other two but did not resemble them, and it was easier to guess her age, which couldn't have been more than fifteen. She seemed delicate but not frail, with exquisite features, a glowing complexion, bright red lips, and silky hair that hung down to her slim waist. Her gaze seemed so pure and innocent that it was positively unsettling.

"Oh, Loorine!" groaned Mairénith.

"Such ugliness!" wailed her companion.

"I can't bear it," moaned Mairénith, on the verge of tears.

"Go away, quickly, you horrid creature!" shouted

Loorine. "Leave us alone! Don't come near these travelers!"

Then, as if appalled by some repulsive vision, Mairénith and Loorine took to their heels.

"They are really something else," said Amber, who would have burst out laughing if she hadn't been so astonished.

"You said it!" agreed Jade.

"Anyway, why did they run off like that?" wondered Amber. "I thought they'd seen some dreadful monster— what a racket they were making! Honestly, I just can't figure it out at all."

Jade merely shrugged, while the newcomer approached and said with a smile, "My name is Janëlle."

"Delighted to hear it," observed Jade sourly.

"The girls you just saw are Nalyss. They're rather bizarre, aren't they?"

Janëlle sat next to the three travelers and began to tell them about the Nalyss, who are not uncommon in Fairytale. They are always female and never live beyond the age of thirty. Extremely narcissistic, they spend their entire lives in passionate adoration of their beauty, an obsession so all-consuming that they have to avoid seeing themselves in a mirror or on the surface of a lake, for fear that they will never be able to tear themselves away from their reflections.

Janëlle neglected to mention that not many people

could actually see them. The Nalyss have an unusual gift that even they do not fully appreciate: they can see a person's inner beauty, and see it even more clearly than simple physical attractiveness. Only people who are beautiful both on the inside and the outside can see the Nalyss, and anyone else is repulsive to them.

The Nalyss spend their lives trying to meet as many people as possible who will confirm their own beauty. They are superficial and unintelligent and they amuse themselves by captivating men they find worthy of their attention in order to drive them insane with love—and, occasionally, to have children by them, who are always born Nalyss.

At the end of their existence, very few of them realize that they have vainly pursued a meaningless ideal, that their beauty has brought them nothing, and that they have quite simply forgotten to live.

Her story told, Janëlle let a long silence fall.

"And you, who are you?" asked Jade, breaking the spell.

"I am Janëlle, and I guide people to their destination in return for food and a little pleasant company."

"In that case, beat it," said Jade, who had no idea why she was reacting so nastily.

"No, don't go!" cried Amber indignantly. "Janëlle, could

you take us to Oonagh? We don't know anything at all about Fairytale, and we're a little lost."

"Of course I'll take you," replied Janëlle, beaming with pleasure.

Saying nothing, Opal simply studied the smiling girl; she wasn't happy about her arrival, but she felt no hostility toward her, either.

The party set out again, with Amber and Opal on one horse, Jade and Janëlle on the other.

It soon became clear that Janëlle was casting a pall on the three travelers' spirits. Not daring to trust her, they kept quiet to avoid giving away anything important. And yet, Janëlle truly did seem inoffensive, so Amber decided to talk to her.

Janëlle quickly showed herself to be a nice, normal girl, and she explained to Amber that, like her three new companions, she was fourteen years old. She was very poor, and instead of moping in her village, she had preferred to explore Fairytale by becoming a guide.

"At your age?" marveled Amber. "I didn't know that such dire poverty could exist here!"

"Unfortunately, yes. Wherever there is life, there cannot always be happiness."

Despite the furious looks Jade gave her, Amber

responded to Janëlle's friendly overtures by telling her own story, from the beginning. She had just reached the part when she had first seen her Stone when Jade interrupted her angrily.

"Be quiet, Amber! You're not supposed to talk about that!"

Amber's sweet face clouded over instantly.

"Jade, it's not for you to tell me what I must or must not do. I can decide for myself. If you can't manage to trust anyone, that's sad, but it's your problem. Not mine. I respect your opinions, so don't judge mine. You should mind your own business, Miss Princess, and let other people take care of themselves."

Although Amber didn't flinch at Jade's wounded expression, she was secretly stunned by her own words.

"It's funny when you realize how wrong you can be," said Jade in a cold, numb voice. "You take the risk of respecting someone, even though she might be an enemy, a real danger to you, but instead of heeding such warnings, you think you're creating a fragile friendship, a mutual understanding. And then you're forced to admit what you'd thought you could ignore: suddenly you discover an enemy where you would have sworn you had a friend."

Startled by the unusually heated argument between

her companions, Opal tried clumsily to bring the conversation back to safer ground.

"What happened while I was still unconscious? How
come I didn't die? And is Adrien all right? Where is he? I
dreamed . . . that he was in a uniform, and I had the feeling
that he was going to leave."

"That's true," said Amber. "I'd forgotten that you don't
know the latest developments."

And although her voice still showed her irritation,
Amber began to tell Opal about everything that she had
missed.

Jade rode along without looking up; although she didn't
want to admit it, she didn't feel like her usual self. She was
gradually growing used to Janëlle and was beginning, not to
accept her presence, but simply to forget she was there.

The girls rode through several villages without incident.
After Amber finished relating to Opal all that had happened
during her coma, there was an awkward silence, which
Janëlle tried unsuccessfully to dispel.

After a few hours, Amber's exhausted horse sent her a
weak telepathic message, asking her if he might rest.

"We have to stop," she announced, and although they all
agreed to halt there in the middle of a rugged plain, they
could still feel a certain tension in the atmosphere.

"Do you think you're special because you can read a horse's thoughts?" asked Jade snidely.

"At least I don't think I'm the center of the universe," Amber shot back.

"Stop it, you two!" exclaimed Opal, growing more and more baffled. "Something weird is going on. Maybe we should use our Stones."

"That's right, you aren't strong enough to take responsibility for yourself," replied Amber. "You always have to ask for help."

"So you think you can hurt me?" Opal asked Amber. "Too bad, you're wrong. I hope you aren't going to start crying—because I know what a sensitive girl you are, so touchy-feely with everyone, and it would be so sad to see you all teary. Oh, sorry—how can I be saying such things to you, when you're just so perfect? Of course, I wouldn't dare mention that you're just a poor, ignorant, and sentimental peasant!"

Opal couldn't believe she'd just spewed out those words—they had poured forth of their own accord, harsh and uncontrollable. But now she wasn't sorry that she'd said them, because blind hatred was starting to grow inside her.

The girls set out once more. Speaking soothingly, Janëlle

tried to start a peaceful conversation, but it was hopeless: the other three lashed out at one another with increasing venom. Things deteriorated when Amber and Jade reined in their horses after two hours, saying it was time to rest again. They had hardly dismounted when they flew into a fury, slapping each other in the face. Opal joined in the brawl as well, giving a few vigorous thumps of her own.

At first Janëlle called out to them, but to no effect. Then she yelled her head off. It was a waste of time. She waded into the fray, receiving a flurry of vicious blows. Her slender body seemed to falter for a moment; then, with unexpected strength and determination, she separated the three girls.

With her jet-black hair in wild disorder, her clothes torn, Jade seemed beside herself, red-faced and menacing. A few drops of blood beaded a shallow cut on her cheek. Opal had come out of it with only a few scratches, and the look in her eyes was more inscrutable than ever. The pain of her wound had flared up again, and she kept her head down to hide her feelings. As for Amber, she was fighting back tears. Her bruised lower lip was split, and she tasted the hot, disagreeable bitterness of blood in her mouth.

They glared at one another.

The situation had become unbearable.

*   *   *

Somehow the girls managed to mount their horses and continue their journey, but the air was filled with palpable tension and bitterness as they struggled to hold their angry tongues.

When night fell, bringing an end to a difficult and tiring day, the four girls stopped at the edge of a meadow, for Janëlle had persuaded the others to spend the night outdoors rather than in an unfamiliar village.

Unable to bear even sharing some food, Jade and Opal stalked off across the field in different directions to spend the night on their own.

Amber was alone with Janëlle. She felt no resentment toward their young guide, whose presence didn't affect her bad mood one way or the other. Janëlle began to tell Amber about her past, how she had come to be alone, working as a guide. Janëlle's story was so similar to her own that Amber found herself opening up to the other girl and pouring out her grief over her mother's death. She was relieved to have found a real friend, after being so let down by Jade and Opal.

When they grew tired, the two friends decided to go to sleep, promising to continue their conversation the next day. Amber slept heavily, without any dreams.

The sky was sprinkled with stars; the moon shone faintly. In the middle of the night, the silence was broken by a stifled cry. Amber awoke suddenly, gasping for breath; she felt a burning sensation spread throughout her body, and slowly, painfully, she struggled to her feet.

"What's happening?" she moaned. "I feel so terrible!"

Janëlle did not reply. Her expression had changed into one of loathing and malevolence. She bent down and tried to pick up something in the thick grass, then straightened up with a shriek. It was impossible to deny: her eyes were flashing with rage.

"Janëlle!" gasped Amber, mesmerized.

"Leave me alone!" cried the other girl in a shrill, hysterical voice.

"What's the matter with you?"

"Can't you tell? Don't you want to understand?"

Janëlle slowly held out her clenched fist, then opened her fingers to reveal a palm disfigured by burns. At that moment, Amber saw her as the Nalyss had perceived her—as everyone would have seen her if her appearance had been the reflection of her soul: oily skin, messy black hair, dark eyes buried in puffy cheeks, a piggy nose, a massive and ungainly figure. Her eyes glittered with wickedness, and all her features betrayed a desire to destroy: she had become the incarnation of hatred.

"It's your fault!" she screamed, as if demented.

"But—what is?"

"Everything! You don't dare see what's right in front of you? I hate you. . . . I hate you!"

Amber felt sick. Her eyes filled with tears. She didn't understand anything anymore, and didn't want to.

"You have everything for yourself, you're the one I should have been!" wailed Janëlle. "You've stolen my place! You've stolen my life!"

"That's insane," stammered Amber.

"Of course, it's easy for you to say that. Me, I'm just a poor miserable girl, I have no right to be important—that's what you think."

"No, no, not at all!"

"You still don't get it? Then I'll help you. Let's go back to the beginning. I meet three girls, so I stop, and from what I hear them say, I realize that they've seen some Nalyss who ran away when they saw me coming! Of course, these three are perfect enough to have seen them, but not me!"

"I—I didn't know," whispered Amber, who felt the burning sensation in her body grow worse as her world crumbled around her.

"So," continued Janëlle, "I decide to make friends with them. I want to show them that I, too, have a right to exist, to be appreciated."

"I never said you didn't—"

"But these three girls ignore me."

"That's not true!"

"They have everything on their side. Life has given them so much, and me, nothing. I feel violent anger growing inside me: it fills me, possesses me, until it takes me over completely. I have to get rid of it. I concentrate, and with an ease I've never known before, I expel my hatred. It overflows . . . into the soul of another."

"Jade!" said Amber.

"But this hatred keeps rising in me, so to control myself I shift it to you, then to the other girl, Opal, isn't that her name? The anger gradually enslaves me and each of you in turn."

"Why? We didn't do anything to you!" protested Amber, choking with misery.

"Then you confide in me. I invent the story of my so-called life and you believe me, feel sorry for me. I hate your goody-goody feelings, your sympathetic manner. I was dying to spit out the truth, to tell you how I've infected people with hatred and brought about deaths, caused wars.

When you told me about your Stone, I realized who you were. And then I thought I was going to explode with rage. I wanted to outdo you, humiliate you, annihilate you."

"No!" cried Amber miserably, still refusing to accept the truth.

"Tonight I tried to steal your Stone, but I couldn't: it burned my hand. And you! You woke up, so trusting, with that perfect, smart, unbearable look on your face."

Amber couldn't say a word.

"What do you think? That I'm some tormented soul? That I turn to evil simply to escape from my problems? No. Evil nourishes me, gives me power! Without evil, I'm nothing. I serve it, but it consoles me, transforms me, makes me invulnerable! I need evil. When I see others suffer, when I feel evil possess me, I grow strong! With no more need to hide behind simpering smiles, to force myself to be someone else, to seem nice. Evil lets me be myself."

"Why are you telling me all this?"

"Because I know that it hurts you. My words wound you, make your bruised soul bleed—and I love that. You thought you were better than I am? You aren't! You thought I was your friend? I was just the opposite, one of your most fervent enemies! Your tears give me incredible joy. You think I've betrayed you? Well, I have no regret: I do as I please, I follow my own nature. I don't flinch at the slippery world I'm forced to live in; I create evil, and I live off it."

With these words, Janëlle smiled triumphantly and left satisfied.

Amber thought she vaguely glimpsed a horseman in the distance, watching the scene, but that image could only have been an illusion, a mirage in the night.

She looked in the grass for her Stone, which had turned warm and comforting again. The bitterness and burning in her heart had vanished with Janëlle, yet her cheeks were still wet with tears, like pearls of deep dismay.

PARIS: PRESENT DAY

I was growing frailer, weaker. I barely touched the food the nurses brought me. For months I'd refused to look in a mirror; I could just imagine seeing myself: thin, shaking, my bones sticking out, my face drawn. I didn't dare confront the despair in my eyes. I wanted to keep the image of Joa, not the specter of an invalid huddled in fear. When I closed my eyes tightly enough, I still saw myself the way I used to be. The image would come to me slowly, and it was growing more and more blurry as the days went by. Then I was somebody else: Joa. . . .

It hurt to remember how things used to be, and tears would sting my eyes. I had tried to forget everything, to file my past away in the depths of memory, and I had thought I'd succeeded. I wanted to accept my fate.

But the dream dredged up the past—the three girls reminded me of how I had once been—and at the same time began sketching out the future. I thought I was strong enough, tough enough to resist the dream. I was wrong. Although I wouldn't admit it to myself,

I felt stirrings of renewed hope. And yet, this whole story was only a dream—this tale that was bringing me back to life was something my tormented mind had invented from nothing. I was almost afraid to think about it, as if my memories, my thoughts, my feelings might change the sparkling colors of the dream, muddling them until they grew pale, faint, and faded away. The dream seemed so important to me that I dreaded feeling it slip away from my memory. I wanted it to continue, forever. Although I wouldn't let myself admit this, unconsciously I believed the dream was true, I felt it was true, I wanted it to be true.

But my illness continued to destroy me. I was in pain, and the dream, which carried me far from my reality, renewed my pain whenever I left it and returned to my hospital bed. The more I wished to live, the more I suffered in my struggle against death. Once again I began to reject that fate and to believe in the illusion of hope; naive, perhaps, but I was happier that way.

19

THE CHOSEN ONE

THE NAMELESS ONE OPENED HIS EYES AND quickly regained consciousness. His injuries had disappeared. He no longer felt any pain or saw any trace of the deep wounds he had sustained. He realized that he was in the same room as before, a narrow room with bare walls. And though he was still sitting on the strange chair of green moss, his limbs were no longer restrained by bonds. Next to him, Elfohrys seemed unhurt as well, although he was still tied up.

"Ah! Nameless One!" Elfohrys cried. "Finally, you've come round!"

"But—the theater, the agony . . ."

"Excuse me? You must still be in shock."

"I didn't dream it," murmured the puzzled hovalyn.

"A few hours ago, after Naïlde left, some Ghibduls came."

"I know."

"They surrounded you and started chanting a strange

spell. You fainted, became agitated, and babbled some incomprehensible sounds. Then they stood around you without a word for about half an hour. I was beginning to get really worried! You were still unconscious when they left. I shouted, I tried to help you. At last, after two hours, the vines imprisoning you untied themselves, and you seemed to become more peaceful."

Perplexed, the haggard young man stared at his intact limbs, unmarked, save for the old wound on his right arm. He took his head in his hands. Was his memory beginning to play tricks on him? After eradicating his past, was it betraying him anew, conjuring up an imaginary present?

Before he could think any further, three Ghibduls entered the room. Their monstrous faces were twisted into affable expressions, while their lips tried vainly to form smiles. Approaching the knight, one of the visitors silently held out to him a long object wrapped in an immaculate white cloth. The young man reached for it with a tentative hand.

"Take it," said a Ghibdul encouragingly, in a harsh voice tinged with humility, respect, and admiration.

Unwrapping the object, the Nameless One was astonished—it was his enchanted sword!

"If you will accept them," continued the Ghibdul, "we

would like to offer you our apologies, honorable hovalyn."

Elfohrys hooted with laughter, which drew scowls from the Ghibduls.

"Perhaps you could let us go now," suggested Elfohrys gaily. "We're quite touched by your sudden change of heart, but—"

"Quiet, wretch!" ordered the Ghibdul who had returned the sword and who clearly had the most authority.

"I forbid you to treat Elfohrys like that!" protested the hovalyn indignantly.

"If such is your wish," mumbled the disconcerted Ghibdul.

"I think that you might offer us some explanation," continued the young man, still bewildered but determined to take advantage of this unexpected development.

"We entered your mind and staged a simulated experience, using images that were already in your thoughts but of whose existence you were unaware. And we added a few elements of our own."

"So everything I thought I saw and felt was false?"

"From the moment you thought you had left this room," confirmed the Ghibdul. "It was a necessary and effective test. We are particularly gifted at this sort of painless manipulation."

"Painless," sighed their victim. "That word may not mean the same thing to everyone, but personally, I did not consider the invasion of my mind to be either pleasant or harmless!"

The Ghibdul was so close to him that the young man could smell the creature's fetid breath, and he turned his head aside when his visitor spoke again.

"There were some doubts about you. What we had at first suspected seemed unlikely, but we were determined to settle the question. And in entering your mind, we were able to confirm our initial suspicions, our hopes. . . ."

"Oh, so you are actually capable of hoping?" said Elfohrys sarcastically. "Well, we learn something every day."

"Hovalyn, you are the one we have long awaited. What is your name?"

"I don't have one," confessed the knight. "I am the Nameless One."

The Ghibduls did not seem troubled by this news.

"You are the only one to have ever completely withstood the, uh, the mental torture we inflicted on you. We are truly sorry to have put you through that."

"Well, you certainly weren't very subtle about it."

"But it was necessary," said the Ghibdul earnestly. "Even among ourselves, no one has ever lasted that long under such a trial. And it's the choice you made that is especially unbelievable. No one, until you, had opted for defiance. No one had had the courage to do so. Except you."

"You think it's fun to practice mental torture on one another?" asked Elfohrys. "That's really . . . entertaining!"

"And why do you think I am the one you have 'long awaited'?" asked the hovalyn.

"For centuries we have lived a secluded existence. We have created a civilization that is still in its infancy. But since the dawn of time, a tradition, a belief has been passed down: that one day a man would come and we would recognize him. He would change our way of life, create fellowship between us and other creatures. And we would follow him, obey him, help him when he asked for our assistance. That man, Nameless One, is you."

"That can't be," protested the hovalyn. "How could I bring you together with other peoples? And besides, I have no intention of leading you!"

"We are going to show you our village, and then you will leave. But one day soon, you will call on us for aid," announced the Ghibdul calmly. "For so it is written."

Seeing that the skeptical young knight was highly confused and unconvinced, another Ghibdul spoke up.

"There is no reason for you to believe us, hovalyn,

except for the fact that, some centuries ago, Néophileus himself prophesized the same event. He wrote in *The Prophecy* that one day, after a victory, a man would discover a hidden civilization living in the depths of the forest. He would endure a trial that would reveal his identity to the creatures holding him captive. Then the man would leave. When the darkness came to blot out the light, he would return. He would ask these forest people for help and would bring them forth from oblivion. Hovalyn, this is your story. And ours."

The Ghibdul paused. One of his fellows now addressed the young man.

"We know who you are. You were not to learn your identity before that day, for *The Prophecy* affirms that we are the ones who will reveal it to you."

Trembling with emotion, his heart pounding wildly, almost choking with anxiety, the young man waited. Would he finally find out who he really was? The Ghibduls stood gravely before him, and in a solemn voice, one of them announced to him at last: "Nameless One, you are the man who has long been expected by everyone, everywhere. You are the Chosen One."

20

THE SEAL OF DARKNESS

AMBER SPENT THE REST OF THE NIGHT TEARY-
eyed and unable to sleep. How could Janëlle have betrayed
her! Amber had thought she was her friend, and in the short
time that this illusion had lasted she had trusted the girl,
opening her heart to her.

At dawn, Jade and Opal came running over, for they had
both strongly sensed a terrible threat to Amber. All their
hatred had vanished, so they were eager to hear what had
happened, and to comfort her. The girls felt uneasy when
they remembered their fury of the previous day, and
Amber's swollen lip showed them how badly they'd behaved.

After exchanging hasty apologies, the girls finally realized how close they had grown since the liberation of
Nathyrnn. Even Jade and Opal, once so hostile to one
another, had been getting along much better.

They ate in silence, then mounted their horses.

In the distance, snowcapped mountains, veiled in mist,
rose into a sky still streaked with the light of dawn.

The three girls rode on toward Oonagh's grotto, which was no longer very far away. Jade told Amber that they might reach it within a week if they hurried, and Amber gently asked her horse to quicken his pace.

"I just remembered something," Amber said. "Last night I thought I saw a man on a horse. I was probably mistaken, I know, but I thought I should tell you."

Jade shrugged, but Opal, who was sitting behind her on the same horse, spoke up as if what she had to say were the most natural thing in the world: "Me too—I saw a shadow before I fell asleep."

"Who could be spying on us?" wondered Jade. "I'm sick of all these mysteries. The last thing we need is some phantom horseman bothering us! If you see him again, tell me, so I can go give him a good swift kick!"

Amber laughed weakly, and Opal gave her a fleeting smile. Opal was recalling the moments she had spent with Adrien before she relapsed into unconsciousness, and remembering the terrible feeling of waking to the realization that he was going away to risk his life. Her heart sank at the thought. Would she ever see him again? She slipped into a melancholic reverie.

Amber, too, was feeling gloomy, and tried to distract herself by observing the countryside. Once again she noticed that no one was working the fields. Men and women with long silvery hair were indeed out amid the crops, but they had no farming tools and were simply laughing and singing. Curious, Amber asked her companions if they might stop and question these people, and the other girls readily assented, eager for a distraction. They dismounted and made their way through a field of sunflowers, welcomed by the peasants' beaming smiles. The farm folk were won over by Amber's open face and friendly greeting, and one of them, a short, stocky fellow, exclaimed, "Your eyes are made of gold, the sky, and flowers!"

The other farmers laughed in agreement, looking at her with teasing expressions. Nonplussed by this unusual compliment, Amber gamely launched into her questions.

"Do you work the land? I don't know Fairytale at all, and I'd like to know how peasants live here, if that's what you are."

Her audience laughed again good-heartedly; these people seemed simple but hospitable, with a joyful gleam in their eyes.

"Since the beginning of time, we have understood the earth," explained one of the women. "Our songs and our rejoicing nourish her, make her happy. When the plants begin to spout, we reap our reward. We live in harmony with plants and the earth. If that means being 'peasants,' as you say, then that is what we are."

"Are you a magic people?" asked Jade admiringly.

"No more than others, or yourselves," replied the woman. "There is magic in every one of us. Each seed is unlike any other."

Seeing the girls' quizzical expressions, the farmers laughed again, and the woman who had spoken to them murmured, "We're pleased to have met you."

Sensing that it was time for them to go, the girls said good-bye to these jovial people, who bade them farewell with melodious songs and merriment.

Once the three companions were on their way again, Amber announced, "When we were leaving, the man who said those strange things about my eyes whispered something to me, something like: 'Nature works miracles that magic can only dream about.'"

"Those people were weird," said Opal.

"But nice," insisted Amber.

"Well, they certainly seemed to like you," said Jade decisively.

"Me?" replied Amber. "Maybe that's because I feel close to them, as if I understand them. . . ."

The girls rode on, stopping briefly from time to time.

After a few hours a town wreathed in a dark fog appeared on the horizon. In spite of their growing distrust of anything unfamiliar they decided to go through the town, because going around it would have taken too much time.

They entered the town that afternoon. Dismounting, they led their horses by the bridle and the animals moved forward confidently.

"Is there any danger here?" Amber asked her horse.

He did not reply but seemed to sniff the air before sending her a feeling not of peril, but of poverty and desolation.

The town was silent, and all the houses were shut tight.

"A few homes have burned down recently," remarked Opal.

And in fact, at the end of the first street several houses had been reduced to a heap of ashes and charred objects.

Amber shivered. Suddenly a fat man wearing something like an elegant silk toga came rushing out of a house and fell to his knees in front of the girls. His face was livid with terror, he was shaking violently, and the despair in his eyes was close to madness.

"Whoever you are," he begged, "help us! I implore you, don't let us perish."

Because she was learning to be wary of everything, Opal was convinced that this was some new trick and she wanted to continue on their way, but Amber held on to her arm and Jade nodded briefly to show her approval.

"What happened?" Amber asked the man.

"You don't know?" he moaned. "Come inside what's left of my home, and you'll understand."

The three girls looked at one another. Amber and Jade decided to investigate, one from compassion, the other from curiosity, and Opal was forced to go along with them. Amber paused to tell her horse to wait there for them, then followed the others into a modest stone house, closing the door softly behind her.

Inside, a weeping, disheveled woman and a swarm of children huddled together, terrified and in a state of shock. The place had been torn apart: broken objects and furniture littered the floor and the unassuming but pleasant pictures on the wall had been slashed to ribbons. The once comfortable home was now nothing but ruins.

"Just look at what they did!" said the man. "What can we do now? No one—except you—has dared set foot in our town. No one will sacrifice their lives to help us."

"But what happened?" repeated Amber.

"They came back," hissed the man, eyes wide with fear. "Ever since the fall of Thaar, they have been showing up everywhere."

"Who?" demanded Jade.

The woman cowering at the back of the room let out a shriek.

"Just ignore her," cautioned the man. "She's a madwoman who wanders our streets. When they arrived I took her in to save her, in memory of my wife, who was killed by them a long time ago."

The woman continued to shout hysterically.

"Béah Jardun, be quiet!" ordered the man, clamping his hands over his ears.

The woman obeyed him promptly, reassured by the sound of her own name.

"So you don't know who *they* are?" marveled the man, turning back to the three girls. "We've always dreaded them. There were periods when they reigned over almost all of Fairytale, and at other times we heard nothing more of them for centuries. They have returned, and now they are more powerful than ever! A hundred Sorcerers of Darkness in command—they have always wanted to rule Fairytale: that's why they have joined the Council of Twelve, which has promised them this territory in exchange for their support and their obedience. They've almost certainly pledged their loyalty so that they can betray their masters after they have conquered us."

"Aside from these Sorcerers of Darkness," interrupted Jade, "who are *they*?"

"Wicked creatures of all kinds," he replied, "including some men, who have chosen the side of evil because they all have one thing in common: the desire to destroy. Some of them even know how to breathe hatred into pure souls—they have the Gift of evil."

Like Janëlle, thought Amber bitterly.

"Ever since Thaar fell to them and the Council of Twelve," continued the man, "they have been running wild in Fairytale. They pillage, slaughtering those weaker than they are. Most of our army, the one that protected us from them, is mobilized around Thaar. As for the Sorcerers of Light, people say that they never existed and are only a legend. Many of us are ready to fight, of course, but the Chosen One has still not come, so we're losing hope and beginning to give up."

"The Chosen One? Who's that?" asked Jade.

The man stared at her in disbelief. Then he seemed struck by something obvious, and coughed, recovering his composure.

"I don't know what I'm talking about anymore—I must be raving, like that poor lunatic Béah Jardun. Pay no attention to what I said."

"Don't expect me to fall for that!" scoffed Jade. "Do these evil creatures have a name?"

"Not really, just the Army of Darkness."

"And who are the Sorcerers of Light?"

"If they exist, they're the only ones capable of opposing the Sorcerers of Darkness. Soon, when the Army of Light is assembled . . ."

"What? What army?" asked Jade. "Why would it assemble? Is there going to be a war?"

"I've said too much," sighed the man. "I don't want to talk about this anymore."

While Jade was questioning the man about the Chosen One, Amber had approached the woman and children, speaking to them in her soft, gentle voice, hoping to comfort them as best she could. A spark of lucidity seemed to flicker in the eyes of Béah Jardun, who leaned forward, tugging on Amber's arm to make her bend down, and whispered nervously, "When you were born, your mother was overjoyed! Frightened as well, but so happy . . . I was there—only a maidservant, but still, I was there. Many people were. Even Jean Losserand, the traveler, who was going home after his many adventures, was passing through that night. He helped your mother to flee, to hide you safely in the Outside. And when he tried to bring her back to Fairytale, before going back to his home, they were arrested. Jean Losserand remained out there, in prison, but your mother—she was killed by order of the Council of Twelve. I went with them too, but, thank goodness, I was luckier; I managed to come back and find your father again, who was waiting in vain for his wife. Later the Army of Darkness killed him as well."

"Is that true?"

That was all Amber managed to say, she was so staggered by emotion.

"Of course it's true," replied Béah Jardun indignantly. "Your mother and father loved you, so did Jean and I, and others, and that's what made you different, Amber."

Then the woman fell back into a stupor from which nothing, not even Amber's desperate questions, could rouse her.

Meanwhile, the man had taken up his story again.

"This town is inhabited exclusively by healers, like myself, and by professional magicians. We use only a rudimentary form of magic to give the necessary strength to our potions and ointments. We're fine, peaceful people! But they showed us no mercy—they took our food, our few bits of jewelry, and they burned our houses. I could save only a dozen potions. Today they returned to destroy almost everything that was left and sealed the town."

"Sealed the town?" repeated Jade. "I don't understand."

"That's what they do in every city and town they invade: they mark it with the Seal of Darkness so that no one will be able to leave for an entire year. We're condemned to die of hunger, and we'll suffer atrociously until Death's strike is over."

"That's despicable," gasped Jade.

"And of course, nobody ventures into a town sealed by the Army of Darkness—they're afraid of reprisals, or simply of winding up a prisoner like everyone else!"

"Which means that we are now shut up inside your town," observed Opal evenly.

"Yes, but . . ." The man began to cry. "From the moment you entered, there was nothing I could do," he sobbed.

"We have a little food that will last us for a few days," said Opal brightly. "We'll find a solution."

Jade was furious: "Great, we're in another trap!" she fumed.

21

No Way Out

WHILE JADE, OPAL, AND THE HEALER DISCUSSED the situation, Amber was silent. She was having trouble following the conversation because she could think of nothing but the words of Béah Jardun.

"So why did this Army of Darkness attack you?" Jade asked the man.

"They spare the villages and fields because they are a waste of time for them. The people there will never resist them and so pose no threat in their eyes. In certain towns like ours, however, they strike without mercy. They're trying to intimidate us because they know that we're against them and that when the Chosen One comes, we'll be at his side."

"You were just saying that this Chosen One doesn't exist, that you were raving," observed Jade dryly.

"Right, of course! I'm—not feeling well," stammered the man, trying to cover up his mistake. "I don't know what came over me, I'm talking utter nonsense. The Chosen One? I've no idea where that came from."

He pretended—without success—to be having a fit of madness.

"By the way, who are you?" asked Jade, giving up on learning any more from him about the mysterious Chosen One.

"My name is Amnhor."

"All right—what we need to do now is find a way to liberate this town," announced Jade.

"There is no way," said Amnhor bluntly. "Don't you think we're tried everything? Once a town is sealed by the Army of Darkness it is doomed. The spell they have cast over us is extremely powerful."

"Well, we're going to try anyway, since I have no intention of staying here more than a few hours," replied Jade.

The three girls exchanged knowing looks and got out their Stones. Amnhor sighed resignedly, convinced that they would fail. Jade, Opal, and Amber concentrated their thoughts on the fine black mist enveloping the town: the Seal of Darkness. As communication was established among the Stones, the three girls became one. They felt that familiar gentle warmth and, with increasing intensity, chanted to themselves: "Break the Seal, break the Seal. . . ."

But nothing happened. The Seal was much too strong for them. They had to admit defeat and put away their Stones in disappointment.

"I warned you," scolded the healer.

Opal began to feel feverish and noticed that she was trembling. She had been having headaches ever since discovering her Stone before the appointed time, although she hadn't attached any importance to this because the pain wasn't usually very serious. Now, however, her head was really throbbing because of her wound.

Seeing that Opal was unwell, Amnhor asked what was wrong, then left the room, returning with a small pot of ointment and a flask containing a transparent liquid.

"This is the simplest potion there is," he explained, "but it's good for all fevers and headaches."

Opal swallowed a mouthful of the cool, refreshing liquid and felt better immediately.

"Take this for your wound and for the cut on your lip. This medicine is rare, but very effective," continued Amnhor, handing her the pot of ointment.

Opal thanked him gratefully.

"You're fortunate that all three of you came away unscathed from your struggle against the Seal," observed Amnhor. "Dark magic is quite dangerous."

"I'm still not giving up," announced Jade grimly. "I've got to go and see Oonagh, and I will!"

"You might be better off looking for a way to survive

for a year without food," replied the healer sadly.

"You look for it, if it amuses you," said Jade, "but I'm definitely going to destroy that Seal."

"So am I," agreed Opal.

"Wait a minute!" cried Jade excitedly. "Amnhor, you said there are magicians in this town, right?"

"Yes, but they only practice magic on a very superficial level," explained the healer. "They would never be able to break the spell of the Seal."

"Summon them anyway!" ordered Jade imperiously. "If they can't do it by themselves, then we'll manage to do it all together!"

"In any case, we're better off trying something than patiently waiting to starve to death," concluded Opal.

Amnhor left, returning in an hour.

"The magicians are in the main square. I have explained to them that you intend to break the Seal. They aren't particularly optimistic, but they came anyway. Follow me."

A mournful silence reigned in the large, crowded square, for the men and other creatures assembled there were overwhelmed with sorrow and discouragement. Jade addressed them in a loud authoritative voice.

"I know what you have endured, but you cannot let yourselves give up! We can still try to break this famous

Seal, and in the end, we will. Alone, no one can do anything, but all together, we can succeed!"

Her listeners seemed unconvinced, and remained silent.

"Sorcery is not practiced collectively," Amnhor explained to Jade. "No one would dare to do that—it's
contrary to our customs."

"So a custom's more important than our lives, is it?"
snapped Jade.

The crowd just stood there.

"It will be a difficult and risky undertaking to try and
attack the Seal," continued Amnhor.

Jade struggled to control her temper.

"They don't want to listen to me," she grumbled under
her breath.

"Let me speak to them," said Amber.

She stepped forward shyly. She wanted to show this
crowd that she wished to help them, to understand them,
but she wasn't sure how to do this. Her audience stared
at her impassively, unimpressed by her friendly expression and fiery red hair. They didn't want to hear any more
talk about the Seal, because it terrified them and they
could not imagine ever attacking it. Although Amber felt
discouraged, she did her best to smile.

"I would like to help you," she began faintly. Taking a

deep breath, she continued with more determination. "We have a common enemy. Whether it's the Army of Darkness or the Council of Twelve, they want to rob us of the same thing: our freedom. We cannot let them succeed, we cannot accept their domination. There have always been those who opposed them and fought back: thanks to them, there have been years of peace. Today, we must resist the oppressors! They have killed your loved ones and they killed my mother, whom I never knew. It's in the name of that injustice, in the name of those who have suffered, that I ask you to attempt to break the Seal."

Amber had spoken movingly, with tears glistening in her eyes at the mention of her mother, and the passionate sincerity of her words had touched the crowd.

"They came a week ago," called out a voice. "They sacked the town, they killed everything in their wake. . . . Then they returned just a few hours ago to burn what was left of our houses and place their Seal on the town. If we manage by some miracle to break the spell, they might come back again and this time their revenge will be much worse!"

A murmur ran through the gathering.

"You cannot refuse to fight; that would be refusing life itself," said Amber stoutly.

While those gathered in the square were talking things

over quietly, Jade whispered to Amber, "I didn't know your mother was killed by the Army of Darkness—I thought she died of an illness!"

"I am talking about my real mother, the one who bore me," explained Amber. "She was killed by the Council of Twelve. Béah Jardun told me about her."

"What about my mother and father?" asked Jade. "I've got a right to know what happened to them! Would Béah Jardun know anything about that?"

"No, I'm sorry, I don't think so," sighed Amber.

Finally, turning to Amber, Amnhor spoke for everyone in the square.

"The magicians will follow you."

"I'm afraid I don't know how to break the Seal," Amber confessed to the crowd. "You must each attempt this in your own way, and if we all try together, something will surely happen."

There was a ripple of assent. The three girls got out their Stones, gripped them tightly, and concentrated on the Seal. With one accord the magicians began to recite an incomprehensible spell.

"The Alypiûmm," muttered Amnhor to himself. "The most powerful, the most difficult spell, and the most dangerous . . ."

However, even joined with the strength of the Stones, the magicians' power was not enough to attack the Seal. Nothing happened.

"What if we simply tried to walk through the Seal?" asked Amber.

The crowd seemed to freeze in horror, and no one would look Amber in the face.

"We would die," said Amnhor.

"But Death is on strike," Jade reminded him.

"Yes, but that wouldn't change anything. If we crossed through the Seal, whatever happened would be worse than death."

"I'm convinced we can break this Seal," insisted Amber. "Don't you believe in the impossible, all of you? Have confidence in yourselves and in me! I promise you we can succeed."

All eyes were on Amber. Everyone waited.

"I have an idea," she said.

Signaling to Amnhor to come closer, she whispered a few words into his ear.

"That will never work," he told her. "You're going to lead this entire town into disaster!"

"If we do nothing, it will be a disaster anyway."

Resigned, Amnhor gave in. He and everyone else knew

that Amber was right: they had to try something. But he also knew what fate the Seal reserved for those who dared to oppose it.

"Are you sure about this?" Jade asked Amber softly.

"No."

"That's exactly what I thought. Well, fine, it doesn't matter anyway, and it's better not to worry yourself with too many questions."

Minutes seemed to turn into hours as the directions Amber had given Amnhor were carried out. Joining hands, all the inhabitants of the town formed a great circle that included the three girls, who held their Stones tucked into their palms.

"Now what do we do?" asked Jade.

"Nothing," replied Amber. "No magic formulae, no magic at all. We don't let go of one another and we walk through the Seal just as we did with the magnetic field protecting Fairytale. If we're convinced that we can cross through it, then we will. If you believe in the impossible . . ."

"And you're sure this will work for the Seal as well?"

"We're about to find out!"

Soon the human chain was so close to the Seal that everyone could smell its acrid odor. They were only two steps away from leaving the town, but between them and freedom lay the Seal.

"We have to believe," repeated Amber.

Her faith ran through the crowd, swelling everyone's heart with hope, and the warmth of the Stones enveloped them all. There were thousands of them, but they now formed one whole, determined to break the Seal. First they managed to sweep aside their fears and then they all stepped forward as one. The black fog engulfed and immobilized them, but they never doubted their victory for a moment. An invisible battle began.

Evil and hunger for power were seeping into everyone, paralyzing them with hatred, fear, rage, and most of all, pain. Their struggle continued, however, for all the inhabitants resisted, setting their conviction, their hope, and all the goodness within them against this stifling wickedness.

Amber was gasping for breath and felt herself change, as if enslaved by a ruthless and irresistible force. Then she realized something obvious.

Just as Janëlle infected us with her hatred, thought Amber, this Seal is filling us with evil—the feelings of the one who created it, one who clearly carries something dreadful inside himself, something destructive: that famous Gift of evil. And the Seal is only the reflection of its creator's soul.

All at once, Amber understood the Seal. She had the impression it had actually spoken to her, confided in her, but she would never know whether this was true.

The Seal injects evil into those who wish to overthrow it, thought Amber, and that's why they die. But Death is on strike, so instead of succumbing, we're all absorbing what's coming from the Seal. It's overwhelming us, even transforming us into people possessed by evil, in the service of that Army of Darkness. That's why the spell is so powerful!

Overcome with exhaustion, Jade, Opal, and Amber felt beaten. The choking, sickening odor of the enveloping fog made them feel like giving up, and as the Stones started to slip from their grasp, their eyelids began to droop. . . . But they didn't give up, they *couldn't* give up. Good and evil were battling mercilessly in their hearts, just as the Seal of Darkness was fighting the inhabitants of the town. These opponents were evenly matched, but everyone was suffocating, and the unbearable pain was making it harder and harder to resist the Seal. And yet a glimmer of hope still lived in every heart: they would conquer the Seal. They could not resign themselves to defeat, not completely.

They all called on their last reserves of strength. The Seal would resist, of course, but they had to try. All together, they took another step forward.

The Seal did not resist: it shattered abruptly and vanished. They had believed that they could break it, and they had broken it.

Jade, Opal, and Amber fainted with exhaustion.

22

THE DARK HORSEMAN

"LOOK! SHE'S WAKING UP AT LAST!"

Amber opened her eyes and saw the faces of Jade and Amnhor hovering over her. She was in a room, and everything was spinning. . . . It was some minutes before she fully recovered consciousness and managed to sit up.

"The Seal—it's broken, isn't it?" she asked eagerly. "Did we succeed or not?"

"Hush, hush," said Amnhor gently.

He held a flask to her lips. She took it, swallowed a mouthful of a nauseating liquid, and felt herself grow calmer.

"You've been unconscious all night and most of the morning," explained Jade.

"That long?" exclaimed Amber, who remembered nothing since the moment she had collapsed while crossing the Seal. "The town—is it still sealed shut?"

"Of course not," Jade reassured her. "We broke it! Just as you said, we simply had to believe we could do it, all of us together!"

"And you? And Opal? You didn't faint when we went through the Seal?"

"Oh yes, but thanks to Amnhor's care we woke up a few hours later."

"When the Seal was broken," added the healer, "a number of people collapsed with exhaustion and many still haven't come to. We're looking after them, however, and they are out of danger. Thanks to you, everything will return to normal."

Opal came into the room and smiled when she saw that Amber was awake.

"Right," declared Jade, "now we can leave this afternoon."

"We have put extra provisions in your saddlebags," said Amnhor, "to thank you for freeing us."

The girls spoke for a long time with the healer, and then they all sat down to a delicious lunch.

"Wait a minute—whatever happened to Béah Jardun and the children?" asked Amber suddenly.

"The children were orphans," said Amnhor, "and families have taken them in. As for Béah Jardun, I can only tell you that she left right after the Seal was broken. In the general confusion, no one paid any attention. That's all I know."

When they had finished their meal, the girls felt that it

was time to leave. Amnhor went to get their horses and also gave them a magnificent stallion, a surprise gift from the grateful magicians.

"The townswomen have made some clothes for you to show their gratitude," announced Amnhor, presenting them with elegant dresses. Then he gave them a tiny blue glass vial containing a thick liquid.

"The healers would like you to have this potion: it is the most precious one to have survived the attack of the Army of Darkness, and its preparation requires months of concentrated effort. Unfortunately, there are only two mouthfuls of it in this vial."

"Thank you," replied Amber as she took the vial. "What is it for?"

"You said you were going to see Oonagh. That magic creature lives in a cave in a dangerous mountain guarded by giant raptors, ghastly birds of prey. As long as you are not afraid, however, they will not notice you and nothing will happen. But they strike fear into every creature's heart, so you will almost certainly panic. Since you must remain impassive to survive, this potion will help you. A single mouthful will suffice, but the effect only lasts for a few minutes—and one of you will have to do without it altogether."

"And how will this potion help us?" asked Jade.

"It will turn you into a being who is neither human nor magical," replied Amnhor solemnly. "Luckily this effect never lasts longer than five minutes. During this period, the potion will erase all your emotions, from terror to even the feeling of being alive."

Jade merely shrugged, while Opal showed no reaction. Only Amber shivered at the healer's words.

"Why are these birds so dangerous?"

"First, they feed on your fear. They savor it, absorb it. Then you stop trying to run away, and that's when they swoop down to carry you off to their lair and make a meal out of you."

"Thank you for the potion," said Jade, trying not to shudder.

"Be careful," advised the healer, "and don't confide in anyone."

The girls promised to heed his words, and Amnhor finally bade them an emotional farewell.

"Remember that you can always count on me and on everyone in this town."

With a smile, Jade, Opal, and Amber thanked him for his hospitality and left.

They rode along quickly, stopping rarely and then only

briefly, and they encountered almost no one. Once again they were traveling through peaceful and sunny country-side; sometimes they passed through a village or town without seeing a single trace of the Army of Darkness.

"Why is everything so quiet," wondered Amber, "when we've just left a place in ruins? I thought war was raging through Fairytale."

"No," replied Jade. "While you were with the children and Béah Jardun, back at Amnhor's house, he explained to us that the Army of Darkness isn't bothering with the fields and villages for the moment. It's concentrating on enemy towns, which it destroys methodically, but it isn't attacking either the knights people here call hovalyns, or places where creatures with higher magic powers live."

"But what does the Army of Darkness want?" asked Amber.

"To rule Fairytale, of course," said Jade. "They haven't begun an all-out attack yet, however. They're moving one step at a time."

"Amnhor let it slip that they're waiting for a Chosen One or something," chimed in Opal. "But he wouldn't tell us more."

The three girls rode all day long. They ate only sparingly and didn't talk much. That night they stopped on a plain.

"I'm glad we spent some time in that sealed town," remarked Jade. "That was our last taste of basic comforts for a while: from now on I'll be forced to start looking like a dirty, slovenly peasant!"

When she heard that, Amber stiffened a little and bit her lower lip to help hide her irritation. That's when she noticed that the painful cut from her fight with Jade and Opal had disappeared, doubtless thanks to Amnhor.

This time they passed a pleasant evening, chatting animatedly. Amber related for the umpteenth time what Béah Jardun had told her, while her two companions listened closely, as if they were hearing the story for the first time, and daydreamed about their own parents. Who were they? Were they still alive? Why had they abandoned them?

Jade would have liked so much to know about her mother and father—yet at the same time, she was bitterly angry with them: why had they let her go when she was just a baby, and without leaving her anything to remember them by, neither marks of affection, nor memories? She knew they had entrusted her to the Duke of Divulyon to protect her from some "danger," but she couldn't help thinking that they hadn't wanted her, that they hadn't loved her. Deep down, she couldn't love them or hate them. She found it simpler to believe that they had been the ones who hadn't loved her. Her true father was the Duke of Divulyon.

As for Opal, she had never worried about her parents. As a child she had sometimes asked Eugénia and Gina about them, only to receive evasive answers. So she had stopped thinking about them and hadn't ever truly understood what a mother and father were. Now, for the first time, she found herself really wondering about them.

When it was time to go to sleep, Jade was the only one who lay awake. She felt uncomfortable on that plain, lost in an unfamiliar world. She missed her easy life, her sumptuous palace, the universal admiration she had enjoyed. And she missed the Duke of Divulyon. Even if he wasn't her father, he had watched over her and loved her more than anyone. Was he thinking of her at that moment? Was he afraid for her?

"I'm fine, Papa," she whispered. "One day I'll come back to see you and tell you how much you matter to me."

She felt reassured, as if the Duke could hear her affectionate words. After all, why not?

Despite missing the easiness of her old life, Jade was actually enjoying her adventure. She was discovering ideas she'd never dreamed of, learning to use powers she would never have believed she possessed. She loved finding herself in situations where she could flirt with danger and challenge the unexpected.

Feeling hungry, she rose, brushed off her clothes, and went over to their saddlebags of provisions. Without knowing why, all of a sudden she felt ill: her vision blurred and her legs almost gave way beneath her. After shivering for a moment, she managed to get a grip on herself again.

And she was sure of it: there in the distance was the indistinct silhouette of a horseman. Jade took off immediately, running at top speed and cursing herself for not having jumped on a horse. She watched the shadow slip away and realized that she would never catch it.

The next morning Jade was eager to tell the others about the excitement they had missed.

"Did you actually feel sick because of him?" asked Amber thoughtfully.

"Yes. For a moment, I felt nauseated and couldn't see a thing. I almost fainted."

"Well then, he's an enemy," concluded Amber bitterly.

"To add to our list," drawled Jade.

After a breakfast of rolls and fruit, the girls rode off, urging their mounts to keep up a fast pace.

Lost in thought, Amber kept going over what Béah

Jardun had told her, as though she might have missed some tiny detail. She remembered Jean Losserand's good, kind face and wondered why he hadn't told her anything at all about her past. She would have loved to hear about her mother. . . .

Jade and Opal guessed what was bothering Amber and tried to distract her, but without success.

Around noon, the girls stopped in the welcome shade of a tree. They felt uneasy, but they ate their lunch, trying to be frugal with their provisions. As they were about to set out again, Opal pointed to a far-off grove of trees.

"Look, over there! I think I see a horseman."

And in fact, a black-clad figure could just be seen in the distance. The girls gathered their things together at once and mounted their horses, but the mysterious horseman had already vanished.

Riding along, the girls could think of nothing but their unknown enemy, and although not one of them admitted it, he terrified them.

The Thirteenth Councilor smiled in the darkness. His face was cruel, stamped by the horrendous power of evil. His plan was working beautifully, and this time he was in control of everything. Opal hadn't died after all. Since the three Stones of the Prophecy had taken refuge in Fairytale, he could no longer reach them by telepathy, but that didn't bother him. He had come up with something even more satisfying.

He cackled in the silence.

At his signal a golden screen floating in the air hummed into life, showing the image of a grim man in an elegant, jet-black uniform, his face seamed with scars. He had blue eyes, black hair, and a fearsome appearance.

"Ah! It's you, Thirteenth Councilor," said the man on the screen in a harsh voice. "I have sent one of my horsemen. Do not worry, all is well."

"I have every confidence in you, sorcerer. But one of your men—is that wise?"

"He is no longer a man. He is a soldier of Darkness. He will not fail."

"Very well."

"He is watching them. For the moment, everything is proceeding as planned."

"Don't forget that the decisive moment is drawing near."

"I will not forget, Thirteenth Councilor. When that moment arrives, be prepared. Our victory depends on you."

"It is not for you to remind me of that."

The Thirteenth Councilor gestured to break off communication. The news was good, but he was irritated by that Sorcerer of Darkness, who was the only one who dared speak to him as an equal. There was nothing to be done about that for the moment, however, because he still needed the sorcerer's help to destroy the Stones so that the Council of Twelve could triumph.

This time he was certain of it: his plan could not fail.

PARIS: PRESENT DAY

I'd begun telling myself that I could live, that I had the right to live. I knew that I could not possibly command Death to back off and leave me alone, but I enjoyed believing that I could. My reality merged with my dream. Naively, I thought that if I begged her to spare me, Death, as a creature endowed with some feeling, would listen to me and go on her way. After all, why couldn't Death be on strike? Why wouldn't she allow herself to be moved by my distress? But then I would let my tears flow freely, and when I wasn't sleeping, I would cry—from rage, despair, sadness, and fear. I tried to convince myself that one day I would not wake up anymore, that I would have moved into my dream, that I would live there, and be happy. If I really wanted this, if I believed it with all my strength, maybe it was possible that this insane wish would come true—and I could cross over into a fairy tale?

Every night I would plunge once more into the magical world of my dream. I lived it in my own way. The images, the emotions belonged as much to me as to the characters living in this unreal world.

I spent my days hoping that the dream would come back while I was asleep. A shrill, disagreeable voice kept suggesting nastily that I was fooling myself with illusions. I knew this, but I wouldn't let myself think this dream wasn't real.

And I did feel hope. Again. As I'd never allowed myself to hope before. Memories surfaced from the depths of my past. I'd worked so hard to bury them deep down, but now here they were, arrogant, as wounding and splendid as ever.

First the images rushed in. I tried in vain to drive them off, to return them to the void where I'd thought I'd stashed them away. But they stayed right there, lively, dancing, vividly colored, whirling before me. I understood then that the only way for me to get rid of them was to face up to them. I remember starting to cry. Then I looked at them, those images, those ghosts from the past.

The first to return were my parents. Tears coursed down my flushed cheeks. My parents were dead. And I couldn't change a thing. Their image kept nudging me, though: smiling, affectionate, treacherous. Their image almost seemed real, and I wept. My parents *were there before me, laughing, teasing me, cherishing me. I was Joa once more.*

I remember screaming to chase away those images and they left, troubled, frightened, but I knew that they'd be back, that they'd continue to torment me. . . .

23

THE NAMELESS ONE'S PAST

THE GHIBDULS SHOWED THE CHOSEN ONE AND Elfohrys around their domain, which turned out to be an unassuming, almost shabby village. The buildings were essentially constructed of wood and most of them were rather rickety. Some were actually falling to pieces.

"We're not a race of craftsmen," a Ghibdul explained humbly to the hovalyn. "Our true talents lie in telepathy and in battle. Ours is a rudimentary civilization."

Still, the Chosen One and Elfohrys were very impressed. The Ghibduls proved to be gracious hosts, and despite their threatening manners and appearance, they could be pleasant if they so chose. The hovalyn was treated with more respect than he had ever encountered before and was greeted in the street with deference and admiration.

He remained among them for more than a week, since the magic creatures kept asking him to prolong his stay and he did not wish to disappoint them.

The two visitors were given one of the prettiest wood

cabins, decorated with a few carved designs, where they slept on beds of green moss under covers woven from leaves.

The food was delicious and each meal was a banquet prepared in honor of the Chosen One. They served him fresh meat, vegetables, and fruits he had never seen before. The Ghibduls hunted all day in the Endless Forest expressly for him, bringing home the finest game. The women gathered wild berries and selected the tastiest fruits and vegetables from their kitchen gardens.

The Nameless One had changed. There was a new maturity in his face, and his eyes had lost some of their sadness. From now on, even though his name and his past were still a mystery to him, he was the Chosen One: he had an identity. He knew that thousands of people were awaiting him, that there was a place for him among his fellow creatures. Yet still he longed to recover his memory, so that he might be whole again.

When the time came for him to leave, an eminent Ghibdul sage came to see him.

"Hovalyn," he said gravely, "we cannot keep you here any longer. You must accomplish great things. But to find your true self, you must go and see Oonagh."

"I know," replied the knight.

"Be careful, for the fiendish raptors of fear rule where Oonagh lives. Take this to protect yourself." The Ghibdul handed him two green vines from which hung small black spheres. "These are amulets," he explained. "One is for you, the other for your friend. Do not place them around your necks until you see the birds of prey. For one hour, these enchanted pendants will protect you from fear, and then will vanish."

"Many thanks," said the hovalyn sincerely.

"You do not yet know what your true role is," continued the Ghibdul with a sigh. "But do not forget that when you tell others that you are the Chosen One, you will provoke as much hatred as you will happiness."

The young man nodded.

"A few of our warriors will accompany you to the edge of the forest," said the Ghibdul. "We will also give you two wild horses. Alas, they are not magical, but you will find them strong and sturdy."

The Chosen One thanked him on behalf of himself and Elfohrys, with whom he left the Ghibduls' lair the same day. They set off into the forest carrying provisions given to them by the village women and accompanied by Ghibdul warriors who flew alongside them.

The travelers had to halt frequently to allow their

escort to rest. The deeper they went into the forest, the narrower the paths grew, and dry branches sometimes whipped across their faces. The Ghibduls tried to make the time pass agreeably, but they could do nothing about the forest.

"You're still quite a distance from Oonagh," said one of the magic creatures. "Once you leave here, you'll be at least two weeks' journey from your destination."

"I think I know the route we must follow," replied the hovalyn.

"It isn't dangerous. That's the safest part of Fairytale, and it harbors the least magic."

"Nevertheless, watch out for the Army of Darkness," warned another Ghibdul. "Even here, we know it has returned. And you must keep in mind how powerful and savage it is."

At sunset, they reached the edge of the forest.

"Our paths separate here," said a Ghibdul. "Do not forget, Chosen One, that we await your return."

Then one of the warriors took from his pack the pearl-encrusted casket the hovalyn had forgotten to reclaim.

"Take back what is yours."

As he put away the casket, the Chosen One reflected ruefully that he still didn't know what it was for.

"Farewell," he said to the Ghibduls. "Thank you for everything."

"Good-bye," they replied. "We will meet again soon!"

Elfohrys and the Nameless One emerged from the forest. Exhausted by their journey, they stretched out on the cool grass and went to sleep.

After awaking, they ate hurriedly, remounted, and swiftly rode off.

"Well, Nameless One," said Elfohrys, "now that you've learned you're the Chosen One, what do you think about it?"

"I know that I have a role to fulfill, even though I'm not yet sure what it is. But I feel changed. I've found a new meaning to the days that lie ahead."

Elfohrys smiled to himself.

The surrounding countryside was still asleep. Far in the distance rose the snowcapped peaks where Oonagh dwelled.

The two companions talked at length, discussing their remarkable stay with the Ghibduls and the uncertain future before them.

The Nameless One had finally found a friend in his companion and spoke to him with easy familiarity.

"But what about you—what are you seeking?" he asked him suddenly. "Why did you decide to help me?"

"I think that I can tell you now," replied Elfohrys. "Many people despaired of ever seeing the Chosen One appear. They are waiting for you. You are important. So I decided to find you, to lead you to discover who you are. And I succeeded."

"But—" stammered the dumbfounded hovalyn, "exactly what is expected of me?"

"Oonagh will reveal that to you. *The Prophecy* says that you must not find out until then. You know, Néophileus, the author of that famous book, was a Clohryun, like me, and I believe in his words."

"He's been dead for centuries! You're not going to take everything he says literally!"

Again Elfohrys smiled, but said nothing.

After a few hours, a small town appeared on the horizon, veiled in a blackish fog.

"A town sealed by the Army of Darkness," said Elfohrys softly.

"We have to go there and save the people!"

"No," replied Elfohrys. "We can't do anything for them. It's too late. The Seal is unbreakable. I know that place, it's a town of merchants: good, simple, honest folk. The

Army of Darkness only attacks those too weak to defend themselves."

Elfohrys restrained his companion, who wanted to rush to the town, and the hovalyn soon realized that he could not help its inhabitants. The young man felt guilty and useless, and Elfohrys was unable to comfort him.

They rode on for another hour. Then the hovalyn spotted clouds of smoke rising from a distant castle, and this time he and Elfohrys instantly spurred on their horses to dash to the rescue.

It was only when they arrived that they realized their mistake: the smoke was not from flames but from the Seal of Darkness settling around the town.

Lined up before them were hundreds of black-clad warriors on dark horses. They surrounded the castle and seemed united by a single force, a single thought. Their lips barely moved as they recited the spell of the Seal.

The Chosen One now faced part of the Army of Darkness. He acted without thinking and, as Elfohrys uttered a piercing cry, the hovalyn drew his sword. He swiftly attacked a soldier of Darkness and cut off his head, which rolled along the ground, its bulging eyes staring reproachfully at the young man.

A few soldiers of Darkness turned their attention away

from the Seal, which began to fade almost imperceptibly.

"How dare you attack one of us!" roared a deformed-looking creature.

"And how dare *you* destroy innocent lives!" shouted the hovalyn.

"Who are you?"

"The Chosen One."

With that, a dozen soldiers of Darkness advanced on the knight, and Elfohrys joined in the fray. Seriously outnumbered, the Chosen One turned to the casket in desperation, hoping that its mysterious power would aid him in this unfair battle. He instantly felt imbued with an unheard-of strength: he had always been an accomplished fighter, but this time he wielded his sword with unparalleled skill. He moved gracefully and with flawless precision as he rapidly and efficiently cut his way through enemy flesh, while his opponents hardly touched him, only wounding him slightly.

Nevertheless, the soldiers of Darkness were powerful, well-trained, and vastly superior in number. The tide of battle was about to turn in their favor when a tall, imposing man called a halt to their attack. The soldiers surrounding the Chosen One and Elfohrys immediately sheathed their swords and stood to attention.

Although he was astride an enchanted black stallion that breathed flames from its nostrils, the tall authoritative man was human. His splendid uniform was jet-black and the scabbard of his sword encrusted with sapphires. His craggy face was seamed with scars and two pitiless eyes glittered like steel-blue jewels beneath his bushy brows. It was an unsettling, arrogant face, thin-lipped, with a straight nose and strong chin. His hair was black.

"Step forward, man," he ordered in a deep voice.

The Chosen One did not move. The tall man seemed not to notice.

"You know how to fight better than only the weakest among us, but that is already quite an exploit."

Silence.

"I am a Sorcerer of Darkness, in command of this regiment of incompetents."

Elfohrys glanced nervously at his companion, who remained stubbornly mute.

"You are clearly a hovalyn," continued the sorcerer. "Where did you learn how to fight?"

The Chosen One said nothing. Still seated on his horse, he stared into his enemy's cruel eyes.

"Why did you attack our army? No one dares oppose us. You are brave."

A soldier of Darkness spoke up: "He says he's the Chosen One."

"The Chosen One?" repeated the sorcerer icily.

"Yes," affirmed the knight quietly.

"You're no more the Chosen One than I am."

With a wave of his hand, the sorcerer lifted the young man from his horse and suspended him a few yards above the ground, but his captive still did not flinch.

"Do you recognize the sign of the Army of Darkness?" asked the sorcerer.

Without waiting for a reply, he uncovered his left ankle: several numbers were inscribed on the skin, and beneath them, a black moon. The sorcerer waved his hand again, bringing his captive floating toward him, and with a snap of his fingers, he laid bare the skin of the young man's left ankle. There was no sign of Darkness.

"Oh!" exclaimed the sorcerer sarcastically. "So, what you are is a deserter."

Unsheathing his sword, he drew the tip of the blade across the hovalyn's left ankle, and to everyone's amazement, a trickle of black blood formed the image of a moon and several numbers.

"As I suspected. A deserter," he sneered.

It was difficult to say who was more appalled,

Elfohrys or the Nameless One.

"According to the numbers, it's been two years since you fled our army."

The Nameless One could not believe his ears.

"Ah! Now I remember," crowed the Sorcerer of Darkness. "At one time everyone knew about you. Your parents had died a few years earlier and you were living with your grandparents, but one night you decided to leave your humdrum little existence behind. You wandered from village to village until we took you in, even though you were only sixteen. Within just a couple of months, you deserted. But you didn't get far. Deserters from our army are punished by death. Since you were so young, however, we simply erased your memory. All of it. The rest of you, we spared."

At a sign from the sorcerer, the Nameless One fell to the ground. He got to his feet, bruised and blinking back tears of pain and dismay.

The sorcerer began to laugh mockingly.

"Ordinarily, I would have you killed. But Death is so inconveniently on strike. Therefore I will let you continue your loathsome and insignificant existence."

Alive, the Nameless One was condemned to bear his shame. Hope would vanish and all eyes would turn away at the sight of him. Meaningless, dishonored, his life would be one of endless wandering.

The Sorcerer of Darkness knew that such a life was worse than death.

"And you wanted to make me believe you were the Chosen One?" he exclaimed, bellowing with laughter.

Then, with a disdainful gesture, he dismissed Elfohrys and the Nameless One.

They had no choice but to obey.

24

THE RAPTORS

THE THREE GIRLS RODE THROUGH THE COUNTRY-side without encountering any obstacles or any sign of the sinister horseman. During the day they kept heading for the snowy mountains in the distance, asking for directions from the people with the long, silvery hair. At night the girls rested out in the pleasant meadows. They had seen no more sealed towns and had found only peace and prosperity along their way.

As the days went by the girls saw fewer villages and fields of crops, and after traveling for a week they arrived one morning at the foot of the mountains capped with everlasting snows. Now that they were so close to their goal, they needed to find out exactly where Oonagh lived. Fortunately, they met an old man riding along on a donkey.

"Hello!" said Amber. "Could you please tell us where to find Oonagh?"

"I've just come from there," replied the man, with a

toothless smile. "I had a lot of trouble avoiding those accursed birds, but I made it!"

"How do we reach her?" asked Amber eagerly.

The old man pointed to a mountain whose peak was lost in the clouds.

"Oonagh lives over there, but don't worry, not on top of the mountain. All you need to do is follow this path. You'll see, the birds are the only problem. Luckily, if you manage to get by them on the way there, they don't bother you when you leave."

The girls thanked the man, then set off for Oonagh's mountain. The winding path was not too steep and led them at first through a hardwood forest. The birds were nowhere to be seen, but when the slope became more abrupt and the lovely forest gave way to lofty evergreens, the horses became skittish, balking and neighing in panic. Trying to read her horse's thoughts, Amber sensed fear but could not discover its cause. Finally, she managed to contact the animal's mind.

"What's wrong?" she asked.

It was some minutes before her frightened horse was able to reply, but when he could, he ignored his custom of not speaking to his rider and said distinctly, "I will go no farther. If I do, the birds of prey will kill me. Leave. I will wait for you here."

Realizing that any argument was useless, Amber explained the situation to Jade and Opal, who resigned themselves to proceeding on foot.

"Let's take only essential things with us, like food," suggested Jade. "We'll pick up the rest when we return."

Each girl packed a small bag of provisions, and they continued on their way.

Now that they were no longer on horseback they quickly felt tired, but they hurried on, resting only when necessary. They did not talk, so as not to waste their breath. Their excitement grew as they drew closer to Oonagh, and their burning curiosity drove them to pick up their pace. They no longer thought of anything but that magic creature and what she would reveal to them.

Night fell at last over the evergreen forest. Jade felt they would get lost if they tried to go any farther, so the girls made camp in a large clearing and began to eat supper. Their nerves were on edge, for the darkened forest had become spooky and hostile. Amber thought she heard chilling cries in the distance. Wolves. She started to shake. Shadows were creeping all around them. Amber imagined shining yellow eyes behind the trees that ringed the clearing; evil eyes that stared at her, glinting ferociously.

When an apple fell from Jade's bag and rolled along the ground, Amber was so tense she screamed.

"Calm down!" cried Jade, with a slight quaver in her voice. "You scared me!"

"Don't worry, Amber, everything's fine," Opal assured her.

"What if—if those birds come tonight, while we're asleep?" stammered Amber.

Jade's blood froze at the thought. Even Opal shivered.

"We can't go without sleep," said Jade flatly.

"Nothing will happen!" insisted Opal, but more hesitantly than before.

By now the girls had lost their appetite. They stretched out, breathed deeply, and tried to rest, but it was no use. Their anxiety was overwhelming, and the silence was unbearable. When Jade at last suggested that they talk, to try and relax, her companions readily agreed.

The enveloping darkness hid their faces, making it easier for them to confide in one another. Jade began to describe her life in the palace of Divulyon and, like the other two girls, she forgot about her fear as she spoke of the homesickness she sometimes felt. For the first time, Amber told her two companions at length about the death of the woman who had been a mother to her, and she admitted how upsetting Béah Jardun's revelations had been. Then she went into great detail about the story of Janëlle's betrayal.

Although Jade and Amber had expected Opal to keep quiet when it was her turn to speak, she did tell them—hesitantly at first, almost shyly—about the ordinary life she had known and, growing bolder, she explained how much she was enjoying her new life, in spite of her distant air. Pausing, she wet her lips nervously and ended by saying how much she had "appreciated" Adrien's company.

Jade and Amber kindly pretended to be surprised.

By the time the girls dropped off to sleep, their anxiety had vanished.

They didn't realize it, but that night, something changed. After talking openly about their deepest feelings, there was no chance they could ever be enemies. The Stones and their shared adventures had already drawn them close to one another, but it was this conversation that bound them together for good.

They spent all of the next day in the vast coniferous forest, breaking the silence with frequent peals of laughter, for the girls were in a good mood and amused themselves by telling stories. However, it was a difficult climb up the mountain, and the three of them soon ached all over.

For the moment, they did not seem to be in any danger. Amber even convinced herself that she had imagined the howling of the wolves the previous night. As for the birds of prey, the girls began to wonder if they actually existed.

And so the whole day passed uneventfully.

Night found them in a clearing where they promptly fell asleep, exhausted.

Opal awoke at dawn the next day knowing only that she'd had a ghastly nightmare, and although she was unable to recall it clearly, she was still terrified, and her face was bathed in tears. She could feel her heart pounding wildly, and it was a little while before she could pull herself together.

Jade and Amber woke up not long afterward, and they were frightened, too.

"I don't feel well," murmured Amber. "My stomach's in a knot. I'm quaking—and I don't know why!"

After a moment's reflection, Jade said grimly, "We must be getting close to the birds. Amnhor said they sent out some kind of wave that makes you frightened. But we must still be quite far away, because we aren't panicking completely yet!"

When she heard that, Amber's heart sank. She had thought she would be able to confront the birds, but now that she was about to do so, her determination was falling apart.

The girls got up, looking at one another in dismay and apprehension.

"Let's go back," suggested Amber abruptly.

Jade and Opal considered the tempting proposition for a moment and almost seemed to waver, but finally Jade sighed.

"We've made a huge effort to get this far. Ever since the liberation of Nathyrnn, we've risked our lives several times trying to reach Oonagh. We're so close to our goal now, we can't just give up."

Amber and Opal had to admit she was right.

"Anyway," piped up Amber, "we've got the potion."

"But we're not supposed to use it except as a last resort," Jade reminded her.

They resumed their journey. This time, though, they felt so shaky that they couldn't carry on a coherent conversation, and they made slow progress, haunted by their visions of the birds of prey. In her bag, Opal carried the potion that Amnhor had given them; she took it out to look at it and felt reassured by the smooth glass vial.

Each minute seemed to drag by as if time were somehow solidifying, as if every instant were heavier with anguish than the one before. Even though they expected the birds to appear at any moment and swoop down on them, the girls didn't spy a single one.

When the sun was at its zenith, they emerged at last from the forest. Now the climb was even steeper. A few shrubs replaced the conifers, and then even the bushes were few and far between, finally giving way to grass, sparsely dotted with spindly flowers. Looking anxiously up at the sky and dazzled by the sun, a fiery sphere in an ocean of azure, Amber could see no trace of the dreaded predators.

Nevertheless, the girls could feel fear growing inside them and knew that soon they would no longer be able to bear this rising terror. They continued on for another hour, but their steps began to drag slower and slower.

Suddenly, Amber spotted menacing shapes up in the bright sky, gliding on long wings. Even though the birds were flying at a great height, there was no doubt what they were. The girls felt engulfed in a whirlwind of fear as soon as they caught sight of the birds, which did not yet seem to have noticed them, for they continued to soar overhead.

The raptors soon made their power felt.

Although she was shivering, through some miracle Opal still managed to stay reasonably calm by convincing herself that she shouldn't panic.

Jade clenched her fists, proudly tossed back her hair, and stood up staunchly to the terror assailing her. She was trembling and her pulse was racing, but she refused to lose her head.

Amber, however, was petrified. She could not help imagining the birds diving down to devour her, and she trembled uncontrollably. She just couldn't tear her eyes away from the birds.

"The vial"— Amber could hardly stammer out the words—"Opal, I need it!"

But Opal would not give in. The birds had not come down yet, and Amnhor had warned them to use the potion only at the last possible minute.

Slowly the birds descended toward their prey. There were more than fifty of them, darkening the sky. Now the girls could make out their gray plumage and above all, their horrifying size. They seemed to be two—or even three—times bigger than a man.

Amber cried out, certain that she was living out her worst nightmare.

Even Opal felt herself falter.

The birds flocked together, uniting their strength. To live, they fed on fear, so it was important that their victims' terror reached its full height. In order to achieve this, the raptors used a method that was almost infallible.

The three girls soon discovered what it was. The birds glided down until they were hovering about ten yards above their heads. The girls were already rooted to the spot after sighting the birds, and were now almost driven out of their minds by those long curved beaks and razor-sharp talons.

The worst was yet to come. The birds reawakened the girls' most terrifying fears, the ones they dreaded above all others. And now many of the birds were no more than five yards away. Their piercing eyes burned with concentration, greed, and the expectation of victory.

Opal was tormented by the image of Adrien in agony, and she thought she saw him dying, his chest a welter of blood, his eyes now closed to this world. Unable to intervene or speak to him, Opal was torn apart by rage and pain.

Jade was confronted with nothingness, with infinite eternity. She staggered, blinded by this dark and endless void. Then the image of her adoptive father—old, sick, lying on his deathbed—appeared to her and made her weep when she saw how thin and frail he was. The image swiftly transformed itself into the malevolent Council of Twelve, planning her death in detail and sending the Army of Darkness in pursuit of her. Jade let herself lose heart without a fight.

As for Amber, so many images and emotions assailed her that they were all a blur. She felt she had touched the very depths of horror.

Then, miraculously, she felt her fear melt away—and had the presence of mind to remember that before finishing off their prey, the birds first absorbed their victims' terror.

"Opal," she whispered hoarsely. "The potion!"

Startled by Amber's voice, Opal got a grip on herself and rummaged desperately through her bag. She found the blue glass vial and tossed it to Amber, who caught it and, in a spasm of fright, pulled out the cork and drank a mouthful of the contents. Her hands trembled so violently that she dropped the vial, which fell and shattered into smithereens. The last mouthful was lost in the grass.

Opal shot a look of despair at Amber, who had just destroyed their only chance at survival.

The potion took effect instantly. The bloodthirsty birds felt their prey slipping away from them as all Amber's emotions and sensations gradually vanished. She just stood there, expressionless, looking around her indifferently. She could see Jade and Opal's agonized faces, but the idea of helping them simply didn't occur to her. She never thought to run away, to hide somewhere, because she didn't even realize the danger she was in.

"The Stones!" screamed Opal. "Get out your Stones!"

Jade obeyed automatically and Amber as well, by reflex, but nothing happened, because Amber was no longer either really alive or human. Now that she had no feelings, she was no longer a real person.

But even lost in her torpor, Amber noticed an opening in the ground. Going over to it, she found a pathway leading into the bowels of the earth, and as Opal watched, Amber disappeared into the underground passage, abandoning her two companions. Opal was almost hysterical by now and tried with all her might to fight off the panic closing in on her.

She looked over at Jade and understood from the dazed smile on her face that the girl's fear had been absorbed by the birds. One predator, which had remained above the others, now plunged toward Jade with stunning speed. Opal at once overcame her own fright, forgetting it to think only of Jade, and without a moment's hesitation she ran to throw herself on Jade, knocking her to the ground and away from the swooping bird's claws. Clambering to her feet, Opal ordered Jade to follow her, but the poor girl couldn't hear her or understand why they had to flee. Opal never knew how she managed to pick Jade up in her arms.

The predator had shot back up into the sky as if it found this scene amusing and wanted to enjoy the spectacle, but it certainly wasn't going to allow its victim to get away. The other birds stayed where they were, for although they could terrify their victims and feed on that fear, only their leader had the right to seize the prey. Opal had hardly taken a few steps before she realized that the predator would dive again, and that this time it would not miss.

She didn't try to run, but as she stumbled along, she struggled to empty herself of everything. She did not reach for the warm comfort of her Stone. She counted only on herself, in a last desperate effort. Anyone else would have believed the bird would carry the girls off, that it was useless to fight on. But not Opal. She told herself not to give up, and focused on gathering her strength; with increasing confidence, she kept thinking that the birds could not beat her. The sweet warmth of hope flooded through her and she felt as though she were in contact with her Stone. Cruel talons dug into her flesh, lifting her slowly into the air. Opal held firmly to Jade and was not afraid. On the contrary, because she did not care, she smiled as her blond curls tumbled in the wind, and blood spurted from the wounds in her pale skin where the bird's claws clutched her painfully. She closed those eyes bluer than the sky, and did not give up.

Then the bird began to fly lower. Opal was still impassive and refused to rejoice, simply holding on to hope. When she opened her eyes, the predator was hovering six feet above the ground and, little by little, reluctantly, it relaxed its grip on Opal. The two girls fell to earth.

In the sky the birds of prey gradually disappeared, clearly suffering from an agonizing invisible, wound; they flew as if escaping a terrible powerful foe. Jade, who had been oblivious to everything, now came to her senses. Opal showed her the opening through which Amber had escaped, and after Jade had vanished down the passage as well, Opal looked calmly up at the sky, once again innocent of all menace, and smiled.

Then she entered the underground passage as though nothing had happened.

25

A Meeting with Oonagh

JADE AND OPAL HAD JUST BEGUN FEELING THEIR way along the dim tunnel when they stumbled over a huddled form: it was Amber, sitting curled up in the darkness with her head in her hands. Startled, the weeping girl gave a cry that reverberated along the passage.

"Amber!" exclaimed Jade. "What's the matter?"

Amber leaped to her feet.

"It's you, you're both alive!" she cried, wiping away her tears. "I abandoned you! And I thought you were dead!"

"Why didn't you come and help us after the potion wore off?" asked Jade reproachfully.

"I just couldn't," sniffled Amber. "I only came to a few minutes ago, and I was sure it was already too late to save you. How did you get here?"

Jade told Amber what had happened right after she'd vanished into the tunnel, and Opal took over to describe how they had defeated the birds, although she didn't fully understand it herself.

Then Jade thanked Opal warmly for saving her life, and Amber, who was still upset, hugged both girls in relief at finding them again.

"Where should we go now?" worried Jade. "If those birds come back . . ."

"Remember, they can't attack us twice. But I think we can follow this underground path," suggested Opal. "It must lead somewhere, and I'm curious to find out where."

After a short discussion they decided to keep going, and so, still a bit shaken by what they had just been through, the three of them headed off along the path. Strangely enough, instead of getting darker, the tunnel gradually grew lighter until the girls could see their surroundings perfectly. This powerful supernatural light seemed to emanate from everywhere, rather than from a little crack filtering in sunshine from outside.

After a long walk the girls stopped short in alarm: footsteps were echoing along the passageway—and growing louder. Their hearts racing, the girls were expecting to see a horrifying creature lunge at them . . . when a little girl appeared. She couldn't have been more than five years old, and although she wasn't human, she was still a sweet little thing and seemed honest and open. Her flared white dress left her slender arms and short legs bare, revealing skin of a very pale blue. Her face was solemn and innocent, with huge blue-violet eyes, and her blond hair cascaded all the way down to her tiny bare feet.

"Hello!" she chirped in a crystalline voice.

The three girls smiled at her.

"What are you doing here?" asked Amber kindly. "Do you live here?"

The little girl simply laughed gaily, revealing sparkling white teeth.

"What's your name?" inquired Amber in a soft voice.

But with a playful and mysterious expression, the child refused to speak.

"We've come here to see Oonagh," said Jade. "Do you know if we still have a long way to go?"

"Oonagh, Oonagh," repeated the girl slyly. "I can help you."

"Thank you," replied Amber. "But how?"

"Come," said the child. "I know Oonagh. Just follow me."

With that, the strange creature went skipping away. Jade, Opal, and Amber set off after her without hesitation. Their guide was merrily singing a song whose words were simply "Oonagh, Oonagh," as though this were the nicest name in the world, and sometimes she looked back with amusement at the three big girls following curiously in her wake.

In several places the tunnel branched out, but each time

the child chose her path with evident confidence and familiarity. At last, after an hour, they arrived at an extraordinary
wall glowing with light. Dazzled, Jade, Opal, and Amber
heard the child's clear voice ring out.

"Enter the light, it will not hurt you!"

And the three thought they saw her pass through the
shining wall.

"What do we do now?" exclaimed Amber in dismay.

"I don't think we have much choice," observed Jade.
"Either we go back the way we came, without our guide,
and risk getting lost—or we try to cross this barrier."

Amber had no time to protest before Jade stepped forward and vanished into the light. Opal made as if to follow
her, but Amber held her back.

"Who knows what's behind this barrier? I really don't
think we should go through it."

"We're not going to abandon Jade," insisted Opal. "If
she's in any danger, then obviously we should be with her."

Resigned, Amber went forward and disappeared into
the light with Opal.

They crossed the wall as though it weren't solid and
were greeted by an incredible sight on the other side: a
great chamber lit up by walls of brilliant crystals sparkling
in every possible color.

Opal and Amber saw Jade lost in the same admiration they felt.

"This is where all the light in the tunnel comes from," thought Amber.

Looking around for the child who had led them to this fairylike place, the three girls saw her half hiding behind a tree.

"Oonagh, Oonagh," she called laughingly. "This is where she lives."

"Wonderful!" cried Jade excitedly. "And where is she?"

The little girl stepped toward them, suddenly serious.

"Right here," she said simply.

She spoke so frankly and distinctly that it was impossible to doubt her words. Seeing her differently now, the three girls noticed the mature intelligence behind her childish smile, and when Jade looked into her gaze she knew at once that the creature was telling the truth. Reflected in those huge blue-violet eyes was a wealth of years, thoughts, madness, wisdom, and experience—of joy as well as sadness. Jade felt as though she might get lost in that gaze, it was so filled with life, and she understood that beneath her frail and youthful appearance, Oonagh had watched more time pass than Jade herself would ever see.

"It's about time you arrived," said the magic child. "I've been expecting you."

The three girls' felt almost dizzy with excitement.

"Who are our parents?" asked Jade abruptly. "Why were we driven from our homes? What danger is threatening us? Why is the Council of Twelve looking for us?"

Flushed and breathless, she was going to continue when she saw the placid look in Oonagh's eyes, and fell silent.

Then the child's clear voice rose in song, filling the entire chamber.

"From the shadows will come the Chosen One
To unify the Realm
And lead it into the light
As a King who must not reign,
Crowned in the name of the Gift.
Three Stones, three young girls:
One will discover the Gift.
One will recognize the King.
One will convince the two others to die.
Of three Stones only one fate will remain.

"People have been reciting this passage of *The Prophecy* for centuries," added Oonagh. "They have been waiting patiently for you. Your destiny has been marked out. Only its outcome is uncertain."

A shudder ran through the three girls.

"I don't understand any of it," sighed Amber.

"One will convince the two others to die," gasped Jade. "What's that supposed to mean? That one of us will make the others kill themselves?"

Frightened by her own words, Jade stopped speaking, and a heavy silence fell. So that was the reason why they were supposed to be enemies: one of them would betray the others and urge them to die.

"That's awful!" burst out Jade. "It can't be true!"

"None of us would do that," insisted Amber.

Oonagh said nothing.

"Who is the Chosen One?" asked Opal, to distract them from that shocking revelation.

"Within two weeks, on the day of the summer solstice, a great battle will take place," said Oonagh, evading the question. "Néophileus specified the date. Good and Evil will clash on the plains of the Outside, in front of the magnetic field of Fairytale. On one side will be the Army of Darkness, with the Council of Twelve and the Knights of the Order; on the other, the Army of Light."

"Who will be in the Army of Light?" asked Amber.

"All those who wish to fight for freedom: knights, men, creatures . . . The Army of Light is assembling even now. But it will never be able to fight if the Chosen One does not appear. It is for him to lead it to victory, to sacrifice his life in battle if he must. It is said in the Prophecy that one of you will recognize him: no one knows who he is; perhaps he himself does not know. People have always thought that he would have appeared long before now, and many have made it their mission to find him. They believed your role was simply to confirm he was indeed the Chosen One. It is not so.

"You must go to the palace of Yrianz of Myrnehl. Part of the Army of Light is waiting there for the Chosen One. Perhaps he will be there. If not, it is up to you to seek him out—you *must* find him!"

"And how do we get to this palace?" inquired Jade.

"Never fear. A man named Rokcdär will guide you there. He is one of Death's councilors, and can be trusted."

The three girls looked at one another in astonishment.

"On the way to the palace you must go and see Death," exclaimed Oonagh earnestly. "She must give up her strike so that the battle may take place. You alone are capable of making that stubborn creature listen to reason."

While Oonagh went to fetch an object in a far corner of

the chamber, the bewildered girls grew more and more uneasy. Go and see Death? Argue with her? How could they manage that? Oonagh returned and gave them a map to help them find their way to the gloomy land of Death.

Jade spoke up suddenly in a strangely subdued voice.

"That's all very nice, this business of the Chosen One, the battle and all that, but what I want to know is, what do I have to do with all that? I want to know who I am!"

"You are the three Stones of the Prophecy," explained Oonagh. "You are the ones who will tip the balance of the world toward good or evil. While the two armies clash, you will go to Thaar, the City of Origins, where you will fight the ultimate battle."

"And that's also where one of us will lead the others into death?" asked Jade sullenly. "I've had enough! Why should I go and see Death, and then look for this Chosen One? Why should I go to Thaar to fight the 'ultimate battle,' which basically means, get myself killed? Why shouldn't I just go on home? What's forcing me to risk my life? I'm tired of being scared. I don't want to keep asking questions without getting any answers!"

After catching her breath, she added more softly, "Just tell me what's keeping me from going quietly back to my palace, seeing my father again, and finally living in peace."

"Jade, the Army of Light needs all three of you to win its victory. If you don't even fight, evil will carry the day."

"So what! It has nothing to do with me!"

"You *must* go to Thaar," continued Oonagh. "Because your parents sacrificed themselves for you. Because knowing that one day you would fight against the Darkness, they gave their lives to protect you. You have no right to betray them."

"They're dead?" cried Jade. "They're dead!"

"They hid you safely before being killed by the Army of Darkness, or the Council of Twelve. By evil."

"But who were they? What were their names?"

"What use would it be to know that? You mustn't live in the past. Don't weep over what cannot be helped. Devote your energies to what you can still change. You haven't the right to give up the struggle."

"And *my* parents?" asked Opal suddenly.

"I'm so sorry," murmured Oonagh. "They were not spared. They were forced to flee, to hide you. The Army of Darkness and the Council were very powerful, and hunted them down. Your parents had guessed what fate lay in store for them, so they placed you in the hands of people whom they trusted absolutely."

"You still haven't answered my question," interrupted

Jade. "Who are we? Why do we have so many enemies?"

"The Chosen One and you three . . . are the Sorcerers of Light," said Oonagh gravely.

Her admission was met with profound silence.

"Ah!" said Jade finally. "And where does that get us?"

"Listen to me. When you were born, you were already clutching your Stones in your fists. These Stones grant you considerable power, but they belong only to you; they are part of you. Until your fourteenth birthdays your Gifts lay dormant in you. They were not yet ready to awaken. It was vital that you should not discover them too soon, and above all, that you should discover them together. Alone, you are vulnerable and your Gifts are useless to you."

Opal coughed nervously. Although she knew she had found her Stone too early, she had never imagined that this might have dangerous consequences.

"Opal," said Oonagh sternly, "your heart is telling me what you're trying to conceal. And what it tells me is bad, very bad. If you discovered your Gift too soon, you must have attracted the attention of the Council of Twelve—which may well have had access to your mind through telepathy." Oonagh sighed heavily. "No matter. What's done is done! Ever since your fourteenth birthdays, your Gifts have been evolving. You had to undergo a good many trials to strengthen them, however, and reaching me was the last stage necessary for these Gifts to develop fully. During these tests, if you had discovered your destinies before the allotted time, your powers would have ceased to grow."

"So," Jade concluded, "we were chased out of our homes so that we could discover our so-called Gifts when we turned fourteen, and we all had to be together to discover them? And then we had to go through terrifying adventures so we could wind up deciding the fate of the world? Don't you think that's a little too much for the three of us? Especially since the finale doesn't sound promising, if two of us are supposed to die."

"So be it," said Oonagh.

"I mean, really," screamed Jade, "do you think we're mad? We're not going to deliberately go and get ourselves killed in Thaar!"

"Do you have any choice? Go home if you like, but the Council or the Army of Darkness will catch you and kill you. The three of you are capable of changing many things. It's up to you to decide whether that's worth it or not. But know this, Jade: if you refuse to go to Thaar and somehow manage to survive, you may escape the hatred of others, but you will hate yourself for ever."

Jade could say nothing in return. Although she didn't

want to believe Oonagh, Jade knew she was speaking the truth.

"And our famous Gift, what is it?" asked Opal.

"One will discover the Gift," replied Oonagh. "So it is written by Néophileus. It is not for me to reveal what one of you, alone, must understand."

Although the three girls bombarded her with questions, Oonagh would not say another word. Wearing her lazy little-girl smile, she began to sing:

"From the shadows will come the Chosen One
To unify the Realm
And lead it into the light,
As a King who must not reign
Crowned in the name of the Gift;
Three Stones, three young girls.
One will discover the Gift.
One will recognize the King.
One will convince the two others to die.
Of three Stones only one fate will remain."

Jade, Opal, and Amber understood that Oonagh would say no more to them, and they turned as one to cross back through the wall of light and pursue their destiny.

PARIS: PRESENT DAY

I woke up panting, upset after a wretched, disturbed night. I remembered in detail the revelations of the magic creature with the blue-violet eyes, and the emotions of Jade, Opal, and Amber overwhelmed me, as if I had experienced them myself.

Once again my dream had been interrupted, returning me sorrowfully to my cold, somber world. I remember that I cried, revolted by the injustice of it: why was my reality so horrifyingly different from my dream? Just then, memories rushed in, desolate and deceitful beneath their golden glow.

This time I was too upset to resist them. They invaded me, glittering with a bitter gaiety. I saw myself: Joa. I recalled how much everyone had admired the exuberant girl I had been. I was rich, pretentious; every girl I met turned pale with envy over my clothes. People put up with my whims, treated them as commands I gave to others. Joa's character was deplorable, but I knew that she was also more sensitive than she allowed herself to appear. I remembered distinctly how some were fascinated by my slightest casual gesture, but also how some would make fun of me. Then I would hide in a dark corner and quietly cry. Deep down, I was fragile, even though I hid this carefully. I liked to have fun, to laugh at the expense of others, and it's true that I was far from being thoughtful and mature. But sometimes, in the midst of my shallowness, I did show myself to be considerate and serious-minded. I was more than just a flighty girl; on the contrary, I had a tender heart. I revealed my feelings only when I was far from prying eyes, far from the effervescence I left sparkling in my wake.

I had believed in eternal happiness. I had thought the girlfriends who surrounded me were sincere and fond of me, but their smiles were only honeyed pretense. When my illness destroyed my perfect life, I'd expected to be bolstered by support—only to see everyone disappear like cowards. What did I have to offer, lying in my hospital bed, my poor face ravaged by sickness? Only my parents still took care of me, but life decided that even this consolation was unnecessary, and an accident erased them, too, from my world. I had gradually understood and accepted that *my friends had abandoned me. But was among those who had deserted me, the one I loved, and who loved me. Although I didn't know what it meant to love, that didn't stop me from caring for him, from loving him in my own way—in my former thoughtless way. He looked like the Chosen One in my dream but, like him, he was just a deserter, a traitor who masqueraded in the light when he served only darkness. He'd visited me once, just once, and then he had run away and never come back. And that is something I still cannot accept.*

26

THE RING OF ORLEYS

THE NAMELESS ONE RODE ALONG BESIDE Elfohrys, despairing over the crushing blow he had just received. He could not understand how he could have handed his soul over to evil. For as long as he could remember he had always considered the Darkness as not just a formidable enemy, but a loathsome one as well. Yet it seemed he, too, had once belonged among those shadows! The sign of that dreaded army had marked his left ankle, where his blood still trickled, distinctly tracing a moon crowned with numbers. The Sorcerer of Darkness had not lied to him, however vile his intentions. Now the hovalyn longed for the time when he had wondered in vain about his past, because now the knowledge that he had once served the cause of evil would torment him all his life.

Completely disheartened by the sorcerer's revelation, Elfohrys did not speak to the young man for several days. The two continued their journey, silent and dejected.

Finally, at nightfall on the third day, Elfohrys asked a question. "How is it possible that you, whom I considered a friend, could be a soldier of Darkness with innocent blood on your hands?"

The Nameless One did not reply, but he flashed a look of profound distress at his companion.

"I know you don't remember anything," Elfohrys continued less harshly, "but I really believed in you! I was sure you were the Chosen One! And you were claiming you wanted to save lives, when you've actually taken them! How can I convince myself that you've changed, that your soul steeped in darkness has now been flooded with light? What's the point of going to see Oonagh now," he asked, gazing accusingly at the hovalyn, "just to have her read what's in your cruel heart? I think that our ways must part here, and I hope never to hear of you again. And if our paths should ever cross, I trust that I will already have forgotten you!"

With that, the magic creature wheeled around and made as if to gallop off, but the Nameless One called out his name hoarsely.

"Elfohrys! Before deceiving you, I was betrayed by myself. I never would have imagined that I'd served the Darkness. How I came to do that is beyond me, but I can promise you that today I would rather die than go back to that sinister army. I don't know if my soul crossed over suddenly from evil into good, but the blood staining my hands makes me suffer more than I ever would have believed possible."

Hearing these words, Elfohrys turned back, and when his golden eyes looked deeply into the knight's sapphire blue gaze, they still saw strength and nobility behind the sadness.

"Even if that were true," replied Elfohrys curtly, "why should I follow you? You're not the Chosen One, and I must continue to seek him. I cannot remain with you without thinking of the atrocities you must have committed. You are a murderer—and I cannot forget that!"

"So you think I should carry the burden of my crimes until I die?"

"You even deserve to die for them!"

"But I've become someone else," protested the hovalyn. "I'm not going to let myself be haunted by my past all my life! I feel remorse, I'm sorry for what I did, even if I don't remember any of it. Will I never be allowed to be rid of my mistakes?"

"Will your regrets bring back those who begged you for their lives?" replied Elfohrys disdainfully. "A man doesn't change overnight, and the deaths you caused demand your own!"

"So I must suffer all my life?"

"That would be the only just thing!"

The Nameless One found himself alone, bereft, abandoned to his misery. He rode on like that for an hour before he finally saw an elegant manor house in the gathering evening shadows and decided to seek shelter there. When he knocked on the door, it was opened almost immediately by a plump, jolly woman.

"I humbly beg your hospitality," he said. "I am a hovalyn, lost and hungry."

"Welcome!" exclaimed the woman. "Sleeping under the stars would not be sensible on such a dark night. Do come in, sit down at the table, while I take your horse to the stable."

The Nameless One thanked her and felt somewhat comforted by the warm atmosphere inside the manor. He went down a corridor, observing with curiosity the portraits decorating the white walls, and followed the sound of happy laughter until he came to a vast banquet hall. There, about fifty people laughed and talked while servants plied them with delicious-looking dishes. When those at the table noticed the stranger, they gradually grew quiet, until a pleasant, round-faced man, simply dressed, rose to greet the new arrival.

"Here is an unexpected guest!" he announced in a kind voice. "Let me introduce myself: Tivann of Orleys. You are welcome, do come and join us. Aren't you a hovalyn?"

"I am," replied the Nameless One.

"Now, that's interesting. Come, sit down, and let's talk for a while!"

The young knight sat next to Tivann of Orleys and helped himself to food. Warming to the relaxed atmosphere, he tried to forget his troubles.

"So, you're a hovalyn?" repeated the man, who was clearly the lord of the manor.

"Yes," his guest replied again.

"Well, we have something here that will certainly be of interest to you," continued Tivann mysteriously. "It's been handed down in my family from father to son. It's an enchanted ring, and there isn't anything special about it, except that—" Tivann of Orleys broke off dramatically and then, lowering his voice, said, *"Except that it can ..."* But the man suddenly seemed to change his mind and merely added, "You'll see tomorrow morning."

Intrigued, the Nameless One ate his meal in silence while he studied the other guests. Seated across from him was a dainty girl dressed more carefully than the other diners, in a long, sky-blue dress that gracefully showed off her figure. Her thin lips curved sweetly, and eyes of a limpid, almost unnatural green shone out from her pale face. Meeting the stranger's gaze, she looked him over in return, and smiled.

"Hovalyn, this is my daughter, Orlaith," declared the lord of the manor. "She is the youngest of my children, and the most sensitive. She is my pride and my despair, for ancestral tradition demands that her hand be given in marriage to the man destined to possess the enchanted ring I just mentioned. Unless he declines the honor—which would truly astound me, for Orlaith is a pearl."

Unable to think of a suitable reply, the hovalyn finished his meal in silence. When he confessed to his host that he was very tired, Tivann courteously had him shown to a room, where the young man donned the nightshirt laid out for him, stretched out on the bed, and gratefully inhaled the fresh smell of clean sheets. Burying his head in the feather pillow, he tried to rest, but his troubles kept him awake for hours. Once asleep, he dreamed that Tivann of Orleys kept saying, *It's an enchanted ring, it can . . . It's an enchanted ring, it can . . .* Then Orlaith's face appeared while her father repeated, *She is a pearl. . . .*

At dawn, the sleeper was woken by two strong arms shaking him vigorously. Opening his eyes, he saw his host bending over him.

"Hurry, hovalyn," said Tivann briskly. "In ten minutes we will expect you in the great hall where we dined last night."

The Nameless One moved to get dressed, but sank back on the bed, feeling crushingly depressed. He felt buried under the burden of his past, and could no longer bear to go on. He drew his sword, as if to thrust it through his own heart. . . .

It was sheer curiosity that saved him. Why put an end to life when there were so many questions still to be answered? Who were his parents? Why had he chosen to join the Army of Darkness? Sheathing his sword, he hurriedly dressed and rushed off to the great hall where Tivann was waiting for him. What would he learn there? Something about that strange ring, perhaps?

When he reached the hall he could not hide his amazement: all around the rectangular wooden table stood many humans and magic creatures, some clad in heavy armor, others scarred by battle wounds. Swords hung at their sides, and the same solemn expression was on every face. The Nameless One knew at once that this was an assembly of hovalyns. He saw Tivann of Orleys as well as Orlaith, who looked even more fragile and fairylike amid this soldierly throng.

At a sign from Tivann, the Nameless One advanced and took his place among the others, wondering what event he was about to witness. He soon found out. Smiling broadly, Tivann of Orleys stepped forward.

"My friends, our gathering unites precisely the number of hovalyns required to observe the ancient custom passed down in this manor. Each of you will have the opportunity to try on the enchanted ring in my possession, but I must remind you that this is a perilous undertaking."

After a pause, he went on: "For centuries, whenever anyone has presented himself to try on the Ring of Orleys, tradition has demanded that a meeting of hovalyns take place according to a precise ritual. Today, the first brave youth to risk putting on the ring is Arthur of Farrières."

A conceited knight drew himself up arrogantly.

"If he succeeds," continued Tivann, "he will win my daughter's hand as well as my esteem. If he fails, anyone else gathered around this table may also try his luck."

More and more intrigued, the Nameless One watched closely as Tivann cleared his throat and signaled to his daughter, who reached into the bodice of her gown to pull out a silver chain on which sparkled a ring.

"Only Orlaith can wear this jewel against her skin without suffering atrocious burns," declared Tivann. "According to tradition, only the purest of the daughters of Orleys may have charge of the ring." Then, turning to Arthur of Farrières, who returned his gaze with pompous pride, Tivann asked: "Hovalyn, are you determined to wear this ring, enchanted by sorcerers in times immemorial? Do you accept the risks you run? Weigh your response carefully, for once you have given it before this assembly, it will be irreversible."

"I am; I do," replied Arthur of Farrières, smiling fatuously at Orlaith, who looked away with a faint shudder.

"So be it. Before beginning the test, I will enlighten the few hovalyns among you who are not yet aware of the magic property of the Ring of Orleys. It lies under a powerful spell: the ring can distinguish hearts blackened by evil from those pure hearts that strive only for good. The more darkness a man has within him, the more pitiless the ring will prove toward him, for it tolerates only innocence and justice. But even if an honest man of irreproachable virtue dares place this ring on his finger, he might well also suffer grievous consequences. This is why the Ring of Orleys demands mature reflection from those who would measure themselves against it."

A mysterious shadow veiled Tivann's gaze. "The ring was forged for one purpose only: to recognize the one for whom it has waited for centuries. When it has accomplished its purpose, it will vanish. It is an enchanted ring: it can find the Chosen One."

Feeling a shiver run through him, the Nameless One turned to leave the room, but his legs almost buckled beneath him and his vision blurred. Shaken, he pulled himself together, and his strange weakness passed unnoticed.

Orlaith unfastened the chain from around her neck and took the ring in her white hand.

"I have always known that I am the Chosen One," announced Arthur of Farrières. "I have never considered myself a simple hovalyn. This trial does not frighten me in the least."

Orlaith slipped the ring on to a finger of Arthur's outstretched hand. The ring, a cunningly wrought circle of white gold, soon melted into a whirlwind that began to spin around the man's finger. The knight's face betrayed his growing alarm, while his bulging eyes revealed his pain as the ring gradually became a circlet of silver flames with pearly reflections. The hovalyn shook his hand, his features distorted in agony, and cried, "Take this ring off me! I cannot bear it anymore! Mercy! Help me, I beg of you!"

"It is impossible," murmured Tivann.

The vicious flames kept spreading, licking greedily, and soon strips of charred flesh hung from the knight's mutilated hand. The Nameless One was fascinated by the sight, filled with repulsion yet unable to tear his eyes away.

"Rarely has the Ring of Orleys punished a man so cruelly," sighed Tivann.

At last the torture was over. The hovalyn's finger crumbled into black ashes, while the ring, as smooth again as when it had hung around Orlaith's neck, fell to the floor with a metallic clink. The girl quickly picked it up as Arthur of Farrières returned to his place, grimacing with pain.

"Now," asked Tivann of Orleys, "does anyone else wish to risk wearing the ring?"

Silence reigned over the gathering of hovalyns. Then a man with a rugged face spoke up.

"I want to try my luck."

"If that is your wish," nodded Tivann. "You are a man of great merit, Gohral Keull, and if you are not the Chosen One, then no one is worthy of that honor."

Gohral Keull's face remained impassive. He held out his hand to Orlaith: it was scarred by many wounds. The terrible event occurred once more. As the flames danced wildly around his finger, Gohral Keull made no sound; on the contrary, he stood like a statue, as if the suffering he was enduring were of no importance. Only his dark eyes were shadowed with pain. Soon the ring clattered to the floor. The other knights stared at Gohral Keull in astonishment, however, for the finger on which the fiery ring had burned was intact.

"The ring has judged that even though you are not the Chosen One, you are nevertheless a worthy man," explained Tivann.

Gohral Keull showed no reaction to this compliment.

"Does anyone else wish to try on the Ring of Orleys?" asked Tivann, certain that no one else would step forward.

"I will," announced the Nameless One suddenly, surprising even himself.

"You? But my lad, you are still much too young! What is your name?"

"I have none," replied the hovalyn, now amused by this question that had always tormented him before.

A murmur ran through the crowd.

"The Nameless One," muttered Arthur de Farrières disdainfully. "So you are he! And you claim to be the Chosen One!"

"No," came the reply. "I simply want to know whether I have good or evil in me."

Gohral Keull watched the young hovalyn intently.

Tivann looked dismayed. "Nameless One," he announced, "According to custom I cannot refuse you your chance. But if I were you, I would withdraw your offer."

"I will not," said the hovalyn confidently.

He advanced toward Orlaith. The knights who met his gaze had to admit that it reflected strength and determination. The Nameless One placed his hand in Orlaith's icy palm. He looked at the ring. It was simple, but beautiful. At first it seemed to be made entirely of white gold, but closer inspection showed that its smooth, shining surface was encrusted with minute diamonds. Orlaith slipped it on to one of the young knight's long, slender fingers and gave him a look of encouragement.

The Ring of Orleys changed into a silvery liquid flowing faster and faster around the hovalyn's finger. The pain was atrocious, savage, yet he managed not to groan out loud. Soon silvery flames were pitilessly consuming his flesh; he wanted to scream, felt as though he were fainting, but he resisted, standing tall, controlling his weakness in spite of the odor of burning flesh now filling the air.

The hovalyns watched, commiserating with him. His torture lasted even longer than it had for Arthur of Farrières and Gohral Keull together. The Nameless One forced himself to hold his head high, without looking at his wounded finger. What he had refused to admit had been proved: the pain had been so appalling, so unspeakable, that he was certain that the Ring of Orleys had seen the evil in him and punished him accordingly.

He felt the hovalyns' eyes fixed on him but did not dare to meet their gaze. When one murmur after another rippled through the silence, the Nameless One thought the knights were commenting coldly on his plight.

"You're right," he said bitterly. "I've failed, and my heart is filled with evil. The Ring of Orleys has confirmed your judgments. So let Orlaith pick up that ring and place it on another's finger, but forget me, forget the defeat I just endured, forget even my face. . . ."

He no longer knew what he was saying and no one else did, either, for he was mumbling softly to himself as he looked for the ring on the floor. It was not there. He looked all around him, searching for the silvery gleam in the far corners of the hall, but he looked in vain. Then he dared glance hesitantly at his injured hand.

It was sound and whole.

Orlaith was smiling radiantly at him. The knights were watching him with humility and admiration, even if some looks were mixed with envy.

"Nameless One, there is no doubt," declared Tivann of Orleys, moved to tears. "You are the Chosen One, he whom we have all dreamed of seeing one day!"

At these words the hall erupted with thunderous applause in honor of the Nameless One, who still stood there in disbelief.

Was he truly the man whose very name, the Chosen One, was keeping hope alive deep in the world's heart?

27

THE LAKE OF THE PAST

DISTURBED BY OONAGH'S REVELATIONS, THE three girls retraced their steps and headed back to where they had left their horses. Amber and Opal were worried and daunted, but also fascinated by the importance of the roles they had to play. As for Jade, she was too upset by what Oonagh had told them to even know what she felt. At first she had rebelled against such a grim future. These new responsibilities weighed too heavily on her shoulders. But she had to see this through to the end! If everyone had been waiting for her for centuries—well, she couldn't just give it all up now. And yet, how could she accept marching straight into danger? Without admitting it to herself, Jade was paralyzed with fear.

"I swear," she declared, "that I will never betray you. The Prophecy can't be true. None of us would ever urge the others to die. Never!"

"I swear," repeated Amber solemnly, "that I will never do such a thing. I'd rather die than kill you!"

"I swear it as well," said Opal. "That Néophileus was wrong. He's been dead for centuries. There's no reason why we have to do everything he says!"

Jade and Amber smiled, but they were still deeply anxious.

"I can't believe it," muttered Jade. "What's happening to us, it's so—"

"Weird, unbelievable, unimaginable," chimed in Amber. "And to think that we're going to see Death!"

"It's terrifying, but very exciting, too," admitted Jade.

"Besides, so many people will be watching everything we do," said Opal pensively. "Oonagh did say that we've been expected for hundreds of years!"

"I'm scared," confessed Amber abruptly. "How can they ask us to decide the fate of the world? It's crazy. I'd really like to pretend I didn't know about any of this and go back home to live a normal life."

"Me too," sighed Opal heavily. "I don't want to go to Thaar—I can't go there. . . . knowing what we'll find waiting for us. But I realize I have to go."

"Well, if you're going there, I'll go too," promised Amber.

"So will I," said Jade. "We have to stick together. How do we know what horrors lie ahead of us? If so many people are counting on us, though, we can't let them down. Our parents did give their lives for us, and if we're really able to change something, to weaken the Council of Twelve or the Army of Darkness, we ought to do it."

Jade had said her piece. She could not abandon Amber, Opal, and all those people who believed in her. Although Amber found herself longing nostalgically for the carefree days she'd known before her fourteenth birthday, she also knew that she would have to live out her incredible destiny.

Although Opal seemed as aloof and unruffled as always, her feelings and memories were in turmoil. Before she had met Jade and Amber, time had passed slowly and uneventfully for her in a routine existence devoid of passion and adventure. Living out the same day over and over again, she had learned to forget dreams, laughter, emotions, tears. Withdrawing into herself, she had rejected friendship and love. Meeting Jade, Amber, and then Adrien had taught her to discover the world as it can be: astonishing, beautiful, gentle and harsh at the same time. And now that this life she was beginning to enjoy was threatened, it became all the more precious in her eyes.

"How does Oonagh expect us to explain to Death that she shouldn't give up her strike?" grumbled Jade. "What's so special about us that's going to make her see sense?"

"And anyway," added Amber, "going to see Death is *tremendously* weird!"

After discussing their doubts about this eerie mission to the realm of Death, the girls wondered about the mystery of the birds of prey. Why had they spared Opal and Jade? And what was the source of the unknown power from which they seemed to be fleeing?

The trip down the mountain was easy, almost pleasant. Within two days the travelers had reached their horses, who were waiting patiently for them. Amber stroked her mount for a long time, happy to see him again. He had adopted the white coat she particularly liked and tossed his head in welcome.

Before they set out again, Jade studied the map Oonagh had given them.

"Well, according to this map, I *think* the countryside we crossed on the way here is part of a wooded region called Hornimel. The mountain range we're in now isn't very big; it's called the Irog, and according to this map it marks the boundary of Hornimel. Beyond this range there are plateaus and older mountains in the area of Ellrog, which doesn't seem to have any towns or cities."

"Let me see the map," said Amber, coming over to sit

next to Jade and peer at the parchment. "Just what I was afraid of," she sighed dramatically. "Fairytale is huge!"

"But we're fairly close to the territory of Death," replied Jade. "Look, all we have to do is follow a river, the Déâthod, which crosses Ellrog. It leads to a great plain next to a huge lake, into which the river seems to flow. We'll have to cross either the plain or the lake, and then we'll be there." Jade pointed to an elegant inscription in black ink: OKDHRÛL, THE LAND OF DEATH. "If we ever want to reach this famous Okdhrûl," she announced, "then we'd better get going."

"Okdhrûl," groaned Amber. "What a disgusting name!"

As the girls were riding back along the path through the hardwood forest, Opal had a disturbing thought.

"Once we get to the bottom of this mountain and are crossing Ellrog," she said anxiously, "maybe our enemies will come looking for us."

"Yes, I know," said Jade with a shudder. "But in any case, they don't know where we are or what we look like."

"Except that we already decided the black horseman we saw a few times was an enemy," observed Opal. "What if he belongs to the Army of Darkness? Couldn't he be some sort of scout?"

"Let's not think about that," said Amber hurriedly.

"But what if I'm right?" insisted Opal.

"It's quite possible," admitted Jade. "Anyway, it seems as though several people we'd never even seen before have recognized us. There must be something distinctive about us. That means people know who we are—and that's dangerous!"

"Three fourteen-year-old girls riding alone across Hornimel are definitely going to stand out," said Opal flatly.

They were getting too upset to talk much more. If the Army of Darkness found them, what tortures would they have to suffer?

"If only I had a sword," said Jade softly. "Then I'd feel safer. Luckily, we've got our Stones, but will they be enough to defend us?"

"Still," remarked Opal, "if we're so easy to recognize and we have so many enemies, why haven't they attacked us yet?"

The girls spent the day worrying about the threat from the Army of Darkness, which Amber expected to see bearing down on them at any moment in a charge of black-clad horsemen brandishing gleaming swords.

"If the worst comes to the worst," she thought miserably, "if the Army of Darkness does find us, will I be brave enough to fight or will I be just as pathetic as I was with those birds of prey?"

Sensing her anxiety, her horse tried to soothe her with gentle telepathic waves, but Amber could not stop worrying.

Night fell as the girls were leaving the mountain. They looked back at the Irog range they had crossed leaving Hornimel, following the Déâthod's murky waters through the hardwood forest. From that point on, the hills of Ellrog stretched out to the horizon, and the three travelers felt somehow that the desolate region before them would prove hostile.

Jade, Opal, and Amber sat wearily on the ground near the Déâthod to eat a meager supper, and although the sounds of the river rushing along were crystal clear, the water was so muddy that the girls didn't dare drink any of it. Afterward they lay down on the grass. In spite of the calm all around them, they still felt on edge and began contemplating the magnificent starry heavens. Without speaking out loud, they knew they were all three sensing the same thing: their anxieties were gently being washed away by the enchanting spell of nature. Savoring the magic of this quiet moment, Jade, Opal, and Amber cradled their Stones in their hands.

The next morning, bursting with energy, they rode off shortly after dawn. As they set off, they observed the austere landscape of Ellrog: hillocks of short, dry, yellowed grass, a scattering of bare trees, and a few eroded peaks hardly higher than the surrounding foothills.

At first everything was peaceful. The cool morning breeze wafted the scent of a few flowers, birds sang of their happiness, and when a startled doe dashed in front of their horses, the girls admired its sleek coat. They were surprised to find Ellrog so pleasant and, chatting with studied nonchalance, they made an effort to put aside all thoughts of their enemies.

Amber contemplated the winding Déâthod, which had grown broad and imposing thanks to numerous tributaries. Its rapid waters, now clear, sparkled so brightly in the sun that they seemed like molten silver. Warned by a mysterious instinct, however, the girls did not drink from the river.

As the sun rose in the sky the heat became more oppressive. The three companions stopped talking, growing increasingly uneasy. Suddenly Amber blurted out what no one had dared to admit.

"There's something peculiar about this place."

The countryside had gradually changed. Silence reigned, absolute and disturbing. The three horses had grown tense and skittish. The flowers had disappeared, and there were no longer any animals to be seen. As the girls rode along, all forms of life seemed to vanish from Ellrog.

"Maybe this means we're getting close to Okdhrûl, the land of Death," suggested Jade.

"Is that meant to be good news?" asked Amber wryly. "I'm scared. I know you two—you're brave, you'll never admit you're afraid. But I am! I don't want to see Death at all, and this place is already making my skin crawl!"

"Don't worry," insisted Opal. "We're not in any danger."

"Oh, really?" replied Amber in a shaky voice. "Apart from maybe getting sliced to ribbons by the Army of Darkness or some other enemy that's after our hides, right—we're not in danger at all! And then, if we survive, if we *do* get to see Death, hey—we can always head on to Thaar! Great! There, we've got no chance of coming out unscathed!"

Jade and Opal tried halfheartedly to calm Amber down, and the girls talked constantly to keep their fears at bay. Luckily, the black-clad horseman hadn't shown up again, but everything around them seemed threatening. Even the sun had slipped behind grayish clouds, letting the air grow damp and chilly.

When night fell at last over Ellrog, the three girls stopped near the Déâthod, whose waters had grown cloudy again, black with soil.

Trembling, Amber felt around in the darkness for Opal's icy hand.

"When I was little my mother always held my hand so I could go to sleep," she whispered. "As long as she was nearby, I was sure she would chase away the nasty shadows, the nightmares. . . ."

Amber stopped, but Opal gently squeezed her hand in sympathy and did not let go. At last the three girls fell asleep.

They rose the next morning without any enthusiasm for the day's ride and did not enjoy following the river through that gloomy, unfriendly landscape. Whinnying nervously, the horses proceeded slowly. The girls felt increasingly exhausted and depressed. After a few hours a light mist appeared, then turned into a choking fog all around them. The travelers could no longer see a thing, not even one another. Only the Déâthod, glimmering strangely, was still visible. Jade, Opal, and Amber forced themselves to keep speaking calmly together so they would not become separated. They had lost all notion of time. Blinded by the fog, they shivered in a cutting wind.

The fog gradually lifted at last, revealing a flowered plain at the edge of an immense lake.

"I know where we are!" cried Jade. "All we have to do now is cross that plain to get to Okdhrûl!"

"That didn't take long!" exclaimed Amber.

"Ellrog is a small place. Which is just fine with me!"

They were about to ride on to the plain when a man's voice rang out loudly, even though no one was in sight.

"The traveler choosing plain or lake
To Okdhrûl, either path may take.
If 'cross this plain your way doth lie,
Dreams will haunt you till you die.
If the boat you decide to row,
Then this lake the past will show."

The voice said no more. Worried, the girls consulted one another briefly, and all agreed to choose the Lake of the Past. They took with them only some provisions, and Amber ordered the horses to wait with the rest of the baggage. When the three companions stepped into the wooden boat they found at the lake's edge, it rocked precariously, then glided across the limpid blue water, impelled by an unknown power. The girls were dismayed to see the shore vanish behind them into the mist of Ellrog. All of a sudden, Amber screamed: the clear water had become blood red, and Jade now shrieked in horror as well. Amber was the first to see the dark form that emerged from the troubled depths as the boat stopped dead in the water, but her fright soon turned to joy: the shade took on the appearance of a young woman with gentle, loving eyes, and Amber knew it was her mother. The woman stroked Amber's hair affectionately.

Come with me, she urged in a melodious voice. *I've missed you so much. . . . Come back to me, Amber. . . .*

And the young woman held out a white hand. Amber was entranced by the apparition and took her hand, intending to obey her. The figure was invisible to Jade and Opal, who cried out in alarm when they saw Amber stand up in the boat, ready to step over the gunwale and fall into the lake. Desperately, Jade pulled back on Amber, who fell on top of her, tipping the boat and pitching all three girls into the lake. Opal and Jade grabbed hold of the boat as Amber, lost in a daze, began to sink. Hesitating for a moment, Jade looked at Opal, who mumbled, "I feel too weak—I can't go and get her."

And Opal truly did feel her head spin as she saw shadows all around her acting out the cruel death of her parents. She saw blood spurting from her mother's heart, heard her scream for mercy; she could see the pitiless face of a Sorcerer of Darkness. . . .

When she began swimming toward Amber, Jade

accidentally swallowed a mouthful of the water, which tasted like blood. Thousands of smiling faces immediately swarmed disturbingly around her. They seemed eager to explain who they were, and abandoning Amber, Jade swam over to them. She heard them murmuring: "We lived so that you might live. We fought so that you might fight the ultimate battle. We are in you, we are with you. You are here because we came before you. . . ."

Jade was running out of breath, but she barely realized this. Then, suddenly, she could feel her Stone safe in her hand, and a voice inside her said: *Those shadows calling to you belong to the past. You must save Amber, you must live!* And Jade turned away from the kindly faces to swim as fast as she could to Amber.

Jade's lungs felt as though they were about to explode, and she could only hope that she would manage to rescue Amber, who with one last effort had taken out her Stone. But now Jade was exhausted and already resigned to giving up and sinking to the bottom of the Lake of the Past. When she felt new energy surge through her, she understood that Opal was holding her Stone as well. "You're alive," said a voice, and Jade couldn't tell anymore whether it was Amber's or Opal's. "You're alive, and as long as you are alive, you cannot stop hoping to stay alive."

Then Jade found the strength to bring Amber up to the surface, where she gasped for air. Although Amber was regaining consciousness, Jade kept holding her up because she was obviously too weak to swim.

Jade's head was spinning. Her vision began to fade. Failing rapidly, she was about to abandon herself once more to the reddish waters of the Lake of the Past.

Then out of nowhere, she felt two strong arms take hold of her, lift her up, and lay her down on dry land.

Paris: Present Day

I opened my eyes. My heart was beating painfully fast, and I was distraught: this time, I realized without any doubt that my dream was complete fiction, the product of my unbridled imagination. I'd been deluding myself when I'd almost managed to believe that this dream really did exist in some other dimension. I'd been wrong, and I knew it. All my hopes had come to nothing.

In the deep waters of the Lake of the Past, among the faces calling out to Jade, I had seen my own. Or rather, Joa's. Joa, even more smiling and beautiful than ever. That vision tortured me, but it was my own fault, for I had put my own image into my dream to remind myself that it was merely my own invention. And I could still see Joa, her face framed by auburn curls, her blue-green eyes twinkling with mocking laughter. She didn't say anything, but her indulgent smile seemed to tell me how naive I'd been.

So the dream was nothing. I created it, I controlled it. It was nothing, nothing—except a failed attempt to go on living. The brutal truth was right in front of me. Why had I wanted to prove to myself how mistaken I'd been? Why had I wanted to destroy the only chance I had left?

Death, which I'd hoped to stave off, was stalking me once more. This time there would be no escape: my dream, my last defense, had weakly fallen apart. All I had left were pain and sorrow. Death was too good at her job, and would be coming for me soon. Shaking, I closed my eyes, but the vision of that shadowy creature draped in black pursued me, growing more and more clear. And real.

I wanted to feel the sun break through the clouds in my heart. I wanted to hear the wind humming its sweet melody. I wanted to smell the intoxicating perfume of spring, the rich scent of summer. I wanted to savor life the way I'd never dared to before.

I'd thought that when the time came to leave, I would be brave. But I wasn't. How could I be? There were so many things I hadn't done when I'd still had the chance. And now I was sorry. Tears streaked my face, although I hadn't even known I was crying. If only my dream would dare reach its climax and give me one last moment of grace. "I'm begging you," I said to Death. "Give me a little more time. One night . . ."

28

A MEETING WITH DEATH

JADE AND AMBER SOON CAME TO, AND FOUND Opal beside them.

"It's incredible," said Opal. "When I held tight to my Stone I felt a powerful force flow through me, helping me to swim here. We were way out in the middle of the lake, but it seemed as if I swam only a few yards to reach the shore!"

"We're in Okdhrûl?" asked Jade incredulously. "On the other side of the Lake of the Past?"

"Yes," replied Opal.

"How did we get out of the lake?" asked Amber in bewilderment.

"As soon as I got here, I tried to figure out how I could save you—and then you both appeared. You were unconscious, Amber, and Jade was swimming with her arm around you. When you were almost at the edge of the lake, I saw that Jade couldn't go any farther. You were within reach, so I lifted you out."

"But how did we make it all the way from the middle of the lake?" wondered Jade.

"It's an enchanted lake," said a deep voice behind them. "Once you have overcome its mirages, you may enter Okdhrûl."

Jumping almost out of their skins, the girls turned around to see a melancholy man dressed in black sitting on a black horse.

"Help!" yelled Amber. "It's a soldier of Darkness!"

"You don't frighten us," announced Jade fiercely and not very convincingly. "We'll fight you!"

The man smiled in amusement.

"I'm sure you would, but don't bother. I am Rokcdär, one of Death's councilors, and for her own good I have decided to take you to her."

"Of course! Oonagh told us about you!" exclaimed Jade. "She said you would lead us to the palace of Yrianz of Myrnehl."

"For the moment, however, I will lead you to Death. In a manner of speaking, naturally!"

Amber was pleasantly surprised to see her horse quietly cropping the grass a few yards away.

"I brought your horses here for you," explained Rokcdär. "The palace of Death isn't far, and I'll take you there now."

Still somewhat wary, the three girls mounted their animals without a word, but when Death's councilor took off at a gallop, they followed him. The surrounding countryside was spectral and desertlike, with scrawny bushes littering the dry, black soil. At last an imposing palace emerged from the pervasive gloom of Okdhrûl.

"This is where Death lives," announced Rokcdär.

The girls looked up at the dusky building flanked by several large towers whose summits vanished into the sky. The palace gave an impression of sinister power and was surrounded by a macabre silence. A regiment of soldiers in black uniforms stood guard, but when they recognized Councilor Rokcdär, they saluted and allowed him and his party to enter the castle. Servants all in black rushed up to take the horses away to the stables, while Jade, Opal, and Amber followed their guide through endless corridors of unsettling twilight.

"I have no doubt that you possess mighty powers," said Rokcdär warningly, "but all the same, be careful. Arguing with Death is quite an undertaking."

Sudden, wrenching sobs rent the air, and now, so close to their goal, the startled girls began to feel their courage failing. The weeping was coming from behind an ebony door that Rokcdär opened without knocking. He led Jade,

Opal, and Amber into a rather large room decorated entirely in black. There were heavy velvet curtains over the narrow windows, which shut out all sunlight. A dozen solemn men, clothed in the same manner as Rokcdär, were sitting around a wide bed on which lay a dark form, crying pitifully.

"You have visitors," Rokcdär announced to Death.

The girls closed their eyes in mortal fear, expecting to see a creature out of their worst nightmares rise to meet them. When they dared to look, they stood before a short young woman staring at them and sniffling. She had smooth, close-cropped, light brown hair and skin of a deathly pallor. Her hazel eyes were suffused with sadness. While her shell-pink lips were delicate and thin, her cheeks were chubby, and she was a trifle plump. She wore a knee-length, full black skirt and a pretty blouse of the same color, decorated with jet beads. She was rather attractive, but her face was etched with an infinite distress that betrayed the never-ending burden she had been shouldering for so long.

"You're all afraid of me," she wailed in a clear voice, in between sobs. "You curse me, you beg me day and night to stay away. . . ."

Utterly disconcerted, the three girls had no idea what to say.

"Everybody's happy that I'm on strike, so why come to complain about it? You, Opal, you know we should have met earlier and you say it's a miracle that you're still alive! Nobody loves me, except for the suicidal ones—and even they sometimes dread me at the end." She pointed imperiously toward the door. "Everyone out!" she ordered. "Leave me alone with these girls!"

The councilors obeyed. Death was alone with her three guests.

"I truly don't know why everybody hates me. Even the privileged ones I take the trouble to go and fetch personally scream their heads off when I show up. The others, whom I put to death with a single fleeting thought, are even more aghast to meet their end."

"And where do you take them? Is there a life after death?" asked Amber boldly.

"You see!" railed Death in a wounded voice. "Life, life, life! That's all you ever talk about, or think about—all of you fawn over my sister Life! As for telling you where I take the dying, don't expect me to reveal that. You may well be the three Stones of destiny, but I'm still the most mysterious of all creatures: the one most feared by humankind. It's impossible for me to speak to you of secrets the world has tried so long to discover."

"I would give anything to see my mother," pleaded Amber, "my mother whom you stole from me before I even knew her!"

"That's what all you mortals demand of me. You accuse me of cruelty, you want to see the dear departed—but it's not my fault, I'm just doing my job! Since time immemorial, even before magic creatures appeared, men have been busily killing one another. They created evil, they watered it with their blood. I didn't drive them to commit their murderous deeds! I simply bring rest to the dying. I follow the paths laid out by men."

"But why are you on strike?" asked Jade. "We all need you. Without you, life wouldn't exist, and the world would get lost in eternity."

"Thank you," sniffed Death, touched enough to smile faintly. "It's been a long time since anyone complimented me. People offer poems to Life—but me, I only get complaints. Why? Am I so hideous? Tell me!"

"It's not *you* people detest," explained Opal. "They're just afraid, they wonder who you are, what you bring. They dread you because they don't know you, and the unknown is frightening."

"You separate families, friends," continued Amber, "and that's why people curse you, call you cruel and unjust. But deep down, people know that you must come sooner or later, that it's necessary, that the death of a loved one and their mourning are an unavoidable trial that allows them to reflect, and move on."

"Then why am I treated like a misfortune, as if I were some kind of terrible curse?" moaned Death, who had wiped away her tears.

"Because everyone would like to keep their dear ones close to them forever," replied Jade sadly. "They know that's not possible, but they keep hoping, anyway, and they can't help suffering when their loved ones disappear."

"So my strike is a good thing. That's just what I was saying: no one loves me."

"No, really, that's not true," insisted Amber. "Many people wait for you to bring them rest, even though they also wonder what you have in store for them. And you must continue your work, to allow the world to survive. You contribute to life, you're part of it!"

"Really!" said Death more cheerfully, feeling reassured. "Although so many people get scared when they see me. . . . I think it's all this black, and the color doesn't do much for me, either. But if I don't wear it, I lose my credibility."

Jade, Opal, and Amber exchanged amused looks.

"I'm too fat," lamented Death. "That must be my main

problem. I try to diet, but it's impossible, I'm just so greedy. I absolutely must lose weight."

The three girls burst out laughing. Surprised by a light-heartedness she rarely had the chance to inspire, Death smiled as well.

"Don't worry," spluttered Jade. "You're fine the way you are."

"Am I? You think I'm pretty, and nice?"

"Of course," insisted Jade.

"I can't believe it, no one's ever told me that and I've been waiting to hear it for centuries."

Death was so delighted, she clapped her hands. Then she tossed back a lock of her chestnut hair and smiled even more broadly, lighting up her winsome and still youthful face.

"Fine," said Jade. "Now, you're going to stop your strike, right?"

"No. If I go back to work, I'll be sick of it again within three days."

"But people are in agony, suffering dreadfully while they wait for you," said Amber pleadingly. "They were about to die when you announced your strike, and they're begging you to come and get them."

"They're waiting for me?" asked Death in surprise.

"Well! If they want me to, I'll come, I'll go back to work. But only on one condition." Death looked deeply into the girls' eyes, and her gaze was unfathomable. "No mortal has ever come here before. I will call off my strike only if you promise me that when we meet again, perhaps after many long years, you will follow me without cries and weeping. As if we were just good friends, happy to see one another again and who will go together to a pleasant place."

"We promise," chorused the three girls.

"Well, then, I won't try to keep you here any longer," continued Death, "because I sense that you are in a hurry to follow your destiny. Rokcdär will guide you to the edge of my realm. Although I cannot read the future, I do feel that you are in peril. I can wait patiently until we meet again and I trust that you still have many happy years ahead of you." After a pause, Death continued gravely, "For a long time I have been associated with evil, and yet I am beyond that. I belong neither to good nor to evil, and I do not judge either one. Nevertheless, I do know, see, and sense good and evil. You should be aware that the power of these two forces has reached its peak and that the battle between them draws nigh. One or the other will be annihilated, temporarily, but they are both too strong to disappear completely from the world. In the human heart, these two enemies will be linked together forever."

Then, with a worried look, Death asked in a faltering voice, "Are you absolutely certain that I don't need to go on a diet?"

"Absolutely," insisted Jade in a firm voice, before giggling helplessly.

After affectionate farewells, Death smiled sadly at the departing girls.

"I'm unhappy that you're leaving. If fate weren't always in such a rush, I'd try to keep you here with me for a while. But I know I'll be seeing you again. . . ."

29

Elyador

THE YOUNG HOVALYN COULD NOT BRING himself to accept the evidence. How could he be the Chosen One? He, who had served the Darkness! It was impossible. The Ring of Orleys had made a mistake. The other knights tried in vain to persuade him to attend the celebrations Tivann had organized in his honor throughout the day, for he remained cloistered in his room, brooding. Late that evening someone knocked at his door, entering in spite of his protests. It was the stalwart Gohral Keull.

"I know what's eating at your heart," he told the young man. "Go and see Oonagh. She will help you."

The Nameless One seemed lost in thought.

"Tivann of Orleys is already preparing your marriage to his daughter Orlaith, but I sense that you do not love her," continued his visitor.

"I'll leave. I'll go and consult Oonagh. All these people, here in the manor—they believe in me. I don't deserve it. I have to go." After a moment, he added, "I am not the Chosen One."

"I know," replied Gohral Keull. "I know about your past."

Startled, the young man looked up.

"You know who I was?" he asked softly.

"Yes. And I also know that you have changed. Let me go with you to Oonagh. I know many things about you of which you yourself are ignorant."

After a brief hesitation, the Nameless One made up his mind.

"I'll leave when it's completely dark. I'll run away like a coward, and if you wish to join me, then come along."

"I will," replied the older man firmly.

The two hovalyns spent the next hour preparing for their journey and then slipped out to the stables. Like thieves in the night, they mounted their horses and galloped away from the manor of Tivann of Orleys. From time to time the Nameless One glanced curiously at his companion, who maintained a stubborn silence, content simply to breathe in the invigorating air.

"I know some shortcuts," said Gohral Keull finally. "They will bring us rapidly to Oonagh, where you will learn what your destiny is to be and submit to your fate."

"What do you know about me? Can you tell me my name?"

"It isn't your name that makes you someone; it's what you are, what you do, what you feel. You've had your share of names, but I cannot tell you the one your parents gave you."

"Then tell me what you know about my past!"

"The present is more important."

For many hours after that, Gohral Keull refused to speak further. The two hovalyns rode across Hornimel all night long, and at dawn, when the colors of a new day blazed in the sky, the Nameless One spoke meekly to his companion.

"You know who I was, before. . . . You know I served the Darkness."

"I know," repeated his companion.

"And you don't hate me? Even though I don't remember, I have blood on my hands. I'm a criminal."

"You're a man. So am I. Who am I to judge you?"

"Before becoming a man, I was a monster! I was a soldier of Darkness!"

"You are no longer. When you deserted, you renounced evil. When you lost your memory, you became someone else: the Nameless One, a hovalyn in the service of good. You suffered. You fought. Today, even if evil is still inside you—for it's inside us all—it has been vanquished by goodness."

"How do you know? What do you know about me?"

"I met you several years ago. You ask what I know about you? I never saw your parents, but you told me that they died when you were a child."

"So they're dead. . . ." murmured the young man slowly.

"You were living with your grandparents," continued Gohral Keull impassively. "You never wanted to talk about that time and never mentioned the name they called you by. You left home at sixteen because you were eager to see the world. That's when I met you, and you possessed a strength and courage that simply astounded me. You wished to fight, to combat injustice, and were not in the least afraid to risk your life."

Surprised, the Nameless One listened avidly to his companion's words.

"You burned so brightly with audacity, with bravery, that all who met you called you Elyador, 'the one who has been chosen.' You laughed about that and didn't care a whit for glory."

The Nameless One no longer knew what to believe. Gohral Keull spoke with great sincerity, but the young man was haunted by the mark on his left ankle.

"Then your path crossed that of the Army of Darkness."

The Nameless One desperately wished to know what had happened, to discover why he had gone over to darkness. He wanted to see his past clearly at last, forget his doubts, his questions, and understand what faults he had committed so that he might be rid of them. But Gohral Keull now mysteriously refused to say another word, as if he dreaded to evoke those shadowy soldiers.

After another day's riding the two knights saw the mountains where Oonagh lived silhouetted against the horizon and decided to stop. It had been dark for a few hours and they were worn out. Speaking little, they shared their food, then lay down to sleep. The Nameless One did not dare ask any more questions, feeling that his companion would continue his narrative only when he wished to, but he wondered if, at long last, he would soon learn *everything* about his past. . . .

The hovalyns finally reached the Irog range and began to climb the imposing mountain where Oonagh lived. They halted for the night in the dense conifer forest; it was already pitch dark, and both men could sense the anxiety emanating from the birds of prey. They did not fear them, however, for the Nameless One had kept the amulets given him by the Ghibduls. Just as the young man was drifting into sleep, Gohral Keull began to speak.

"Nameless One, I have been a coward and avoided telling you this, but tomorrow we will reach Oonagh, and I want you to learn everything I know about you." After a deep breath, he continued hurriedly, "I don't understand why you crossed over to evil. At the time I was your friend, and we were inseparable. One day we encountered the Army of Darkness. I don't know what happened to you— you were fascinated by the power of those sinister soldiers. Something drew you toward evil. You had always been good, as you are today—yet you joined the black army. I tried to reason with you. You wouldn't listen. Why? You were so young, still innocent. Why does evil tempt men so much? Once a man has tasted its power, once he has known hatred, it's so hard to return to the light. . . . Darkness carried you off into its depths. I lost track of you."

Mortified by these revelations, the Nameless One asked in a shaky voice, "If I was good before becoming a soldier of Darkness, it means that evil could still regain its grip on me! If I gave in to it once, would I be able to resist it now?"

"That is a battle everyone fights at every moment. We are never safe from Darkness."

"Why are you coming with me to see Oonagh?"

"In memory of Elyador, the youth you once were. I do

not believe you are the Chosen One. But neither are you a soldier of Darkness. Many people know the rest of your story, and it finally reached me by word of mouth. You deserted the black army. Why? Perhaps because you wished to return to the light. You were caught, however, and as punishment your memory was erased. You then became once more the man you really are, a hovalyn."

"But how could I make up for my mistakes? Atone for the blood I shed? Will people still trust me when they learn who I was?"

Gohral Keull did not answer.

With a lump in his throat, the Nameless One stared up at the starless heavens. So the Sorcerer of Darkness had told him the truth. He'd been a criminal, then a deserter. One thing still intrigued him. He took from his pack the casket he'd received from the mermaid at the Lake of Torments and showed it to his companion.

"Do you know anything about this object?"

"No, absolutely not. But ask Oonagh about it, perhaps she can tell you."

After their conversation, the young man then spent a wretched night, dreaming of blood and violence.

The two knights continued on their way in the morning. When they caught sight of the birds of prey, which looked like scars in the summer sky, they slipped the Ghibdul amulets around their necks and shed every last twinge of fear. Gohral Keull had already consulted Oonagh once before, so he confidently led his melancholy companion into the winding tunnel. It took them more than an hour to reach the wall of light, and stepping through it boldly, they entered the vast grotto of Oonagh.

"Ah! Here's the youth called the Nameless One," piped a fluting voice.

The young man turned, and there was Oonagh.

"Help me," he asked simply. "What is my name? What am I fated to become?"

"So you want to redeem yourself? Very well. Hasten to the castle of Yrianz of Myrnehl. That is where the bravest hovalyns become soldiers of Light by pledging to fight the Darkness on the day of the summer solstice."

"But I don't understand," confessed the Nameless One. "What will I do there?"

"You served the Darkness. Now, serve the Light. Take the oath of a soldier. Fight when the battle so long awaited by everyone takes place. As it will, within two weeks."

"But the people in that castle—they won't ever accept me when they learn who I've been! They'll hate me!"

"If you wish to stand up to the Darkness, first stand up to the hatred of men."

"I'll go with you, Nameless One," announced Gohral Keull. "I, too, want to fight in the Army of Light. And all those who have the strength for it will join us! Fairytale has been expecting this battle for such a long time. . . . At last the Council of Twelve and the Army of Darkness will be reunited before us. We will annihilate them! On the day of the summer solstice, thousands of people will be there— pouring in from everywhere to fight for the Light!"

"But do not forget that the Chosen One has not yet appeared," Oonagh reminded them softly. "He is to lead the Army of Light. Without him, I fear that the battle will not take place."

The young man looked down. He was not the Chosen One.

"Go to the castle of Yrianz of Myrnehl," repeated Oonagh. "Perhaps you will find the Chosen One there— and perhaps you will find yourself there as well."

"What does that mean? Will I learn my name there? Or what I must become?"

"I read people's hearts, not the futures," Oonagh reminds him.

Resigned, the Nameless One carefully withdrew the

casket from his pack and held it out to Oonagh.

"I was hoping you would show this to me," said the magic creature. "A long, long time ago, when you were just a child, your parents sensed that your destiny would be threatened by shadows and danger. Guided by their instinct, they knew that evil was lying in wait for you and they feared for your life, so they came to see me to tell me of their plans. I tried to dissuade them, but they did not listen to me. They sought out the deepest part of the forest and found the Lake of Torments."

The Nameless One shuddered and caught his breath.

"There your parents asked the mermaids, who are powerful enchantresses, to cast a spell they alone may perform. 'As you wish,' they answered cruelly, 'but you will have to pay with your lives.' Your parents accepted the bargain."

The young man thought he was going to suffocate.

"What was the spell?" he asked, his voice quivering with emotion.

"The mermaids swore to give you this casket when you appeared at the edge of the lake. Inside the casket they placed your parents' love for you."

The Nameless One felt tears spring to his eyes. His parents had sacrificed themselves for him. . . . He took the casket from Oonagh's hands and caressed it, trembling.

"Whenever you open this casket," explained Oonagh, "you will be protected by the undying love of your parents."

"Unbelievable," murmured Gohral Keull.

"Nameless One," said Oonagh sympathetically, "do not regret the choice your parents made. They are not dead, not really. Every time you open that casket their love will live in you, and they will be there, always."

The hovalyn smiled sadly.

"Now," declared Oonagh, "you must go. Cross Ellrog, go around the land of Death. Not even the Army of Darkness dares go there. Go to Yrianz of Myrnehl. If you encounter the three Stones of the Prophecy, convince them to go to Thaar. The battle they will wage there will be decisive for us all."

"But—" began the young man.

"Good luck!" said Oonagh abruptly. "Perhaps we will see one another at the battle!"

"What?" exclaimed Gohral Keull, staring at the frail creature. "You are going to fight as well, on the summer solstice?"

"Do not judge by appearances," replied Oonagh curtly. "Magic is a powerful weapon—" Breaking off, she took leave of them. "Don't waste any more time."

The Nameless One and Gohral Keull turned back toward the light.

30

THE KING AND THE GIFT

FOR SEVERAL DAYS ROKCDÄR LED THE GIRLS toward the far boundaries of Okdhrûl. When the castle of Yrianz of Myrnehl loomed up before them one evening, Rokcdär bade farewell to his charges. After his departure, the travelers washed their hands and faces in a stream, and Amber told their horses to wait for them.

The girls took turns hiding behind a tree to change into the lovely gowns given to them by the women of Amnhor's town. The gowns suited the girls perfectly, and although they did not know this, the seamstresses had stitched a bit of enchantment into their work so that the dresses made their wearers even more attractive.

Delighted with their elegant appearance, Jade, Opal, and Amber walked through the gilded entrance gate on to the grounds of the castle and followed a path of white pebbles across a vast, carefully tended garden. The girls were enchanted by delicately colored flowers, which gave forth intoxicating perfumes. A few trees laden with ripe fruit stood at a bend in the path.

Forgetting their past perils, the three girls laughed gleefully. Jade looked like her old self again: the daughter of the Duke of Divulyon. She was wearing a long dress of finest Prussian blue silk that rippled and fluttered as she walked. Her black hair tumbled fetchingly about her shoulders, and her jade-green eyes gleamed proudly. And yet, many in her father's palace would never have recognized her now, for her adventures had changed her: she had lost her haughty air, her pretentious manners. Her features reflected a new seriousness and maturity, although there was still a rebellious twinkle in her eye.

The three visitors knocked on the palace door. The servant girl who hurried to open it was momentarily speechless at the sight of these creatures bathed in glowing light.

"You're here at last," she said, smiling in admiration. "The three Stones . . . enter!"

She led them to an immense room lit by imposing crystal chandeliers, where hundreds of guests were talking animatedly. They were mostly men, wearing swords at their sides, but there were also magic creatures and even some women who had come to join the Army of Light. Not all the future combatants were there; messengers had been sent to the four corners of Fairytale to assemble the army and lead it, on the day of the summer solstice, to the battlefield designated in the Prophecy. Néophileus had written that the Chosen One as well as the three Stones were Sorcerers of Light. The boldest and most renowned hovalyns had gathered in the castle of Yrianz of Myrnehl to pledge to fight the Darkness, and everyone in the castle was hoping that the Chosen One would arrive and that the three Stones of the Prophecy, sent to the palace by Oonagh, would be able to identify him. Jade, Opal, and Amber would then proceed to Thaar, leaving only the Chosen One to fight the Sorcerers of Darkness. No one could take his place. Without him, the battle would not begin. . . .

When the three girls made their entrance, the great hall became quiet. All stood motionless in amazement. Some were dazzled by Jade, whose eyes shone like stars; others admired Amber, dressed in flaming red muslin; still others saw Opal, splendid in white tulle, as the very incarnation of purity. Opal's once cold and distant air had given way to an expression of regal self-confidence, and the girl who had once kept her eyes downcast now held her head high.

Soon cries resounded through the great hall: "Long live the three Stones of the Prophecy! Long live liberty and the Army of Light!"

Jade, Opal, and Amber smiled. It was then that two forms appeared in the doorway. The first was a knight who looked rugged and valiant; the second, a young man with an aura of mysterious power. The youth gazed solemnly around the assembled throng, and yet he seemed not to see them. His brown hair was disheveled, his clothing untidy. There were deep scratches on his careworn face, which seemed ravaged by some hidden pain, and there was an infinite sadness in his eyes.

A hovalyn who had come from the manor of Tivann of Orleys recognized him and shouted, "It's the Chosen One! That young man is the Chosen One!"

Another knight who had also witnessed the ritual of the Ring of Orleys called out, "Long Live Elyador, the one who has been chosen! I will fight beside you!"

In the ensuing tumult, cries of joy rang out, but one voice was raised in dissent.

"That man is not the Chosen One! He's a soldier of Darkness!"

In the sudden pall of silence, all eyes were on a magic creature with pale blond hair, black eyes, and silvery skin: it was Elfohrys who had spoken, and now he addressed the Nameless One.

"Tell them who you are! A murderer . . ."

Everyone expected the young man to deny these accusations.

"It's true," he admitted. "I belonged to the Army of Darkness. I was a murderer. But I no longer am. I have changed. And I would like to become a soldier of Light."

"And you think we're going to trust you?" cried a hova-lyn, his voice full of hatred. "How can we tell if you've really changed? You can't go from the Darkness to the Light! You have shed innocent blood!"

"And now it's your blood that ought to be shed!" someone else yelled.

The crowd began to shout at the young man, heaping abuse on him. Jade joined in, yelling insults, and Opal felt the same way, although she remained silent.

As for Amber, she pitied the young man. Pale and dignified, he said nothing, made no effort to defend himself, and simply stared wretchedly at the angry throng. Then his eyes met Amber's: they looked at each other, and immediately understood. They felt as if they had always known one another, as if they had lived only in the expectation of finding each other again someday. The Nameless One no longer saw Amber in her fiery red dress, he saw further—he saw her heart. And he realized that she would possess his own. There was only one word to describe what he was experiencing. In fear and trembling, he considered that word. Impalpable, stronger and more maddening than any other emotion, the word lay in his golden casket as from now on it would lie in his heart, and in Amber's eyes: love.

From the shadows will come the Chosen One
To unify the Realm

Amber could hear Oonagh's voice . . .

From the shadows will come the Chosen One.

Amber lowered her eyes and reflected: this young man— if he really had shed blood . . . Of course, he had changed—he must certainly want to forget his past, atone for his misdeeds. But, still . . . was he truly a murderer?

One will recognize the King.

She heard Oonagh's voice . . .

"From the shadows will come the Chosen One," murmured Amber, almost without thinking. Then suddenly she understood, and shouted, "From the shadows will come the Chosen One!"

Her cry silenced the astonished crowd.

"Are you feeling all right?" asked Jade.

Amber ignored her, and went to the Nameless One. Then she addressed the crowd.

"The one who was chosen, Elyador, the King, whatever you wish to call him—this is he. This murderer, this deserter whom you so despise. It is precisely because he comes from the shadows that he is the Chosen One."

Jade and Opal stared at her open-mouthed. Amber was transformed, with passion in her voice and fire in her eye.

"It's impossible," called out Elfohrys. "A soldier of Darkness can't be a Sorcerer of Light!"

The crowd muttered in agreement.

"It's written in *The Prophecy*. 'From the shadows will come the Chosen One,'" repeated Amber. "This man belonged to the Army of Darkness, but he had the strength to leave it. Who among you would have been able to leave the shadows to go toward the light?"

The assembled throng remained doubtful.

"This man deserves your admiration, not your insults. He has dared to come here to join the Army of Light. He did not try to lie to you: he admitted that he once served the Darkness. He knew that no one would trust him, that you would hate him. But he came anyway. Who here would have done as much?" After a pause, Amber continued gravely, "Those who have always been on the side of the Light are good. But those who have known the shadows, who have suffered, who have endured the contempt of others yet have continued to walk toward the Light . . . they are truly great."

The lofty hall was still.

Then the crowd was startled by the hiss of a sword drawn gleaming from its scabbard. Elfohrys advanced toward the Nameless One. Standing at the young man's side, Amber tried to cry out but could not make a sound. To everyone's amazement, when he reached the Nameless One, Elfohrys dropped to one knee and laid his sword before him.

"Elyador, to the one who was my friend, I offer my apologies. To the one who is my king, I offer my homage."

"Rise, Elfohrys," said the Chosen One. "I am not a king. I am only a man. And I forgive you."

Elfohrys got slowly to his feet and picked up his sword. Brandishing it, he shouted, "I pledge to do battle against the Darkness! I pledge to serve the Light and its King! I swear it!"

Then all the men drew their swords and in a single voice promised, "I swear it."

"I'm not fit to be a king," said the Chosen One in a faint voice.

No one heard him, except Amber.

"A few moments ago," she whispered, "you were a murderer. Now you're king. All in all, it's an improvement, right? Stop complaining and accept their homage."

Elyador smiled. From now on, he had a name. And his life had a purpose. He looked at Amber, then at the assembled throng. Oonagh had been right: in this castle, he had found the Chosen One. And at the same time, he had found himself.

"I will lead you to victory," he promised everyone. "The Army of Darkness and the Knights of the Order are powerful. We can be still more powerful. All we must do is believe this. Gathered together in the Light, we will defeat them!"

His words were greeted with shouts of enthusiasm.

Opal, who had hardly ever cried in her whole life— Opal was weeping with happiness.

Staring at Opal, Jade remarked, "Something very strange is going on this evening. First Amber, and now you! What's wrong?"

"I understand," gulped Opal between sobs. "I understand! How did we break the Seal of Darkness?" she continued, her face bathed in tears. "Do you remember? Because we believed. We were convinced we would succeed. And the birds of prey? We hadn't a single chance, but I *believed* we'd make it through—I *believed* we could. And the lake? It's the same thing! And the battle—we'll win it in the same way. It's obvious!"

Jade gave Opal a pitying look.

"Well, you'd better *believe* me: you're not your normal self at the moment."

"But you don't understand!"

"What? That all we have to do is believe? If you say so . . ."

"No!" insisted Opal. "That's it, the Gift."

"The what?"

"It's what allows us to believe. What can transform absolutely any man. Make a murderer into a king. Don't you see?"

"No. What I do see is that you don't seem well at all!"

Opal took a deep breath.

"Our Gift . . . is Hope."

One will discover the Gift.
One will recognize the King.
One will convince the two others to die.

31

THE BATTLE OF THAAR

AMBER AND ELYADOR REMAINED TOGETHER FOR
the rest of the evening. They talked about everything and
nothing, and shared their fears about the future. The
Chosen One would be risking his life on the battlefield,
while Amber would do the same in Thaar. They promised
to meet again when it was all over. Amber resolutely
refused to give in to tears.

The next morning Elfohrys asked Elyador to go with
him into the forest. The Ghibduls had said that they wished
to join his cause, so the Chosen One was forced to leave
Amber. With heavy hearts, they tried to pretend that neither of them was in any danger and that they would soon
see each other again.

That afternoon Jade, Opal, and Amber had to leave as
well. Thaar was several days' journey away, and they had to
hurry. When they set out this time, however, they knew that
the end of their adventure was perilously close. Opal told
Amber about her discovery.

"Our Gift is Hope?" exclaimed Amber. "That's incredible! How did you ever discover that?"

"But it was completely obvious! What about you? How did you know who the Chosen One was?"

Amber simply smiled.

Jade looked miserably at her two companions. All night long the words of the Prophecy had haunted her dreams: *One will convince the two others to die.* Amber had recognized the King. Opal had understood the Gift. Jade was the only one left. She felt trapped in a nightmare. Impossible, it was impossible. She would never urge Opal and Amber to die! And yet, until now, the Prophecy had always spoken the truth.

The three girls rode along in an uneasy silence, for Opal and Amber could guess what was worrying Jade. They didn't dare talk about it, however, because they had no idea how to help her. Of course they knew that Jade would never lead them into death, but their silence led Jade to suspect precisely the opposite.

The girls were traveling through Lionëral, crossing plains as monotonous as those of Hornimel but dotted with towns and villages through which they rode without stopping.

One evening Jade couldn't stand it anymore and blurted

out, "I won't betray you. Believe what you want, but I will nev—"

"We know," interrupted Opal.

"The Prophecy must be mistaken about this, that's all," said Amber soothingly.

Jade burst out sobbing.

"You know perfectly well that there's no mistake. But I can't even imagine . . . I mean, I'd never do—" She was crying too hard to continue. After a moment she said abruptly, "Let's not go to Thaar. I'd rather have everyone hate us than keep hearing those words in my head: *One will convince the two others to die.* . . ."

"Elyador is going to risk his life leading the army," replied Amber gently. "As for me, I have no right to abandon the journey to Thaar. It would be as if I were abandoning him, betraying him. If we fight, we'll be united in the same battle against the Council of Twelve, against the Darkness."

"What?" said Jade. "Say that again?"

"Let it go," intervened Opal. "She's in love, don't try to understand. But she's right: after all we've gone through, we can't stop now, so close to our goal! If everyone needs us to conquer evil. . . ."

"Yes, but Elyador—at least he knows what he's

supposed to do," objected Jade. "He's going to fight and lead his army. But what about us? Once we get to Thaar, what do we do?"

"You're absolutely right," agreed Amber. "Even though Death is nice, I'd rather not see her again so soon! I've so many things I want to do. . . . Thaar scares me. But I'm going there anyway."

"Fine," said Jade, resigned. "But if the Prophecy is true—"

"You won't betray us," said Opal firmly. "We know it."

The three girls felt that if they remained truly united, nothing bad could happen to them. And perhaps they were right.

All the way through Lionëral, they saw the Army of Light assembling, guided by messengers, and the sight reassured them, giving them courage to continue on their way.

Once, Amber thought she glimpsed a black-clad horseman and closed her eyes in fright; when she looked again, however, he had vanished. She mentioned this to Jade and Opal, but since the horseman did not reappear, the girls finally forgot about him.

After riding all night they reached Thaar on the morning of the summer solstice and were dazzled by the grandeur of the City of Origins. Towering ramparts protected apartment houses that soared even higher into the sky, their countless windows glittering in the pale morning sunshine. The girls had never seen anything like it—indeed, they didn't even know what an "apartment house" was.

They dismounted in front of the ramparts, leaving their horses there. The soldiers who had formerly surrounded the city—Adrien among them—had left to join the Army of Light. Noticing that one of the city gates was open, the girls overcame their misgivings and slipped into the dark city of Thaar.

At that very moment, the Army of Light was crossing the magnetic field encircling Fairytale. Leading his troops, his shining sword drawn, Elyador opened his casket and was immediately reassured to feel an invisible force envelop him. He thought of Amber. Riding at his side, Gohral Keull and Elfohrys were astonished to see him instantly become more imposing than he had ever been before. Behind the Chosen One, the Army of Light spread out across Hornimel for as far as the eye could see and even beyond. So many were there prepared to do battle: the Ghibduls, their friends the Bumblinks, the healers and magicians of Amnhor's town, the country folk with long silver hair,

Owen of Yrdahl, Adrien. . . . A little to one side stood a few powerful magicians, Oonagh among them, who were ready to recite their spells.

When Elyador advanced, everyone followed, all equally resolute, and soon the Army of Light had left Fairytale to come face to face with the terrible Army of Darkness, made up of thousands of Knights of the Order and under the command of a dozen shadowy sorcerers. Their faces wore the frightful stamp of evil. Their numbers were as impressive as those of their adversaries. The two armies stared at one another for a long moment—and then charged into battle.

"We will win!" shouted Elyador and his troops with one voice.

An oppressive silence reigned in the City of Origins. The three girls held fast to their Stones and felt a little of the icy anguish in their hearts melt away.

"Whatever happens, we will win," declared Jade.

Amber and Opal nodded in agreement, because they felt buoyed up by Hope—but in that same instant, they sensed something else invading their thoughts, something insidious. Against their will they were drawn to a tall building, and then on into a brightly lit hall. Although they could tell that the Council of Twelve was taking control of them, they were helpless, unable to resist. After climbing an endless staircase they found themselves on the top floor of the building, in a vast room where the floor-to-ceiling windows had no glass and were open to the air. A man was sitting in a leather armchair, smiling cruelly at them. He wore an ample tunic of purple embroidered with gold. He had a terrifying aura of absolute power.

"Good morning. I am the Thirteenth Member of the Council of Twelve."

Petrified, the three girls clutched their Stones with all their might.

"I see that you are afraid and somewhat perplexed. . . . It's true, I am not a man: I am a spirit. The united spirits of the Council of Twelve."

The three girls *could not* react.

"How naive you are! You reached Thaar without any trouble—and yet you still haven't understood! The Army of Darkness has been watching you since you entered Fairytale; it has even guaranteed your safety . . . so that you would come here to me. I am the only one capable of anni-hilating you. Maybe it's not worth the bother? After all, you have done all my work for me."

* * *

The two armies clashed savagely. The Sorcerers of Darkness muttered evil spells, and the magicians of Fairytale strove to repel them. Warriors fell on all sides as heartrending cries resounded on the Outside. Elyador fought with superhuman strength, with Gohral Keull and Elfohrys still at his side.

If only Amber and the other two girls manage to defeat evil at Thaar, thought Elyador. Because I don't know if we can destroy it. . . .

And in fact, although the Army of Light was battling valiantly, it was largely untrained and was slowly losing ground.

"Thousands of years ago," explained the Thirteenth Councilor, "violence and hatred ruled throughout the world. The magic creatures hid themselves in fear, and mankind did not even believe they existed. One day, though, these creatures decided to appear to men and help them resolve their conflicts. For a few centuries, there was peace. I should mention that this was in the time of dear old Néophileus. Human nature eventually reasserted itself, however, and the world was again torn apart by wars. That was when the Council of Twelve was elected for the purpose of making the world into one country, at peace."

"That's not true," retorted Jade. "Peace already reigned among the magic creatures and mankind before the Council of Twelve imposed its rule!"

That was in fact what Jean Losserand had told the three girls.

"No," the Thirteenth Councilor insisted. "I'm not lying to you. There's no point anymore. When the Council of Twelve came to power, there were too many weapons and too much technology for peace to be possible. In an attempt to avoid wars, the modern world was gradually swept away. Everything regressed, after a fashion. The cities of yesteryear have disappeared. Thaar is the only one that still remembers its glorious past."

The three girls listened, quaking with dread.

"The Council of Twelve has stood strong, passing on its power from father to son. In spite of all these changes, there were still rebels and troublemakers. The Council of Twelve managed little by little to deprive people of their freedom by telepathically controlling their minds without their knowledge. It was so much better that way! The result was universal calm and prosperity. But the magic creatures also knew how to practice telepathy. They understood what was happening and they revolted. That's when Fairytale was created—the only defeat the Council suffered in all those years."

The Thirteenth Councilor paused.

"From generation to generation, the Council of Twelve has maintained its rule and its power has grown steadily stronger. The world of long ago has been forgotten, replaced by a life in which people are controlled by the Council—without revolution, without warfare."

Jade, Opal, and Amber felt their blood run cold.

"Only Thaar remains as it was thousands of years ago. Now it is known as the City of Origins. It has had so many names. . . . For centuries, when mankind believed itself alone on this earth, it was also called Paris. . . ."

The battle was raging. The sight of blood spurred on the Army of Darkness, who were thirsty for evil, while Elyador, surrounded by a halo of love, encouraged the Army of Light to keep fighting. Everyone was growing weaker. Mutilated corpses lay scattered about the blood-stained ground, and hundreds of wounded lay dying in atrocious agony. There was butchery everywhere. Elyador's sword streamed with blood, yet it still gleamed brightly. The Chosen One thought only of Amber, and her image appeared to him, urging him on.

All of a sudden, one of Elyador's adversaries managed

to unhorse him, and he dropped his sword. In the chilling certainty that he was about to die, he looked up at the soldier of Darkness who was about to strike him dead—and saw the soldier himself run through by a sword. Retrieving his weapon, Elyador thanked his savior, who seemed quite young. The brown-haired youth with the determined look in his passionate eyes was named Adrien of Rivebel.

Having lost sight of Elfohrys and Gohral Keull, the Chosen One battled on alongside Adrien, who fought with such surprising agility that none of his adversaries had managed to wound him.

The Army of Darkness seemed sure to win in the end, however. Trained killers driven by hatred, its soldiers were skilled in brutality, unlike the many peasants and villagers in the Army of Light who did not know how to fight.

I must see Opal again, thought Adrien. I *mustn't* die. . . .

As for Elyador, he was exhausted. But he would never give up.

"And you, the three Stones of the Prophecy," continued the Thirteenth Councilor, "you dare to threaten the reign of the Council of Twelve! Because of you and that accursed

Néophileus, the seed of revolt grew in people's hearts, and numerous minds have escaped our control. And yet, you are nothing! I could kill you here and now. But first I wish to make the most of your defeat."

"You'll never manage to beat us!" exclaimed Jade. "Our Gift, Hope, is stronger than anything!"

The Thirteenth Councilor roared with laughter.

"Is it stronger than that?" he asked with a sneer, waving toward a large window.

The three girls cried out in dismay. From the top floor of the building, they could see the battlefield strewn with thousands of bodies. The Knights of the Order and the soldiers of Darkness were clad in gray and black, while the Army of Light wore silver armor. There were still thousands of dark soldiers, but only a few hundred soldiers of Light remained, a pale spot in the center of a black mass.

"Now what do you think?" asked the Thirteenth Councilor in an icy voice. "You cannot defeat evil. It is everywhere: in each person's heart, in the air, in life itself."

"So is goodness," Amber replied firmly.

But she looked out at the battle and began to shiver as anguish gripped her heart. Was Elyador still alive? She knew that the outcome of the struggle was obvious: at Thaar, as on the battlefield, the Light would be defeated.

"Thank you, my dears, thank you so much," gloated the Thirteenth Councilor. "Without you, no one would ever have recognized the Chosen One, and the battle would not have taken place. I would never have had the opportunity to annihilate all my enemies in one fell swoop. What a nice touch that was, to have gathered them all up and sent them off to be killed! They will die, every last one of them. How could they hope to triumph over my Knights of the Order and the Army of Darkness? Tomorrow, and for evermore, the power of the Council of Twelve will be absolute. Nothing will ever threaten our domination again."

The three girls stared at the Thirteenth Councilor in despair. What could they do?

The soldiers of Light knew that they had lost. They had almost ceased to resist. The Sorcerers of Darkness were still chanting their dark incantations, which had no effect, thanks to the persistent efforts of Oonagh and a few magicians. Only about a hundred experienced hovalyns fought on valiantly, along with a handful of common folk. Elyador, Elfohrys, Gohral Keull, and Adrien were the champions who caused the most trouble for the Army of Darkness. To everyone's surprise, the boldest combatants were the

Ghibduls. Flying a few yards above the battlefield, they would choose a soldier of Darkness, swarm down on him, slash him to death with their claws, and fly off to attack another victim. The dark army had succeeded in killing only a few of the Ghibduls, but unfortunately there were not enough of these forest warriors to make a dent in the enemy ranks.

Still fighting courageously, the Chosen One was growing weak and knew that he could not hold out much longer. Then he found himself surrounded by several soldiers of Darkness, and summoning his last reserves of strength, he prepared to defend himself.

"So, you're the Chosen One?" snarled one of the shadowy creatures. "Seems that before, you used to be one of ours."

"Before he deserted," cackled another soldier of Darkness. "The Army of Light—do they take our cowards to make kings of 'em, or what?"

"A king—that?" The speaker laughed contemptuously. "Bah! Let's kill him, that way at least we can say we shed a king's blood. I bet it's no different from ours. King or Chosen One—that won't keep him from dying!"

Seeing Elyador in danger, the Ghibduls quickly gathered together, flew to his rescue, and sliced his attackers to ribbons without mercy. Then one by one, they landed on the battlefield. They had decided to fight in hand-to-hand combat so that they could do more damage to the forces of Darkness—even though they knew this would surely cost them their lives.

"Now, what will I do with you?" wondered the Thirteenth Councilor. "Kill you?" He pretended to ponder the question. "No—I have a better idea. Go."

The girls started suddenly, then looked at one another, aghast.

"Yes," crowed the Thirteenth Councilor. "Go! What could be worse than the disappointment of Hope deceived? You did not understand at all, you kept your Gift for yourselves. And when evil has triumphed, when you sink into bitterness, your Gift will sink with you. Hope will become hopelessness. The sight of you will inspire discouragement. Everyone will hate you because you failed. Wherever you go, despair will follow you—until Death releases you at last."

Amber felt tears sting her eyes. But Jade cried out:

"You said we didn't understand, that we kept our Gift for ourselves. So, all we have to do is offer it to others in order to win the battle? To give them the Hope that's inside us?"

The Thirteenth Councilor concealed his irritation. In his excitement, he had said too much. But in any case, it didn't change a thing.

"You have figured that out a little too late," he told Jade pointedly.

"Maybe not," Opal shot back.

Like Jade and Amber, she was still holding tight to her Stone. The Thirteenth Councilor made no move to stop the three girls when they went over to an open window, but as they drew back their arms to hurl the Stones toward the battlefield, the Stones themselves became burning hot. The girls tried to ignore the pain, only to discover that something was preventing them from letting go: they felt a kind of invisible bond between themselves and their Stones, a bond that could not be broken.

The Thirteenth Councilor laughed lugubriously.

"You still haven't realized that yet? Your Stones are a part of you. They represent your Gift. You can never be separated from them. You are tied to them just as you are tied to one another. If one of you were to die, Hope would die with her. Do you know how it came to you? Ever since time began, someone has held your power, which was fragile at first, but it has grown with each passing generation."

The faces, the faces in the Lake of the Past, thought Jade. They were all the people who transmitted our power to us!

"In each generation a single person has held the Gift," continued the Thirteenth Councilor. "This person was said to have a kind of small scar shaped like a sun in the palm of their hand. When you were born, the power had reached its full potential and divided into three, and so the scars became Stones. A long time ago, Hope chose the one who would bear this Gift and carry out the life-long mission of giving it to others. If all those people had failed, if they had kept Hope locked inside themselves, it would have flickered out. But the Gift was passed on, through great endeavor, until it reached you. And obviously it was all for nothing, since you have failed! Your Gift will leave you only with your death, and who knows what will become of it then? It will certainly be extinguished. Or, transformed into hopelessness, it will spread throughout the world. In that case you will have served at least two purposes: gathering all my enemies together so that I may easily crush them, and assuring the reign of evil for all eternity." The Thirteenth Councilor smiled nastily. "Now, get out."

The girls did not move. Even knowing that all was lost,

they still could not bring themselves to admit defeat.

They held on to their Stones with all their strength. Amber thought of Elyador with every fiber of her being, because only his image could still help her. Opal saw Adrien's face in her mind's eye.

As for Jade, she was concentrating on Oonagh's voice, ringing ever louder and clearer in her ears: *One will convince the two others to die.* And she slowly understood that she had no choice. If she obeyed the Thirteenth Councilor and left, evil would win. If her Gift became despair, and were to invade the world after she died . . . Well, then, she had to give Hope to the Army of Light—and give it to them now. But how could she, since she could not be separated from her Stone? Except through death.

Jade tried to repress the truth that was dawning on her, but she couldn't. With a deep breath she admitted to herself that if she were to die now, sacrificing herself voluntarily, then maybe her Gift would reach the Army of Light, and evil would be defeated. But Hope might also simply die with her. . . . How could she be sure what would happen? And how could she accept death?

She simply could not leave without doing something. What would her life be like if she did? Evil would reign. The few survivors of the Light would hate her, and they would be too discouraged to plan any future rebellions. All her life she would carry the burden of her failure and be sorry that she hadn't acted when there was still time. She just could not walk away like a coward. And yet, wouldn't that be the simplest thing to do? But just the very thought gave her sickening pangs of remorse.

She looked at Opal and Amber. She knew that alone, she was nothing. Her death would be of little use. If the three girls wanted to transmit their Gift they would have to do it together, but Jade could not accept that. She would never ask Opal and Amber to sacrifice their lives, even if she were ready to sacrifice her own.

Resigned and resolute, she stepped up to the open window, holding her Stone. There was a strange light in her green eyes; she seemed like a soldier about to wage the last battle, or rather, like a Sorcerer of Light facing her worst enemy: fear. She was so afraid of jumping, of seeing Death again, and of leaving life behind for good this time. . . .

Without guessing her intentions, Opal and Amber followed her, anxious to remain together.

The Thirteenth Councilor did not intervene, for he was certain that these three fourteen-year-old girls would never have the courage to sacrifice themselves. And besides, surely even that wouldn't change anything: he was sure he had won the battle.

"But he hasn't won the war," murmured Jade to her companions, a fierce, entranced look on her face.

"Only last night you were telling me that *I* wasn't behaving normally," said Opal, "but now you—you are acting really weird!"

"For hundreds of people, the sole aim of their life was to pass the Gift on to us," explained Jade. "Thousands more have waited in the hope that we can conquer evil. Our parents were killed. The Army of Light is being shredded before our eyes. Freedom and happiness will disappear. Until now, even on the Outside, there was a chance to change everything. Tomorrow that chance will be gone forever. And you think we should just stand by and let all that happen?"

"But what can we do?" pleaded Amber.

"You don't understand," whispered Jade. "The war isn't over, not yet. We are here, the three of us, and everything depends on us. Either we listen to this monster and accept defeat, or we offer our Gift to the others, to the Light. And then, without any doubt, victory will be ours."

"That's all very well," countered Opal, "but we can't separate ourselves from our Stones!"

Jade looked out the window.

"Yes, we can," she said quietly.

Opal and Amber realized where she was looking and what she intended them to do.

"You don't really mean—" gasped Amber in horror.

"Dying is the only way to let go of our Stones," insisted Jade. "Then our Gift will be scattered over the battle." With a rueful smile, she added, "Which goes to show that the Prophecy will turn out to be . . ."

"Well," joked Opal, "at least Death will be glad to see us again."

But they weren't quite ready to die just yet.

Although Elyador was on the verge of collapse, he could not bear to lay down his weapon. His parents had loved him, and loved him still; Amber loved him, he loved her, and love sustained him, drove him to fight on.

Suddenly the sky grew dark. Everyone looked up to see huge gray forms soaring over the battlefield: the raptors. Sensing the dense waves of fear emanating from the combat, they had rushed there to feed on it ravenously and finish off the last survivors.

Amber and Opal shrieked at the sight of the birds of prey,

for they knew that even if Elyador and Adrien were still alive, they would certainly succumb to those monsters.

They looked at Jade. All three girls held tight to their Stones. They had never felt so frightened. They had never been so determined. They smiled faintly at one another. Then, before the incredulous eyes of the Thirteenth Councilor, they leaped into the void.

As their Stones vanished from their hands, their Gift left them. Blinded by a dazzling light, they felt themselves falling, falling. . . .

The Hope they had finally given to others became a rain of shining gold that touched everyone's hearts. The soldiers of Light and of Darkness all ceased fighting and lifted their eyes to the sky, their faces bathed in a shower of gold and happiness.

The three girls falling to earth had sacrificed themselves, had sacrificed their Gift, and yet more than ever they were filled with Hope.

A few yards from the ground and certain death, Jade, Opal, and Amber felt the sudden grip of claws digging into their flesh: the raptors had seized them. The girls were not afraid, though—on the contrary, they felt no more panic, only the relief of knowing that they were very much alive. The rain of Hope had transformed the birds, giving their plumage a golden glow, and the girls sensed that the predators meant them no harm. They had saved the girls' lives.

The birds headed straight for the battlefield, where they delicately deposited their burden before wheeling back into the sky.

Still stunned by what had happened to them, the three girls saw Elyador, Adrien, and Oonagh coming toward them. On every side, all the adversaries had stopped fighting and seemed lost in a blissful daze.

Opal and Amber ran to the two young men, overwhelmed with joy. Jade went to meet Oonagh.

"Did we succeed?" she demanded breathlessly. "Did we conquer evil?"

"Yes," smiled the magic creature. "You have beaten back evil. One day, however," Oonagh warned solemnly, "it will return. It can never be completely defeated."

"B-But th-then," stammered Jade, "everything we did— it was for nothing!"

"Thanks to you, evil has been driven away. Now peace will reign for a few centuries. And if we continue to struggle, at every moment, against the anger, the fear, the intolerance in our own hearts, perhaps evil will never return."

Jade could have wept. And here she'd thought she had conquered the Darkness forever!

"Now what will happen?" she asked.

"Outside and Fairytale will be reunited into a single land, the Realm."

"And the Chosen One will be our King?"

Hearing his name, Elyador came over, with Amber at his side.

"No," he said softly. "I will not be King. I don't want to rule."

"In the beginning," explained Jade, "according to the Thirteenth Councilor, the Council of Twelve wanted to ensure peace. Corrupted by power, they gradually deprived the people of their freedom. I don't know if that's true, but—"

"It is," said Oonagh firmly. "And that's precisely why Elyador is right. He was King while the battle raged and will remain so until the Realm has been united. Then, to all those people who have never known freedom he will give liberty. We must not repeat the Council of Twelve's mistake. Power changes men. Elyador must cease to be the King."

"And me?" asked Jade. "And Amber, and Opal? What will happen to us?"

"That's up to you," declared Oonagh. "You are now free to decide your own destiny."

Jade thought of her father, the Duke of Divulyon, whom she would soon see again.

Out of the blue, a nugget of gold fell at Elyador's feet. Picking it up, he saw that it was shaped like a seed.

"Is this yours?" he asked, showing it to Amber.

"No," replied the young girl, laughing. "Our Stones don't exist anymore. They were transformed into golden rain."

Opal and Adrien came over.

"What's going on?" asked Opal.

"We found this," replied the Chosen One, showing her the golden seed.

Oonagh looked at it thoughtfully.

"Put it in your casket, Elyador," she told him.

"What is it?"

"A seed of Hope," murmured Oonagh.

Elyador did as the magic creature told him.

"Now, bury the casket."

Intrigued, Elyador followed Oonagh's instructions. A tree sprang up immediately, with a trunk the color of pure silver, and within a few moments it had grown long branches bearing sparkling golden leaves.

"Thanks to this tree," explained Oonagh, "the memory

of today's battle will live for centuries. As long as the tree remains bright, it will mean that the country is at peace. When its trunk blackens and its leaves fall, Darkness will again be at hand. Today, good has triumphed. So let's rejoice!"

Jade, Opal, and Amber gazed at the tree of Hope, shining in a halo of glittering gold.

PARIS: PRESENT DAY

I woke up. This time, it's over. Death is coming for me. But . . . I have to live, so that my vision becomes reality.

I look at my right hand one last time. In the hollow of my palm, majestic rays of light shine from a sun. Hope . . . I kept it for myself; I let my illness defeat me. I'm going to die, and Hope will die with me. I close my eyes. It's much too hard to leave.

That's it. I hear Death's footsteps, her cold breath drifts past my cheek. I feel like crying. The tears don't come. I feel like screaming, but I no longer have the strength.

I would have liked to leave without fear, without regrets, but it's impossible.

I'm suffocating. Everything around me is fading away. Only Death and I are left. She holds out her hand to me. It hurts so much. . . .

The nurses are bustling around in the room. The

door opens. Dr. Arnon comes in, impassive.

"What's going on?" he asks.

"It's the girl, the one who lost her parents," replies a nurse. "She's in trouble."

Dr. Arnon comes over to the bed. The sick child's wasted body is shaking spasmodically; her lips are dry, and she's moaning.

"It's the end," he observes quietly.

A sudden flash of lucidity seems to rally the dying girl.

"The telephone!" she wails. Then, in a tremulous voice, she whispers, "I have to—I have to . . . call . . . someone."

Dr. Arnon nods to one of the nurses.

"It's her last wish," he sighs. "We can't refuse her that."

I mustn't die! I must pass on the gift of Hope. And what if it isn't too late? Death is here—and yet, I still believe in my vision, in the impossible. That's all I have left, Hope. I should have given it to others. But I didn't. Why shouldn't I still believe in it? As long as I still have Hope inside me, can Death really take me away?

The doctor and the nurses leave the room. The patient feverishly picks up the receiver, dials a number. She still knows it by heart. The voice that has haunted both her dreams and her nightmares now answers.

"I'm going to die," the girl says weakly. "I forgive you. But now, the choice is yours. Either you forget me, or . . . You know what you have to do."

"Joa? Is that you, Joa?"

But the patient has already hung up.

There, it's done. I called him. Eli Ador, the one I loved, the one who abandoned me. Why did he run away, the first and last time he came to see me? It made me think I didn't matter to him. But perhaps he was scared. Of the hospital, of Death prowling the halls. Of what I had become.

Now it's not important anymore.

In the end, the Nameless One emerged from the shadows. The blood on his hands did not prevent him from becoming the Chosen One. If the people of Fairytale were able to forgive him, even make him their King—why shouldn't I forgive Eli?

My breathing is becoming more and more shallow.

I can hardly hear my heartbeat anymore. Death is waiting for me. Impatiently.

"Listen to me, she's very weak," the nurse is saying. "She hasn't got long now."

"You can't keep me from seeing her!" the young man protests anxiously. "I have to be with her. She has to live!" There was a burning determination in his eyes, perhaps even mixed with a faint flicker of hope.

"I'm afraid it might be too late," explains the nurse.

She looks at the young man. He has tousled brown hair, desperate eyes.

"Didn't you ever come to see her before?" she asks.

"Once," he says bitterly. "Let me see her," he pleads.

The nurse thinks about it for a moment.

"Go on in," she says gently, "but don't be long."

I don't know if Eli will come. But I look at the sun in the palm of my hand and I believe. I believe in the impossible, I believe in my dream, in my vision of the future. I believe in Elyador. I'm still hoping. Simply hoping.

Death is nearby. Too bad. She'll wait.

I'll live. Because I have to. Because I want to. I've been dreaming. Now, I'd rather live, even if it comes to the same thing.

My dream gave life back to me. Now I must give dreams back to life.